Taking Care of Mrs. Carroll

a novel by

Paul Monette

St. Martin's Press
New York

TAKING CARE OF MRS. CARROLL. Copyright © 1978 by Paul Monette. All rights
reserved. Printed in the United States of America. No part of this book may
be used or reproduced in any manner whatsoever without written permission
except in the case of brief quotations embodied in critical articles or reviews.
For information, address St. Martin's Press, 175 Fifth Avenue, New York,
N.Y. 10010.

Design by Chris Benders

Library of Congress Cataloging-in-Publication Data

Monette, Paul.
    Taking care of Mrs. Carroll.

    I. Title.
[PS3563.0523T35   1987]   813'.54   87-28365
ISBN 0-312-01515-1 (pbk.)

First published in the United States by Little, Brown & Company

Designed by Chris Benders

*Published simultaneously in Canada
by Little, Brown & Company (Canada) Limited*

PRINTED IN THE UNITED STATES OF AMERICA

To Roger

Liking that world where
The children eat, and grow giant and good,
I swear as I've often sworn: *"I'll* never forget
What it's like, when *I've* grown up."

RANDALL JARRELL
"The Lost World"

Taking Care of
Mrs. Carroll

1

WHEN MRS. CARROLL DIED, at seven-thirty, my friend David was lying naked in the tower bedroom, watching the gardener put on his shirt. He nearly said something flattering about the boy's tan, as if it might stop him from getting dressed again so fast. David could lie there until dark, he thought, and watch the muscles play on the gardener's back, while Mrs. Carroll, wild for her nightly egg, went slowly mad with hunger. But he bit his tongue and didn't say it, having thought better of getting too personal with the gardener days before.

"John," he said, because he thought he ought to say *something*, "why don't you take the morning off tomorrow?"

The gardener turned and faced him as he rolled up the sleeves of his work shirt.

"Why?"

"Because you've stayed so late. It must be after seven."

"Are you my boss?"

"Well, no," David said, sorry he'd gotten started in this.

"So don't tell me when to work. I finish up at five. What I do after that is my own business."

And he sauntered out of the room, making so much racket

as he thumped down the stairs in his gardener's boots that David decided he must have stirred Mrs. Carroll out of her nap and started her hungering. David propped himself up on his elbows. From where he lay, he could look out the tower windows in every direction. To the east, the marshes, the beach, the sea, and then Africa (though Mrs. Carroll's property presumably *stopped* somewhere as well, at one edge or another). To the west, Mrs. Carroll's forest, a range of wooded hills, on the lowland verge of which was throned the house, close on the marsh and the dunes. The woods went west for a couple of miles, darkening and thickening, until they seized at the borders of Mrs. Carroll's dairy farm. The cows that trooped and huddled there did not seem to know that the sea was so near. Nor did the milkmen, who drove out to the farm every day from as far away as Boston and suited up in white duds and drove off in white trucks. The sea was a secret in Mrs. Carroll's domain.

But the view, it seemed, had lost its shine. Though at last he was not horny, David was cruelly bored. He had been with Mrs. Carroll since the beginning of May, and it had taken him the five weeks since then to defuse the nervous collapse he had been convinced he was coming down with. He had stayed busy from the moment he arrived, finding a hundred things to do around the house. Mrs. Carroll, it appeared from the beginning, would not require half enough of his time. So he polished the dullest silver and rearranged the Fitzhugh cups and Rose Medallion bowls in the china closet. He alphabetized the north wall of the library. With two quarts of lemon oil, he polished the bowling alley on the upper floor of the carriagehouse. But it was inescapable, he thought as he got dressed himself. He was bored, and, what was worse, he had just bedded the only available man in the county, only to discover it wasn't going to be a regular thing. The dark and sullen gardener was a wonder in bed, but David knew from the pressure of his hands and the pace of his coming that he wasn't on the lookout for something steady. And David *always* was.

I don't remember how it came about that David told me all of this. Because of Mrs. Carroll's dying when she did, because we all got so caught up in it, I never gave a thought about what David must have felt *before*. It happened that Mrs. Carroll's death set the summer in motion. When David told me the story of the gardener, all I could think of was Mrs. Carroll herself, still lost in reverie in her overstuffed bedroom, still at the center.

"They never fall in love," I said to David about the boy. "They're in love with their roses."

"Do you think so, Rick?" David said. "I just decided he wasn't gay."

"If he wasn't gay, why did he go to bed with you?"

"I don't know. Maybe to make sure he was straight."

I looked at David then and found I was frantic to be thirty again — was anyone ever so young? — and I didn't like to envy him. It must have been after the first of July, because he reached over and undid a button on my shirt. We were on the grass, and there was a row of tangerine poppies, open wide, all around the sundial. It was the poppies, in fact, that brought the gardener up.

"He's a kid," David said, finishing the gardener off. The gardener was twenty-six or twenty-eight, so that in one way it didn't make any sense. But David felt a good deal older because he thought he was so wise. He thought so because he had slept around a lot.

But to go back to the night the summer began in earnest: David came down the tower stairs two at a time, calling out as he passed her door on the second floor, "I'll be there in a minute, Mrs. Carroll." In the kitchen he had to turn the lights on, and he guessed it was later than he thought. He was glad the daylight lingered high up in the tower. He had already set out the linen and the heavy service on the bed tray. From the refrigerator he took a tomato he had stuffed with chicken salad and laid it on a bed of lettuce. A sliced egg. A glass of Pinot Chardonnay. A finger bowl. Mrs. Carroll was not given to toast and tea. At eighty-two, she was down to one glass of wine a day and a single cigarette, but she enjoyed them extravagantly. Even David, who had never smoked, would take a Gitane when she offered him one. And they would sit there in the smoke and get stoned as the night fell.

Properly decked out, the tray weighed about fifteen pounds. David staggered across the kitchen and through the swing door, reeling under the weight of it. Damn the gardener, he thought. David had been slow and subtle about seducing him, arranging to bump into him when they came around corners, setting up a chance to talk in the potting shed, say, or out by the hedges. David loved the courting dance. He spaced the ceremony out over several days, so that he watched it happen when it dawned on the gardener what David was getting at. David was ready at just that stroke of the late afternoon to drop to his knees and undo the gardener's pants. And so they went on up to the tower. Now David thought he would have made a pass the very first day if he had known they would stop at two hours' coupling.

Not that David had wanted anything permanent, he was quick to assure me. He was afraid he didn't have the strength to get serious. Or he didn't believe in it anymore. Like all fanatics and the more professional lovers, David was always changing and refining his beliefs. He suffered as well from sudden conversions.

"And it wasn't just him," David said. "He reminded me of someone I always thought I should have slept with."

"Go ahead," I said, though I was tensed to hear only one thing now, what it must have been like to come upon the dead woman with no warning. But everything about David entails a story, and he seemed to feel that he couldn't get to the body in the four-poster before he had gotten it exactly right about the gardener. David always tells too much of a story. It is as if the accretion of detail itself will settle the problem of motive. He likes to feel that he is held in the grip of his life, and not the other way around.

The gardener, John, reminded David of a brief and long-gone man he had never gone far enough with — the elevator operator in the Hollywood Roosevelt Hotel on the six-to-two shift. David used to stare at him from behind as they went up and down eight floors. David had gotten himself entangled with a television writer who had lived on the eighth floor since 1961, who looked like he had never left his room in all that time and who said he *lived* in New York, whether anyone asked or not. David hung around for about three weeks, and he would size up this lean and smoky elevator type on his way down to the lobby for cigarettes. He would lean against something or other, a stucco palm, and light a cigarette and stare at the man as he stood at ease, waiting for a fare. In his brown and orange, lightly braided uniform, he looked half like an organ-grinder's monkey and half like a colonel in a banana republic.

This had gone on for days and days, and David was fairly sure that the elevator man had lost his heart to him; but he didn't know what to suggest. This was not like a taxicab, after all, which you could pull in under a viaduct for ten or fifteen minutes in the backseat, the meter still running. The Hollywood Roosevelt Hotel would miss an elevator that took a fifteen-minute break. And yet that is what the elevator man must have been suggesting. It was a Tuesday night, about eleven o'clock, and David had been walking in the Hollywood hills with his hands in his pockets, feeling the weight of the fifties he thought he would never shake. He gave the colonel a surly look as he got into the elevator.

"Eight," he said, for about the thousandth time.

They started up. David slouched at the back of the car. After three or four floors or so, the elevator man flexed his shoulders against his monkey jacket and turned around. Staring back at David for the first time, he reached up and flicked the STOP switch. It was just the two of them now. He unzipped his fly and reached into his pants while David waited politely, settling in for a mad heat, his eyes narrowing. And then out of the uniform came this tiny button of a cock, about the size of the first joint of David's thumb. The elevator man grinned and kind of held it out, although of course it wouldn't come out very far and was as soft as a gumdrop. David shook his head no and stared as well as he could into the middle distance while the elevator man got dressed and got them going again.

He felt terrible. He knew he would have jumped at it if it had been as big as the uniform and the punky style had led him to believe. He didn't like to lead people on and then not deliver, and he thought he should try to say something nice so as to end things nicely. Except not *too* nice, or else he would be leading him on again. And here they were, at the eighth floor already. David passed out of the elevator and turned.

"I've thought who it is you remind me of." He paused for effect, but there *was* no effect. "Cornel Wilde. It's been at the tip of my tongue ever since I saw you."

Nothing happened. The doors closed on the elevator man staring into the middle distance, and the elevator started down. David stood in the eighth-floor hall, wondering where it had all gone wrong. He wondered still, lying in a damp swirl of summer sheets in the tower bedroom. Perhaps, he thought now, he had made the mistake of thinking that every faggot in LA wanted to know who he looked like. Perhaps he had just said the wrong name. The gardener certainly didn't look a bit like Cornel Wilde. He was, however, just the right size.

So, in a sense, it had taken him years to go to bed with the gardener, but it didn't feel as if he'd tied the past up after all. If the gardener looked like the elevator man, it was only a trick that the past played on the present, to prove to him he shouldn't make love to men who were merely beautiful. He wondered why he was so depressed. He paused for a moment on the landing, propped the tray on the banister, and stared out the great hall window at the stone pool in the rose garden. As time went on, he thought, he was coming to feel that the past he had accumulated was a set of evasions. Even today he was thought-less and young, wishing the gardener had loved him back. And he was doomed to feel, day after day, that today he was better and wiser, when it only turned out to be time for the next wrong move.

Oh, he thought as he heaved the tray up again, I should never get laid at dusk. I never get weepy late at night. I just turn over and go to sleep.

Expertly, he turned the doorknob and swept into Mrs. Carroll's bedroom. What always touched him about her at the dinner hour was her lady's disdain for the appearance of hunger. She greeted her dinner as a diverting surprise, as if the time had flown by since lunch and here she was, only half done with her letters. And she was very positive about David's hit-or-miss cooking. "Why, it looks a little bit like what cowboys eat," she said to him once as she peered at her stew, but she said it delightedly. And suddenly all that ended. He knew she was dead, the minute he saw her. He was that accustomed to her neatness and good cheer, and she looked as if someone had thrown her across the bed. It didn't occur to him that she might be sick or asleep. Even in pain or sleep she would have ar-ranged herself just so. She hadn't had anything to say about this.

She lay on her side, bone white, across the big bed, her arms outstretched among the books and papers she kept in piles on the port side of her mattress. Her little office, she called it. In the first moment, he learned everything he didn't know before about the fact of death. There was the pallor of the skin and the surrender of the muscles in the face. But David did not feel as frightened or as alien as he might have. She must have been reaching for something, he remembered thinking, when it happened. Or she had been reaching for something *because* it was happening. It had not taken long, he suspected, though that meant nothing next to how lonely it must have been.

How lonely it was, he thought. He carried the tray on over to the table and chaise in the bay window and set it down. He sat and absently began to eat, all the while glancing out the window at the last of the light and the gray water. He wasn't especially hungry, and he had enough sense of occasion to know that eating was fearfully out of place here. But he needed to feel the thin rim of the wine glass between his teeth, to sink the heavy fork into the tomato, brush the corners of his mouth with a damask napkin. It was weird to eat with the dead so near, so he made up for it by eating politely. If he was acting like the servant girl on the lady's day out, sneaking her lunch into the dining room to eat it with class, it was because the comforts of a fancy, high-born dinner were very real just then. Everything on that tray was substantial. It was ballast.

"Didn't you think you should do something?" I asked him.

"No," David said, a little too quickly, as if he had been expecting the question. "You see, I was so sure that something would be *done*. If I waited long enough."

I was furious at him all over again because he hadn't changed at all. He owed something to the occasion, more perhaps than he owed to Mrs. Carroll, who was past expecting much well before she died. But I didn't say anything. If I told David what I really thought, that he was a bastard and a coward, he would have shut up. So *I* shut up, since I had to know the story.

He sat there in the bay window, he said, wondering what he

was going to do. The question turned over and over in his mind all the time he was in the room. When he had played with his supper enough and finally had the presence of mind to listen to the question, he realized he meant what was he going to do about *him,* not about *her.* He switched on the reading lamp next to the chaise, and the ocean and the wide sky diminished as the light made shallow the space beyond the bay window. Phidias would know what to do. But he didn't make a move to call him. He had to decide first what *he* was going to do, before the chain of events that would attend Mrs. Carroll's passage into the earth took over. She was dead, after all, and it would only be a minute more.

He lay back on the chaise, cradling the glass of wine, and reached over and took a Gitane from the cigarette box on the windowsill. The only way he knew how to do it was to go through the story, starting at the beginning. He lit the cigarette. The story would tell him what to do. After all, the story had gotten him here. He had landed in Boston during the last week in April, in a snowstorm. He had been away five years, the last two in Miami, and he was so undone by the sudden end of him and Neil Macdonald that he instinctively fled to Boston, as if he were creeping home. Leaving Boston had been his watershed move, and yet he always swore he only left because of the weather. That is what he said in the beachy watering holes he landed in during those five years. Winter in Boston was ten months long, he would say, and spring and fall were parlor tricks. But when Neil threw him over for a toothy Cuban tennis pro, the white, whining Florida heat began to make him throw up. He took to going out only at dusk. Boston, with its tulip trees and fruit blooms aching for the first warm day, promised to be sober and pure. Better to weep for his lost youth, he thought, than for the likes of Neil Macdonald.

His real mistake was thinking his life was a story. When he

told me about him and Neil or him and the gardener, he introduced them as the supporting cast in an ongoing drama, like a TV series with guest stars. One of David's stories had ended just before he went to Miami, when he lived in the Hollywood Roosevelt with the writer. I heard about it when he called me from the LA airport, about to flee to Florida. But it was already behind him. He'd started a fresh page.

"Why Florida?" I asked him.

"The Pacific is too cold to swim in," he said. "The surf is too rough." And he wasn't sorry about the experience, because he had asked all the questions about television that he had been saving up.

So it is all something of a story. I have decided it is none of my business. To think your life is a story may be just the right illusion. What was more important was this: in all this talk of leaving Boston and coming back, he made no mention of me. He was talking fast, as if I might not notice. I noticed.

As soon as he walked off the plane in Boston, he said, he knew he had misinformed himself. The first bite of the wind brought back every sullen winter day he'd ever spent here. He walked through slush to a taxi stand, his bare toes frozen to his sandals. He had figured to stay at the Y and not make contact with anyone he knew for several days, not until he had a job and an apartment, neither of which he was going to be fussy about. But the weather rooted in his guts so fast that he decided he had to have a drink. He gave the driver the name of a gay bar on the west end of Beacon Hill. "Having a drink" was one way of putting it, but he really wanted what he always wanted when it snowed. He didn't care if anyone recognized him or not. And then, when several people did, wondering where he had been all this time, he cared too much. He had been wrong, he saw, to think his five years away had been a lifetime. They barely noticed he had been missing, and they knew he'd come back. It was just a half hour, but already he felt like he'd never been gone. Then he went home with a man who had a tattoo of Santa Claus on his right forearm.

The next morning, he saw that his tan had begun to shred off like eraser shavings. The tattooed man had gone to work and didn't care if David stayed. So he slept until noon, full of shrill morning dreams about Neil. Then he stood in the kitchen window, naked, and stared out at the gray sky and the ankle-deep snow. He picked up the *Globe*. He read the classifieds and found the same jobs listed that he couldn't get in Florida. Until he came to Mrs. Carroll, whose ad had a purple ring to it and seemed like a misplaced personal.

YOUNG MAN WANTED as live-in companion for an
old lady who doesn't want to be bothered. Come and go as
you please. Indiscretions and irregularities acceptable.

With a telephone number that turned out to connect him with Mrs. Carroll's lawyer, a Mr. Farley, who felt compelled to provide the job description with the rigors and good breeding the advertisement lacked. David agreed to everything. He knew the name of the town she lived in meant shorefront and what he called "megabucks," and that seemed the safest method of reentry after two years in a condo in Miami Beach. At least it was the same ocean.

"All I want to do is get through the summer," she told him on the day he arrived for an interview. "I came with Mr. Carroll to this glacier of a coast because I fell in love with it in June. The rest of the year it's like Poland. You don't like weather, do you?"

Oh no, he had said, and because she saw he was telling the truth under his flaky tan, she hired him. Now he thought: that is all I really wanted myself, to get through the summer. And now it didn't appear as if either of them would. Somehow it hadn't mattered when he lived in a place where summer went on and on. One always got through in the tropics by getting by. On gimlets, on Coppertone and Chapstick, on filmy Roman shirts unbuttoned to the belly. What he wouldn't give right now, he thought, for an air-chilled car on a hot, still night. He didn't know, as the image leapt at him, whether it meant he wanted to go back to the tropics — to Florida, say — or on to the next improbable harbor, set on a summer angle to the sun. He looked over at the dead woman and tried to think what he could do for her. Then he lay back and shut his eyes to keep from crying. He couldn't think of a thing.

He must have fallen asleep, because he knew it was late when he heard the knocking on the french doors. Ten o'clock. For all he knew, there was a law in Massachusetts that said you had to report a death within three hours. Because he was groggy from being asleep, it didn't seem odd at first that some-one was knocking at Mrs. Carroll's balcony doors. He had been enough of a servant long enough to feel that a knocked door had to be answered. He got up, stretched the muscles in his face and grimaced as he passed the mirror, trying to wipe the sleep away, and went toward the door.

"Beth," a voice called from the balcony, "are you there?" And David woke up and whirled around and saw the body again. This was someone Mrs. Carroll knew out there. Some-one who was going to get upset. I don't want all this to start so soon, David thought. Give me a minute more. He stood still, wishing the intruder away, determined to wait it out. Slowly he turned back to the doors and tried to see in the half-light how they were locked.

"Beth?" The voice was louder, the first ripple of panic rising in it. Then, suddenly, as if to prove that nothing would wait for very long, the doors opened toward David, and Phidias strode into the room.

"David?" he said, stopped in his tracks, and David could tell he knew something was wrong. But unlike David, he wasn't going to wish it away. For the second or two before he walked past and saw Mrs. Carroll on the bed, he stared into David's eyes and silently demanded to be told.

"Phidias, I was going to call you."

But David's moment had passed, and now Phidias had moved past him and stood at the foot of the bed and took it in. "Oh Beth," he said, and the mildness coming into his voice shamed David and shook him so that he began to cry. He turned to the bed and watched Phidias shake his white head as if to say no, his unbrushed hair as wild as a sailor's. Phidias seemed to mean, when he called out Mrs. Carroll's name, that he had to scold her first. Beth, why didn't you tell me, he seemed to be saying, at the same time saying that it was all right. As if she might feel guilty or sorry to go without a word. Death, Phidias made it clear, was something that had to be put in its place. Is *this* all it is, he seemed to say, that you're *dead?* He sat down on the bed and rested his hand on hers where it had disarranged a tidy stack of papers at the end. The intimacy of his touch lay in its lightness. His hand sought in hers its proper repose, and lightly he let it be known that nothing had changed.

"Were you with her, David?" he said. He was crying easily, and David wasn't.

"No. I came in with her dinner." David was standing at the dresser, his hand darting from one to another of the curios, the porcelain boxes and ivory brushes, the hand mirror face down on a folded scarf. He flushed as he looked over to the bay window, where Mrs. Carroll's dinner sat, half eaten.

"Did you know about us?"

Did he know *what*, David wondered. Then, when it dawned on him, he saw how far behind he was. He should have wondered from the first why Phidias came in from the balcony, up the spiral stairs from the garden. And why so late at night. David looked at the old sunburnt farmer and thought: the worst part is happening now. If Phidias was somehow her lover, then he, not David, was the most alone here. David had always survived by being the most alone in a given crisis. He had expected Phidias to help him, and he realized that he was not the one most in need of help. When he answered "No," he let out a sob, and he knew he was crying for himself.

"Well, now you do," Phidias said. "Will you leave us alone for a minute?" Mildly. As if to say: "I'll get back to you in a minute, David. Everything is going to be all right."

David went out through the french doors and pulled them closed. On the balcony he could look down on the garden court, the marshes, and the dark acres of the sea, but he stayed close to the door and looked up at the starred sky, his hands behind him gripping the door handles. He stopped crying almost at once. He still didn't know what he was going to do, but his release from the death-room had stopped the question whispering in his head. The silver polisher in him, the dustman and short-order cook, had been living day by day since he arrived at Mrs. Carroll's. And that, he promised himself, was what he was going to continue to do as long as he could. Finish up the night. Get up in the morning and see what had to be attended to. The present, he knew from practice, was all that was safe.

"I don't understand," I said, pillowing my head on my arms as I lay back and looked at the sky. The unexpected turnabout had already blurred the simple fact of Mrs. Carroll's death. It was hard to keep it in focus that, in the middle of this growing comedy of lovers, someone died. That is what David was trying to tell me, I suppose. I don't know why, but I got madder the more I knew.

"Why didn't you figure it out before?" I asked him. "That's the sort of thing you're good at."

"You mean I'm nosy and a gossip," he said tartly. "Just because you aren't."

"I didn't say it was bad. I've always said it. You have a real gift for other people's secret lives."

"Rick, what do you want from me?"

"Nothing. You said they were lovers. I don't understand. Why did they have to hide it from *you?*"

"They were *always* lovers. For fifty years or something. Their meeting at night didn't have anything to do with *me.* From the time they were young, they were together only at night, because Phidias had his work on the farm, and they both had families. Their being lovers was a whole extra life."

"They must have got by on next to no sleep," I said.

"Can you imagine?" David said, and for a moment he sounded as sad as the story might have been. "No wonder Mrs. Carroll took so many naps."

"It's the sort of thing people used to do."

So it happened that David had never seen Phidias and Mrs. Carroll together before. Phidias had run the dairy business before he retired. The work was done now by his three milk-fed, big-shouldered sons, and Phidias had moved on to become the overseer of the whole estate. Where once there had been a staff of eleven in the main house and a work force of thirty-five for the gardens and the cows, now there was only one here and one there, and Phidias had to keep it all together. Since there was so much of the Carroll place, no one else but him knew where anything was. So he was always putting his head in at the kitchen door, armed with his list of projects.

"Tell her," he would say to David, "that I've got someone coming to rewire the boathouse. Tell her the gray pickup is all wore out. My boys are going to junk it for parts."

David would make a mental note, and he passed it on when he went up with her lunch. Mrs. Carroll would not eat until this business was over. "Fine," she would say. "Ask him to leave me the literature on trucks. I told him that pickup was too cheap the day he bought it. Tell him I remember that. And ask him isn't it time we took down the boathouse. We won't be having any more boats, and it's an eyesore on the beach. He won't agree." And David would nod, knowing that Phidias would turn up at some point during the afternoon, and then he would relay Mrs. Carroll's answer.

Because he liked the two of them so much, it delighted him to be their go-between. He didn't know why they preferred to do it that way, but he had fallen in with enough British novels all rafted with servants and intrigues to know that it had *always* been done that way. As the weeks passed, the nuances of disdain and irony in their messages were as tidal as the sea limit that circled their land. Sometimes Phidias would send up a local irony with David on the lunch tray. "Tell her they voted at town meeting to thank her for the rhododendrons she put in the park. Now they want to know will she pay to have the Carroll fountain in front of the library sandblasted. Someone wrote SHIT on it two feet high."

And she said, "Tell him to say I have nothing against SHIT. Say we will negotiate if it ever comes to sexual organs, and not before."

Long ago, David decided on the balcony that night, a charade must have been worked out to establish the gulf between Phidias and Mrs. Carroll, and at some point the two of them had become infatuated by the charade. It was meant to fool the two families and the staff of eleven. It grew to outlive them. David felt how far away it was from anything he had been on the lookout for. When he settled in from Florida, he was so drained from the crying and accusations in Neil Macdonald's kitchen that he wouldn't have noticed if she'd been making it with a whole troupe of acrobats. He couldn't keep his mind on anything. Even Mrs. Carroll had fretted about him a couple of weeks before: "Don't be so harmless, David." What? "You can't survive," she said, "without ulterior motives. I think you ought to start stealing the silver instead of polishing it all day long."

He walked over to the spiral stair and sat down to wait for Phidias, resting his cheek on the cool wrought iron and looking down the beach. If they needed no ruse with David, who was suspicious only of himself, then they played the game for the game's sake. He wished he had known about them before now, if only so that he could have been a better go-between. It was too late to discover that the best thing he had been doing here was done for the two of them. Uninvolved himself, his days reduced to a seamless net of habits, he had gone about the business of taking him and Neil apart. He stopped the pain by ridding himself of love, and sure enough, he was improving. The gardener proved he was almost ready, give or take a pang, to shiver at sex for its own sake. He could have used the secret Phidias and Mrs. Carroll kept, just to show what might be done with fifty years. If he was harmless, he decided, it was because he didn't believe in time. It required too much attention.

The balcony flooded with light as Phidias came out. He walked over to the railing and stood over David, taking in a long breath of the sea air.

"David," he said, "I'm going to tell you what I have to do." His voice was as strong as ever, even his irony somehow intact. "*You* don't have to do anything, but you have to know. I'm going to bury her on her own land. We discussed it, and I promised I would do that for her. She wasn't afraid to die" — as if that was beneath contempt — "but she was terrified of cemeteries and funerals. She thought all that was what hell was." He paused, locked in on every side by what he and Mrs. Carroll had come to at last. David was scared. Then for a moment Phidias spoke more distantly. "I think she was afraid I would die first, but she never said so. I make it sound like we *talked* about it. But even when you bring it up, you don't talk about it long. Whatever you say hurts."

"Won't they stop you?"

"Who? The police?"

"No. Her children. Mr. Farley. They'll say it's crazy."

"I'm not going to tell them, David." There was a touch of irritation in him now. David could see that there were a thousand impossible steps in this, but he understood right away that Phidias wasn't interested in hearing them. He was not so much irritated as bored. There was something he had to do, and that was that.

"Do you want me to help you?"

"Yes, David, but you don't have to."

"She hated her children."

"Every one of them. Because they come back at Christmas and tell her to sell off the land. They want her dead."

"And now they've won?" David asked, though he could see they hadn't, not yet.

"We'll see. Do you think it's crazy?"

"No."

"We didn't think you would."

We? In that case, it wasn't crazy, but it wasn't fair. They had been implicating him all along, deeper and deeper, and they never gave him a chance. Although they didn't mean it, they were demanding that he take a stand about love. He figured the one he had assumed with the gardener was good enough, because the pain was minimal. It would not do now. If he went along with Phidias, he would be face to face for a long time with this tenacious love of theirs. Then he might not be able to go back to his hard-won detachment. The jitters and the bad stomach would start again. They would bury her, and he would be no better off than he was the night he followed Neil and sat weeping silently under the tennis pro's window in Coral Gables, listening to the two of them inside. But somehow he felt he ought to trust the trap Mrs. Carroll had led him into. After all, he wasn't feeling harmless as the night wore on, and he wasn't scared anymore. The summer was not going. There was all of July and August yet.

"Tell me what to do," he said.

"Go to sleep if you can," Phidias said. "I want to sit with her tonight. In the morning we'll all go up into the woods."

"Okay. I know this isn't the time to ask you this, but I want to know more about you and her." I have a right to, he thought. He tried not to sound as if he were striking a bargain, but he was.

"Of course," Phidias said evenly, sizing him up. "Don't worry about the time. We'll have all the time we need."

"You don't know how much I need."

"No. I'm sorry, David. It's because I need it less and less. I just meant that the time will take care of itself."

"Say you don't get arrested," David persisted. "Somebody's going to turn things upside down eventually. Once we get it done, we have to start dealing with everybody *else*. That's all I'm trying to say. I don't even know who everybody else *is* — "

"We'll tell them when we're ready to," Phidias said. He was leaning on his elbows on the railing, and he seemed out of pain, through with it and on to something else. And though Mrs. Carroll was gone, she seemed intact in everything he said.

But *then* what, David thought. He said: "But how long can we wait?"

"As long as we need to, David. You have to stop thinking about that. Go to sleep."

Phidias walked back into Mrs. Carroll's room and shut the light in. David sat still for another minute. It was warm, and the breeze that blew about his face was temperate as a human breath. He couldn't have said why it happened now, but he felt the full summer break on him for the first time. The other summer that never seemed to come — the one he waited for and kept imagining, weeks of cold at either end, lit by the light of the long gray spring — had given way.

He savored the pace of things as he began to move. Leaving Mrs. Carroll to her proper witness, he spiraled down the stairs, walked across the terrace to the library, went through the cool and paneled hall and jogged up three flights to the tower. He opened all the windows and fell asleep in his clothes.

"But David," I said. "You never figured out what *you* were going to do."

"I know," he said. "It didn't seem the appropriate time anymore. I've put all that off till the end of the summer."

The other questions, then, were still in midair. What he was going to do about me. What I was going to do about him. Things as basic as this: whether or not you can just die and be done with it. Now that I knew what happened, I suddenly didn't know what anyone's motives were. That is why this is a story after all. It is about how we got through the summer.

2

I HAVE IT DOWN SOMEWHERE that David called me on the twenty-second of June. But I must be mistaken. Madeleine's performance was on Friday night, the twentieth, and David would have had to call the next day, because we drove down to the Carroll estate on Sunday, and *that* was the twenty-second. I may as well get the facts straight where I can. I don't understand yet, and here it is September, who was making plans at the beginning. Had any of us — perhaps *without* thinking — thought ahead quickly and led us to where we are now? I see that I wrote down the twenty-second because of David. He was twenty-two when I first met him; and now when I think of him, that is always the age he is in my head. Mothers must suffer from this.

I had been up most of the night when the phone rang. In the five years since he left Boston, since he left *me*, David had called perhaps three times a year, so I had gotten very good at it. But the calls always came at midnight, sometimes as late as two or three in the morning if he was drunk, stoned, or abandoned. At ten-thirty in the morning, I knew we were not dealing with long distance. I have succeeded in being what David

was trying to be after he left Florida, a man well rid of love.
David is nothing if not a lover and doesn't stand a chance of
coming to the steely place I sleep in. But I still shook when
David called. And I am not easy with local calls, no matter
who they're from.

"Where are you?"

"About twenty miles south of you. I've been here since the
spring. Rick, I have to ask you something."

"Where's Neil?"

"Florida. That's all over. Rick, I have to see you."

David always began by talking as if he were in the opening
episode of a soap opera. This had been true always, even when
we were together, because *his* lonely years had been a child's
years, high school and college, and he spent them in front of
the television. He knew what people said when they loved and
lost, or when they wanted something tawdry. The writer he
moved in with in Hollywood usually wrote medical dramas.
About alcohol and wife-beating and the like, where the doctors
are mostly in the wings. But I don't think, to be fair, that
David came by his manners in the Hollywood Roosevelt Hotel.
There is a feel for this sort of thing or there isn't. I was brought
up to say what I meant, and it had to be something serious. I
was given no more stories by my parents than David was, but I
played the piano and go now to the opera. David was given a
television of his own when he was fourteen. When he was
twenty-two and I met him, he lied the way a fourteen-year-old
lies. Now he was thirty and didn't think one way or another
about it, I suppose, but I made a dangerous mistake and relaxed. By the time you are thirty, I figured, you can at least
mean well when you lie.

"Can you come down here?"

"I can't," I said. "Someone's staying with me."

"Bring him."

"Her."

"I mean her. OK?"

"Is it very swanky and very pretty?"

"Yes."

"All right," I said. "We'll come on Sunday afternoon."

We said a good deal more than this, and we were gentle enough with one another. But he never said a thing about Mrs. Carroll, dead *or* alive. I had the impression, partly from knowing David and partly because of the way he *didn't* talk about where he was, that he had picked up with an older man, older even than I and very well heeled. I assumed he needed the sort of advice one needs when the closet is rainbowed with Gucci and Mr. Guy and the pool is warmer than the air. That was all right. Besides, Madeleine was in ruins and needed a day in the country.

"Madeleine, we've been invited to the South Shore tomorrow afternoon. I gather the arrangements are first class. Do you feel up to it?"

"Will they know me?" she asked absently.

"Maybe not. Maybe they're autistic."

"Sure. Let's go. When is my plane to LA?"

"Nine P.M. It's not even an hour away from here. We'll be back."

So we went. Madeleine had been with me for three days, and we both enjoyed them. She was the only houseguest I had anymore. I even found it a luxury to avoid the press, which she insisted on doing in the most flamboyant ways. She gave a single concert a year in Boston, and in thirteen years no one had ever succeeded in finding out how she got there and where she stayed. The Boston press has been slow about celebrity, though. There is no indication during any other week of Madeleine's extravagant year that there is a story to tell about her and me. Perhaps there isn't. Well, there is *now*, but in June, when she was just a day short of a flight home after thirty-two curtain calls in Boston, we had fallen into our old way of saying hello, calling ourselves survivors, and kissing good-bye. I see now we were not satisfied with that. Put another way, we weren't altogether sure we were surviving.

"How old are you?" she asked me.

"Forty-five. Do you know what you just said?"

"What?"

" 'How old *are* you?' You used to say 'How *old* are you.' Don't you think the shift in emphasis is sinister?"

"You're too sensitive," she said.

Madeleine says she does not like my car, an old Chevy convertible I cling to in one of my few mild protests against the corporate inevitable. She says I live like a one-lamb-chop secretary who tidies through life without making a ripple. And she moves me when she talks that way. One year I took her with me to the store and bought a blue velvet sofa to please her, around which I made resolutions to pull things together, but it was delivered after she left and was a shambles the next spring when she blew into town again. I am moved to do something for *her*, not for me. Her years of private planes and sloops, the beach properties in Malibu and Puerto Vallarta, are behind her. She should live like a countess, but her career, like that of a high-roller financier, has peaked and valleyed. I don't blame her for preferring the days of the sealskin slipcovers in the custom touring car.

Not that she complains. She lives all right in her seventy-fourth year. (The figure is an approximation, of course. I am right about how old the rest of us are, but none of the rest of us has tampered with the evidence. That urge comes later in life, I expect, though it has been stirring in me too for the first time, on bright sunny days all summer.) I bet she makes fifty thousand a year, and she doesn't have to make more than eight or ten appearances. The recordings are reissued, and she has lately had a careful manager, an elderly queen in LA named

Aldo who is a giant in computer softwares. I expect he turns to
jelly when she sings

> *I don't know who you are,*
> *I have no memory for men.*
> *Was it in Paris? No? New York?*
> *I've never been there at all,*
> *Is it as lonely as they say?*

The old recordings, the seventy-eights, sold seven or eight
million copies altogether, but she had lousy contracts and
managers who were bums and cleaned her out. They were not
even her lovers, as far as I know. They were like baby brothers. She is taken better care of now. The audience is smaller
but more intense, mostly gay, faithful as postulants, pande-
monium-prone when she does the bridge for this or that famous song. There might be as much as a hundred thousand a
year. But she doesn't make bids any longer at Swiss jewelry
auctions, and that upsets and saddens the faithful.

"You told me you didn't see David anymore," she said as we
threaded our way along the expressway. "Why don't you put
the top down?"

I pulled over. She was not accusing me of hiding anything
from her, but I think she was afraid I wasn't being honest with
myself. She knew all about him but had never met him. David
was the most important person from whom I hid the fact of
Madeleine's visits. In June I would tell him my mother was
coming for a weekend, and he fled gratefully from my apartment. If he returned and found a stray bottle of makeup, a
stocking or something, he would throw it away with a shiver.
Apprised of the fact that they belonged to Madeleine Cosquer,
there is no telling how fanatically he would have souvenired
them. David, unlike the Boston press, was as swift as a whippet

about celebrity and gossip. He would have skywritten the knowledge that Madeleine holed up in his lover's apartment during the weekend of her concert.

I was not being innocent in bringing Madeleine with me on my visit to David and his seamy sugar daddy. I knew he was going to faint with complexity when he met her. I didn't want to hurt him (though here I expect I am straining after innocence). I just wanted to break the set of his expectations about me. And Madeleine too seemed to understand that she was to be party to a showdown. For that reason as much as any, she had a right to ask about David. From all that I know about her life, I know she does not shirk a showdown, but she likes to be armed with the evidence to date.

"I have nothing to do with David," I said, snapping the folded top into place behind the backseat. "I haven't seen him since the day he walked out. I don't think about him anymore, even to hate him and wish him dead. It's all over. But he does call me sometimes. And now he's in Boston again. I said yes. I could have said no."

She was wrapped in a scarf and dark glasses and looked terrific because there was only the hint of Madeleine Cosquer in the shape of the head, and what it hinted at was how she looked in her youth, which lasted well into her sixties and which certain lights still caught. She looked at me as I got back into the car, listening for something else.

"You're testing yourself," she said. "I hope I provide the right diversion, because nobody ever passes that sort of test. Maybe I'll sing."

"I didn't think you sang a note anymore for under a couple of thousand an hour."

"You're being testy because I'm right. He's a bastard. I want you to come out of there alive."

I don't know why Madeleine was being so loyal, and I don't remember mentioning David more than two or three times to her, and those lightly. In any case, David is not a bastard, and I expected that she would find him delightful as long as he didn't go idiotic about her celebrity. But I see that I am cornered into talking about David and me. I can do that. It will help to explain what has been so alive in David during this summer when he finally stopped running. It is *I* whom I would rather leave out, I know. But if I do that, I expect I would be trying to say, to *believe* really, that I have not been involved. And I am as guilty of having loved us all — David, Madeleine, Phidias, and Aldo — as any of us.

I am forty-five, and I have lived in Boston during all of my adult life. I inherited some money early, more than was good for me, and I came to the city from my drunken, monkish home on the North Shore and began to make love. (I have to draw the line somewhere, so I am not going to drag my parents in, nor anyone else's. In one way, gay men are forever in the grip of their fathers' wishes and their mothers' lonely afternoons. More truly, though, they have no parents at all, or their parents are ghosts, like the children they never father.) That is all I really did for fifteen years. There was a time when there wasn't a man in Boston I hadn't slept with, though of course it only seemed that way. Of a certain *kind* of man — thoroughbred, beautiful, hard — I had my fill. I felt discriminating and in control. To be more accurate, then, there was a time when I had cruised every gay man in Boston and either slept with him or looked through him and let him know I was after better things. It didn't make me feel trapped or played out that I knew everyone who was gay and good in bed. I was alert and sexy every night about what might turn up in the bars I drank in, and I always took the first or second turn with anyone fine and ripe who did turn up.

I make it sound at if I were always rid of love, and that is one way of putting it. But fifteen years lived in units of one or two nights go very quickly, like a string of weekends. Heady

Friday nights, the calm and aimless hours of a long Saturday, and then the head-on rush to Sunday night, blank and pointless. We all fall into time. To understand how a gay man executes his fall into the day-by-day, one must try to see how wildly he falls in love with his own body, once it becomes his own. Sex is self-inflicted for so long, and a gay man burns to carry out in lust the years he lost to guilt and shame. Fifteen years seems long and tenacious, but in the end it really didn't take. David showed up.

And for a few years, love won. It is not that David and I spent an uninterrupted time together. He ran away a dozen times, and he brought home half-wit numbers who fucked him in my bed. But for a few years the quality of the affection was steady in me. I mean that. And on the Sunday in June when Madeleine and I drove off to our new survival, on that perfect sea day when the Band-Aid-beige Chevy zinged along like a sloop itself, those three and a half years had been balanced by the five years since. Loveless and pure. My bed blissfully empty, like my mailbox, unlike my bank account. I believed I was testing David, not myself, and I believed I was doing it for his own good. It has not proven to make any difference because, as Madeleine says, these tests are all loaded, and so one feels guilty and lets the other fellow win.

I met David on horseback at Sea Island, Georgia. I had driven down from Boston with two men I had met a few days earlier at a bad party. They were lovers, more or less, and they had taken me onto the terrace and brought from among their toys a vial of cocaine. Even aspirin gives me a headache; but I will go to considerable lengths, usually three-quarters of the way through a fifth of Dewar's, to wall myself away from a holiday of faggots. My head had an aerial view of things, like a kite strung out from my body. It seemed like a marvelous idea to pack us all three into my gleaming Chevy, put the top down, and head south on a real holiday. (I see there is bound to be an arc in everything. The fawn-colored Chevy was just bought, and it possessed its body as wholly as I did mine. But see, I am a man of reversals. The newer things were then, the less complicated they seemed. General Motors, far from being a bandit then, was more like the tooth fairy.) They wanted me to make love to both of them. The widowed mother of one had abandoned her Georgia house for even warmer waters because the dead father haunted its tiled halls in his banker's grays. The son did not suffer the same ghosts as long as he arrived armed with a lover and a stud.

I don't care about the sea. I let them go off sailing by themselves during the day, and they were that much more ready to court me at night. I had a chestnut horse. I dressed in high riding boots ($200. Their gift. The boots must have danced in their heads while they sailed) and my beloved Levi's, and the feeling was very like being naked. Better even, like being naked in bed. The Easter sun was hot at midmorning. I rode north on the sand to the preserve at the upper third of the island; and when the houses fronting the water stopped, the jungle began in earnest. Pelicans flew low over the sea, and the herons perked their heads up in the marshes. There was talk of deer playing and chasing on the beach this far away, but I never saw any. Nor any people, until the morning I saw David standing naked in a foot of water, in a tidal pool.

We came around a spit of land where the view was blocked by a high tangle of rushes. He was about a hundred yards from me, facing away, and he didn't hear us approach for a long time. I have thought long about the length of that moment. I have extended it in my head, the coming together of the rider and the shipwrecked boy, and slowed it down until it is a set of stills. Only the horse moved, and David and I were frozen there, hanging back as long as we could in separate spaces. I don't know how to tell it offhandedly. I was, after all, caught unprepared for the end of my fifteen years. And yet I didn't think of turning back because there wasn't enough *time*. That is the long and the short of it, but how do you figure it? Every spring when I go to see *Casablanca* in Harvard Square, I think about how long Bogart and Bergman hold each other's eyes on the edge of the tarmac. It gets longer every year. That is what I mean.

Burnt and brown, his hair gold and stiff with salt, he seemed nearly a sea creature — ambiguous, amphibious. Something in him rose out of the water in the morning to bask in the sun, and something else detached itself from the jungle and came down to cool its heels in the surf. What brought him back to earth was the luminous band of flesh that girdled his ass, where he slung himself into a bathing suit on those days when he could not cavort like a wild boy. The body's whitest flesh, withheld from the body's turn to summer until the body's dreams and needs uncover it. I can't talk about this. I think: if I can bring it into words, I can know exactly what he was and put him to rest in me at last. But he has always been for me a creature of two worlds. My cock swelled against the saddle because of the given of David's flesh, the full white curve behind and then, as he turned, the reach and sway of his own cock. That was as it had been for fifteen years. But the clash of myths, the sea-god taken by the cowboy, aroused in me the will to break the mirror that two men who couple become. Be something with me, I thought as I came up to him. What I called love was measured in minutes. When David turned and squinted at the sun that rode toward noon behind my head, he tipped me over into the world of years. I have lasted so long, I thought. But for all that I had held out, now I could not go back.

As I rode closer, we looked hard at one another and established right away what sort of men we were. He walked out of the water to meet me, his eyes still locked on mine, a half-smile coming and going on his face. When we met, he brushed his shoulder against the horse's neck and reached his hand up and drew it along the front of my thigh, letting it rest on my knee.

"I thought this island was exclusive," he said. "I thought you had to sit on a corporation to live here. Unless you're married to someone who does."

I leaned my bent knee away from the horse, and his hand dropped between my leg and the horse's flesh. I watched his cock begin to lift.

"Do you sit on a corporation?" I asked.

"No," David said. "And I'm not married."

"Then I guess we're both stowaways on this island."

"Good. We'd better stick together and make a plan. There may be bounty hunters."

I dismounted and stood facing him. I pulled him close, and we rubbed against each other. Then he undid the buttons on my pants, licking at the hair on my chest. As he slipped the Levi's halfway down my thighs, he reached his hand around my cock and held it out tense, so that the pressure of his holding it doubled the heat of it as it swelled. Then he dropped to his knees and began to suck me. I gripped his head in my hands and brought myself farther and farther in as his mouth went up and down and he opened his throat. Then he pulled back, shook my hands from his head and, grabbing my wrists, fell back into the sand. I came down hard on the beach next to him, and we kissed and groped until he pulled back again.

"Get naked," he said. He lay back and put his hands behind his head to watch me. I had to stand up to take my boots off; and as I hopped on one foot, I looked up to see the horse cropping at the marsh grass. I threw one boot down and began to pull at the other. No more than a moment could have passed. But this time when I glanced over to the horse, there were deer all around him. Perhaps a half dozen, their eyes riveted on me to see what I would do. I couldn't believe they had come so close, fifty feet from us, without making any noise. And I remember being happy and wanting to laugh that they and the horse stood the same ground and caused one another no trouble. I held them there as I took off my pants, or they let me think so. It is probably the only time I have ever slipped off a pair of Levi's in front of a waiting lover without making some show of it. I tried to think of what to say, to tell David to sit up and look, when just as suddenly they leapt away in a single motion and were gone into the woods. So I looked down at David and saw, falling to his side again, that the time to tell it would have to wait.

I turned him over. He gasped as I inched into him, and I held him tight around the chest as we lay connected. And we heaved and buckled on the beach, rolling about as we began to feel there was no limit to the space we had happened on. Our legs splashed in the tidal pool. At last, still inside him, I hunched back on my knees and rotated him slowly on my cock, bringing him all the way round so that he faced me. When he came, he wiped the cum from his stomach and held his wet hand against my mouth, and the first smoky taste of it took me over the edge. I came staring into the sun.

In the quiet that followed, we exchanged names, keeping things in the odd order of gay love. But I have said enough about love. Once started, of course, I could flesh out in detail all the succeeding passions of that day on the beach, but I can see too that I have to *stop* talking about David and me as well, although I am perverse and find myself now reluctant to. But here is the skeleton of the flight from Georgia. David was staying at Sea Island with the mousy, clean-handed dean of his college, a closet case who had invited David there during the spring break of his senior year. Not to fuck him. Just to see him stripped down to a bathing suit. David understood the bargain he had struck and knew that he could cheat as well. So he spent his naked days miles from the house of the longing queen and came back late, giving the dean only the briefest glimpse of his dark and loaded body as he slipped into his room to dress for dinner. If David seems here like a mean whore, like the bastard Madeleine took him for, it has less to do with him than with the business of gay life. In one of the crueler customs of that country, the men who have made it out of the closet walk all over the men who stay in. It is the *closet* they are raging at; but the college deans and the priests and the live-in sons, paralyzed by their hidden wish, get beaten because they are in the way.

We rode back together in the late afternoon, David holding on behind me, his head resting on my shoulder. I tethered the horse at the front gate of the house, leaving it to my cocained sailors to lead him back up-island to the stables. I threw what little I had into the backseat of the Chevy, and David and I drove over to the dean's little cottage. I do not know what David would have said, but there was no occasion to explain, because the dean was fast asleep, getting through the day until David came back. While David packed, I stood in the kitchen door and waited. The dean had baked a cake and frosted it. He had arranged a tropical bouquet on the kitchen table. On a wheeled table, a clutter of bottles and glasses attended the cocktail hour, when he would unveil an intricate plate of hors d'oeuvres and lead the way to the terrace.

We drove all night and stopped along the road to make love at dawn, in North Carolina I think. I held back about mentioning the deer and have kept it a secret after all. I think now that I wanted something wholly my own out of that enormous act of change. They had waited in a circle around my horse to see what I would do, and because they ran when they did, they never found out. I know I have kept them to myself for my own reasons, but I have been true to their modesty as well. The deer have stayed free in my heart for knowing when to go. I knew I was doing the opposite. I gave up my freedom freely. You know that without knowing why, and you drive for a day and a half up the East Coast to see if it will come clear. It doesn't. But by then you are home, and you think you can accommodate the changes. There, after all, is your own bed in your own room. You've been *there* before.

"Madeleine," I said, coming out of a silence in which I tried to see what Madeleine wanted to warn me of, *couldn't* see it, and started to shake. "I haven't had a very easy year."

"Rick, I don't think you ever do."

"This is different."

"Is it?" she asked, sharper than she wanted to, or sharper than we are accustomed to, she and I. "Ever since that boy left, you've suffered like a goddamned widow. When the pain went away a little, you got angry. For years you've been trying to prove the pain is different for you. But it isn't."

I steered straight. My hands stopped shaking on the steering wheel. In *Bad Dream*, in 1931, Madeleine gets into a taxi at the Place de l'Opéra; she is leaving Charles Boyer for the last time, except he doesn't know it. "I'm out of cigarettes," she says through the window, and he takes out his case and offers her one, and then he lights it. The taxi driver seems to know that the scene is not over yet. "You know, Philippe," she says through the smoke, "I haven't been a woman for two years now." She means she has been a whore. "I feel so happy when I'm with you, but when I'm not, I feel like a widow. I have a dream where I open my closets and the clothes are all black." The cab drives off. Boyer is going to tell his wife tonight that he is leaving her, and he is going to meet Madeleine at the train tomorrow morning. But we already know she is on the way to the station now. It cannot be. And so I didn't expect to win this argument with Madeleine, but I had it out anyway. I wanted the warning where I could hear it plain.

"Then you think David is dead for me, and I just cling to it out of pride. But if there's nothing there, why are you so worried about me seeing him again?"

"Oh Rick, because you want the pain *back*."

"Well, then help me."

"I will."

"Sing if you have to."

We had been driving south for forty-five minutes, and we had just turned off the main road. For a long time the highway had seemed to parallel the sea, edging a marsh at one point, blowing here and there with a sea wind. But now we had come into deep forest, the sea nowhere near. I do not like woods at all, and I have twice been trapped in the brute meeting of forest and rocky surf, once in Maine and once in Oregon. I have not revisited either friend who tricked me there. Madeleine was right that I was being testy, and I was probably doomed to feel alien on Mrs. Carroll's land, even if it had turned out to be Capri. But a narrow, tedious little Massachusetts beach was what I was hoping for. Imagine my relief when we nosed out of the woods and drove among the fields of the Carroll dairy. A couple of wide machines were busying up and down, doing the first haying, and the smell of grass was overwhelming. I saw plain, dumb cows in all directions. The pressure of the woods lifted, and I felt light and perky as we turned through the great stone gate and began to move across the fields toward the dairy.

"Rick?" There was something unexpected in Madeleine's voice, as if she were rearranging the songs for a midnight show. "Have you ever been here before?"

"No, dear. No one ever invites me to the country. Can you bear how pastoral it is?" A dairy, I thought. What can go wrong at a dairy?

"I know this place."

"From where?"

"I stayed here."

"When?" I asked. Most of Madeleine's life is public record. It is safest to assume, for any given month of any given year, that if Madeleine is not making a film or doing a nightclub tour, then she is vacationing in certain given places. In Monaco or Rio, Baden-Baden, Mykonos. Not in a starchy sea town off Route 3.

"In the war. An American woman I met in Paris, just after the war. I was out of money. I had to get back to Hollywood, but I was sick. She brought me here for a while."

"Was the name Carroll?"

"Yes. Beth Carroll. Is she still here?"

"I don't know."

Having crossed the fields, we drove among bleaching, rose-colored cow-barns and found ourselves in a kind of square surrounded by garages and the farmers' houses. Larger than a farmyard, and more formal, more architected. It was paved with gray flagstones, and the watering trough in the center circled a stone fountain. Like a little village — and from one screen door a woman with a face deadened by Novocain stared out at us. We were not fired upon. But unless David was shacking up with a sweaty farm boy, it was not clear how we were supposed to proceed.

"You go through that arch, Rick," Madeleine said, pointing between two houses.

"Wait a minute, Madeleine. When did you last see this woman?"

She turned to me and took off her glasses. As she often does, she lowered her eyelids by a fraction to get the effect of irony and disbelief that other people get by lifting an eyebrow. As if to say: I know people ask questions as stupid as this, but when did *you* start doing it?

"The morning I left. We weren't having a good time anymore. As I recall, we stood outside the garage. I wanted to go for a drive, and she said I couldn't go out in the car without the chauffeur. If it hadn't been that, it would have been something else. I picked up a shovel and swung it and cracked the wind-shield. It was a Mercedes."

"Oh." Lovers. I am not in the habit of being dumb about Madeleine's women friends. Sometimes there has been a secre-tary or companion who has remained with her for several months, but for the most part she and her lovers have touched glasses and passed on. She is a solitary woman who does not always keep her distance but who always knows how much she is keeping it or letting it go. She has had two husbands, neither of whom knew her very well, though she loved them after a fashion. She has had at least one friend, me, a decidedly mixed blessing. And then there have been the people she has simply *known*, as different as her escorts at chemin de fer in weary little casinos and the refugees she smuggled out of bomb zones in her entourage. The women she loved have constituted her most truly private life; and that, I think, is why they had to be left behind. Madeleine has not been evasive about being gay, though the world has chosen not to notice. But she has lived her life as a continuous international event, a kind of cultural touchstone, and has never had the time to love at length. She could not otherwise have become, in the rarefied company of stars that go on from sky to night sky — Garbo and Piaf and Marlene — the type of a woman in love. Her beauty endures hand in hand with her sense of the irony in this.

There is some truth in what I've said, and it is what I be-lieved in June, believing that it showed how much I *appreciate* Madeleine. But I have buried the truth in left-handed compli-ments. My insights about her have been colored by my own clock of a heart, which still ticked in June and didn't feel and was the size of a river-washed stone that fits in your pocket. The women she loved were not half-loved. I can sing you (badly) every song she has ever done, but it is as if I have not listened at all.

I know you much too well
To love you like a girl.
It isn't right,
But every night
I grow a little old
Just knowing you.

I am sure I heard that song first on the radio from my cradle (Madeleine, forgive me), but I heard it last on the Friday night before we came here. It was the encore in the middle of the thirty-two curtain calls. The truth does lie in time, as the song makes clear, but it is both harder and more life-giving than I have said.

"She could make you laugh about anything," Madeleine said. "I hope she's there. You'll like her."

I drove on through the arch and out of the village, and from there the road swept down through more fields, crossed a wooden bridge over a trickle of a stream, and went up again, perversely, into deep woods. The house would after all be in the woods and on the rocks, I thought, and then realized I could ask Madeleine all about it. But she seemed given over to her own memories. I kept quiet. To touch wood, I said again to myself that only the mildest things could happen so close to a dairy. Madeleine took off her scarf and stowed it in the bag she carried. Then she made herself up, her hands at her face working with the concentration and abandon of an old clown making himself happy. Madeleine has beautiful skin, and I never feel she uses makeup to cover anything up. (As far as *that* goes, she has worked from the inside out. When she last had money, she had a lift of the face and of the thighs, and she has done Switzerland for monkey glands and drunk the vivid waters of countless secret springs, most recently in Nepal.) She just touched her face with a fat brush that she powdered up on a palette whose dozen colors seemed all the same to me. A pencil at the eyes. A fingertip of burgundy rouge smoothed over the lips.

Mind you, she does this so well that she does this while we are driving. I do not tell her to mind the bumps on the wooden bridge. She has made up in tanks in North Africa. In bunkers between bombs. They say that when Renoir was old and arthritis had frozen his fingers, his model would arrive at the studio in the morning and strap the brush to the painter's hand. It is done with the wrists, he would say, not the fingers. I do not know how painting is done. But I bet it becomes like breathing for those who endure. Second nature. Much of Madeleine's life was lived by this sixth sense. She had done her own face in films before there were makeup men, and when the labor law required that she finally submit to one, he became a kind of consultant only. I don't think he ever touched her face.

As we came up into woods again, she reached over and tapped my arm and said, "We're almost there. Brace yourself, Rick. It's very lonely." The pines oppressed me. But just when I thought I would scream at the pines' dead-needle floor and the toothpaste smell, Madeleine saved me. Her perfume was the final scene. She brought out a crystal flagon and drew the stopper. Even in a convertible in the wilderness, it blew my way like a garden in full flower. This is the formula Patou made for Madeleine in the thirties, and it is locked in a Swiss vault or something. The story goes that she left behind a small valise full of silk stockings when she sang for the liberation army in 1944. A bottle of the Patou was packed inside. The valise became a good-luck charm for the advancing army, and it was passed from company to company. It was so thrown about that the perfume finally leaked all over the stockings. In the last days of the war, an American general got hold of the cache, and he passed out the stockings one by one as medals or battle ribbons to his bravest men. I don't know how it was done, whether he draped the stocking around the neck or balled it up and threw it in a soldier's tent. But the story survives.

The woods thinned, and we could see the house now, perched above the marsh on one side and the dunes on the other. As we approached the garden court, I saw David sitting on the bottom of the spiral stair, his head in his hands. He was hardly dressed, which wasn't fair. He stood up, and he was wearing cut-off jeans and was no longer a fawn, not any sort of boy at all. "Oh my God," Madeleine said, by which she meant he was beautiful. No, I wanted to say, or yes, but he is not the same. Now I was warning myself, and fast, as we pulled to a stop a moment away from him and he came forward smiling. Of course, I thought, of course he is older now, that goes without saying. But with me, if something goes without saying, it goes without seeing. He *was* beautiful, with the full, musky beauty of a grown man. I wanted him. And in the instant before he spoke and began to bring me home, I wanted only him and gave up gladly the boy he was.

"If it had been another car," he said, "I would have blown the whistle."

"I keep it as a souvenir," I said.

He leaned on his elbow along the top rim of the windshield and looked down at us. His chest, once flat and clear, was dusted lightly now with hair, and the muscles were firm. He nodded at Madeleine and smiled what I suspected was a Florida smile. He was doing too good a job of not registering who she was.

"Madeleine Cosquer," I said, "David Rowland," pointing them out to each other, thinking that the two names had finally come together with a click, like billiard balls. But I did not understand what David was doing.

"I hope you'll let us wait on you hand and foot," he said in a breezy voice. "You deserve it after Friday night."

"Were you there?" Madeleine said.

"No, but the news travels. I heard you in Las Vegas three years ago. It was wonderful."

"It was all right," she said. "I hesitate to ask what you were doing at the Desert Inn."

"I was up to no good."

She tipped her head back and let out a short laugh. She often laughs in single syllables. I sat stupidly, one hand still on the steering wheel, as if I planned to drive on.

"But look at you," she said to him. "A man would be crazy to be good if he could look like you instead. I'd better warn Beth Carroll. I'm sure she's never been to Vegas."

Madeleine seemed to double the bet as she threw the dice. She didn't mind him coming on strong. She rather liked it. All the same, she had to show her own armies. She told me later that, since he chose to appear like a naked hustler, she decided to find out how much he was hustling for. He didn't stammer or say gosh, but he lost five years of savvy in an instant. He glanced at me and then looked down.

"I'm sorry, Miss Cosquer. Mrs. Carroll's dead. She died last Monday night."

"I see. Suddenly?"

"Yes. It was a heart attack, I think. Phidias says it was old age."

"She must have been nearly eighty-five. I should be sorry for *you* if you think there's anything sad in that." She spoke easily, willing to go where the road led, the surprises of the last half hour taken in stride. So David seemed to know about Madeleine and Mrs. Carroll; and, since I had just been told myself, he had known it longer than I. I didn't know what might happen now, but I was not getting anywhere sitting still. These two were chatting like neighbors over a garden fence.

"Who is Phidias?" I said.

"He runs the place," Madeleine answered, a little chagrined

that I was not keeping up. "Right, David? He'll live to be two hundred. Where is he?"

"Oh, he's around," David said. "Why don't you come in and we'll have lunch. Someone will bring us horses, Rick, if you want to ride."

He smiled at me a little shyly. There may be monstrous subterranean motives here, I thought, but he is also trying to make peace and do things right. Madeleine seemed so well and so in touch with the past that it seemed wrong not to risk the intricacies of the afternoon. We got out of the car, and Madeleine came around and took each of us by one arm and walked us across the terrace to the library doors. She squeezed my arm. David opened the doors, and we came into the cool room.

"When I was here," Madeleine said, "you never knew where you were going to have lunch. Beth would have a picnic set in the summer house, or out in the woods somewhere. You couldn't second-guess her. We always met here at one for drinks, and then she would tell."

"Would you like a drink?" David asked.

"No no," Madeleine said. "Some mineral water perhaps."

"Rick?"

"Scotch," I said. He knew what I drank and when, but he was a little displaced, a little strained at finding Madeleine so possessed of the place. It delighted me. But by the time I had my drink in hand, I decided the strain had more to do with his perception of me, and I wanted to comfort him. They sounded like they could small-talk all day. Meanwhile, David clearly wanted Madeleine as an ally. He had guessed how angry and locked in I was liable to be, and he was hoping she would intercede for him. Little did he know how predisposed she was to pick him apart for my sake. I felt with a pang how much *I* wanted to be his ally against my anger. I was all Jekyll and Hyde as usual. And it made me want to cry to be in the same room with the two people who understood best how helplessly I werewolved between my angel and my demon. Oh David, I thought, let me know fast how much time you've planned for you and me. Enough for me to rattle around in my rage, or more than enough, in which case nothing will be the same. Because here I am, the man for whom everything is exactly the same. I dare you.

"I'll bet you've set us a formal lunch," Madeleine said to him as I clicked my glass against my teeth and studied the spines on a set of Dickens. "In the dining room, with the Spode and the Baccarat and the Belgian linen. We're going to have our lunch in a magazine, aren't we?"

"Actually," he said, wet to the skin with Madeleine's irony, "I set us up on the front porch, above the dunes."

"Why, that's my favorite place."

"I know."

She had to admire his persistence. She smiled to let him know he had gained the point, then turned to me.

"Rick? Do you want something to read with your lunch?"

"No, dear," I said. "I'm going to be witty and riveting. I'm going to thrall you both with the tale of my adventures in the Vale of Kashmir."

"It's not a love story, is it?"

"No."

"I knew it." She came up close to me and took my arm again. "That's what I love about you, Rick. You're the only man left with any discretion."

David stood waiting, as lovely as a statue. Madeleine led me over to him. And the right question finally came to me: *how had he known Madeleine would be with me?*

"I guess we're all ready," she said to David. "Should we take off our clothes, or are you going to put some on?"

He grinned at me, and I cracked a smile in return. Somehow we had all three caught up with one another. It is something to discover that you have had the good fortune to be marooned with people who are old enough to be ironic. Then, if things go one way, you have fun. If they don't, you get very, very sad. But no one is going to get hurt.

"I'll get a shirt," David said.

"Well, hurry," Madeleine said. "We're starved."

3

PHIDIAS ARRIVED the instant the last fork was laid down. David and I had nominally split the bottle of wine, but I was deferred to every time he poured, and so I bloomed with the good fellowship of an afternoon drunk. Incredibly, David had succeeded in getting Madeleine to talk about her films. How the boy *studies*. He knew the budgets and the cameramen, the locations, the wardrobe changes, even the problems with the nuns in the Hays office. Madeleine rewarded him with anecdotes so ripe they fell off the trees and rolled in the summer grass, where the bees buzzed and sucked at them. We stripped bare her leading men, and we laughed as she squashed the ingenues one after another like grapes between her forefinger and thumb. It was a loose, delicious hour, and I was boozy with gratitude to Madeleine. I wasn't even afraid of having some time alone with David. But then I felt safe that it wasn't going to happen.

"So!" Madeleine cried as he came up the steps to the porch. "How long am I supposed to wait, Phidias?"

"One thing at a time, Madeleine," he said, smiling, folding his arms as he leaned back against the banister. "I wanted you to get your sea legs. And I see David is right — I *should* believe everything I read. You didn't get old."

"I am a miracle of modern science, Phidias. Anyway," she said, holding her hands up to frame her face, "some people say this is all a mask."

"What do they say is behind it?"

"Well, opinions differ. Some say the real me is mummified, and what you see is a sarcophagus. Others think I died long ago, and someone has replaced me with a doll."

"So it's all done with wires now."

"Yes. The ones who make me cry myself to sleep, though, say there is nothing behind it at all. They think I *do* look old."

"But you haven't started to listen to anyone else, have you?"

"No. If they get too close, I break their windshields."

This dialogue, rapid-fire and tough-guy, went very fast. It sounded like the scene where the detective is called in by the beauty to find her vanished, very rich husband. The detective and the beauty used to be a thing, and look at them now, not quite over one another. One can be exact about these things because Madeleine wisecracked her way through the very part in *Full House* in 1942. The film is not really part of the serious canon, but it is distinguished by the fact that she smokes about four packages of Camels during the course of events, and does not bat an eyelash when Robert Taylor, having found her out, shoots her from four feet away. She *never* talks this way in public, opting for yes and no and the riddle of her half-smile. She does talk this way to *me* if we are both in a good mood. But as she had not seen this man in thirty years, I couldn't believe she could begin again so furiously, as if in mid-sentence. No bullshit at all. You could tell, for instance, that neither of them had wasted any time in the intervening years missing one another.

There was a pause, and they eyed each other closely. They were gauging what waited to be said, and how long it might take at the rate they had chosen. The death of Mrs. Carroll was the project for this June afternoon, and yet neither of them appeared to feel trapped by it. If they could have been free instead to wander at will, they would have come up against Mrs. Carroll at every turn anyway. And they might have been much less willing, if she had still been alive in her curtained bed and they had found themselves alone together outside her hearing, to give over to each other the unique Mrs. Carroll each had known. If they had been too free, they would have remained tough-guys, very classy and very melancholy. Because she was dead, you could see in their clear-eyed look that they planned to hold nothing back.

"But you don't know my friend Rick," she said, putting her hand on mine and holding on for a moment. It was a gesture meant to fortify her, I think, not me. She looked over at David as Phidias and I measured each other directly. "I know he's *our* friend, David, I'm not being possessive. But I know you by reputation, remember. On the evidence, you aren't my dream of a friend."

You can't say that line nicely. Still, she spoke levelly and with sufficient wryness that she purified it of moralizing and condescension. She wanted to make it plain that she could be as honest with him as she could with Phidias and me. She was warning him to treat me right, of course. But further, she was warning him not to assume that his charm and good humor and swimmer's build could absolve him of the truth here. Her own looks, after all, could have beaten a rap of first-degree murder, so she knew about the uses of power. And since her voice, her sexual pitch, and her social graces had lined her corridors with honors and made her a totem figure for fifty years, she had the wit to urge a man like David on, to wish him

well at seduction and spells. But not here. Here, she was saying, we are among friends. And she wanted him to think over
the gravity of the word.

"I'm working on it," David said.

"Here's your chance. Phidias is about to have his arm
twisted, and it's going to take him a couple of hours to show
me all the places where I used to pout." She stood up and
leaned on one hand at the edge of the table. One of her shoulders was thus thrown into a deep shrug, and then she tilted her
head lazily toward that shoulder. It was a pose she was famous
for, and she could go into it as automatically as a dancer taking Position One. In one of the freeze frames that I carry in my
head, Madeleine stands just so when Yves Montand walks into
the bar in *A Dollar a Dance*. 1947. She looked straight at
David. "Then Rick and I will race to the airport. And we'll tell
each other what went on, just like schoolgirls. So watch
yourself."

And with that she turned to Phidias and took his arm. They
walked away along the porch, and she began to talk in a low
voice, the words blurring from where we sat. For a moment,
though, the magic vanished and they looked to me like an old,
careful couple taking a cautious walk. From the back, Phidias
seemed to have the slightest stoop. And Madeleine's wide
shoulders and narrow hips were, at this angle, exaggerated and
unbearably frail. The effect of the monument, of the woman
sculpted in stone and immune to change, required the mystery
of her face. It made you sorry that you could see so much. If
you were beginning to get a glimpse too of the winy headache
that waited at the end of the afternoon, starting now in a
hairline fracture, it made you want to go to your room and cry
yourself to sleep. So I turned my back and blocked them out,
forgetting as I did it that David now had to be faced. He was
looking straight at me and had the double advantage of having

me all in focus and of being spared the angle in time that I had just seen.

"Do you want to go down to the beach?" he asked.

"Aren't you getting it all wrong, David? *You* go down to the beach. I go get a horse. The meeting comes later."

Silence. I am playing this by ear; and I see, as it comes out, that I am taking my cue from Robert Taylor about thirty seconds before he pulls the trigger.

"I don't know what to say, Rick. No matter what I say, it's going to hurt. You have to help me."

No perceptible whine. Apparently he wasn't going to duck the difficult part. He was getting older every minute.

"David dear, it's all I can do to help myself. Just try to remember that this isn't being televised, so I can feel more than one thing at a time. I know I've avoided you and played with Madeleine and eaten my lunch, and you think I'm going to beat you. But it's wonderful to see you too. Just wonderful."

He looked down and smiled an old dreamy smile of his that has always made him look as milky as a shepherd.

"Now," I said, "a couple of questions. You knew Madeleine was with me when you called on Saturday, is that right?"

"Right."

"Well, you haven't answered the question."

"You mean, how did I know?"

"Right."

"I always knew that. That she stayed with you when she was in Boston."

"Is that so? You know, if my flesh could still creep, it would make its way to the Chevy and get out of here. Why do you suppose you never told me before?"

"I figured it was something private between you and her. And I liked it that you had a secret that you kept from me."

"As long as you knew it."

"I guess so."

"But here we are. Centuries have passed. Why bring it all up now? Don't you think it might *still* be something private?"

It wasn't, of course. I had never cared who knew Madeleine came to me once a year, but there never seemed any reason to tell anyone. I didn't know anyone that well that I could tell. Madeleine wanted a little privacy, and that seemed fine with me. And then, during the years with David, I kept it secret so as to have a secret from him. He was right about that. But now that he *knew*, we could have had a press conference, Madeleine and I, as far as I cared. Something private indeed. What the hell was that supposed to mean?

"I did it for Phidias," he said. "He needed to talk to Madeleine Cosquer, and I knew how to get hold of her. That's all."

"That's all."

"Except for you and me. I know it involves us too now."

I stood up and walked over to the railing and leaned out and looked at the Atlantic.

"David, you have the moral intelligence of a shellfish. You don't know what the fuck you're talking about about you and me." I was so afraid at that moment that I had lost both Madeleine and David. This was why I don't bother with people much. The more time you spend with them, the more you can't follow anything they do. "It doesn't surprise me, of course. All I want you to do now is tell me what this 'it' is that you and I are now involved in. Then I can go about getting myself uninvolved. I'm going to go into the library and read *A Tale of Two Cities* until I fall asleep. And you can wake me up when it's time to go."

He came up behind me and put his arms around my shoulders. He put his face on my neck, letting his lips rest against me. He didn't kiss me. If he had, I would have wrestled him to the ground and slapped him and shouted at him. Instead, because he just stood there holding me, I started to cry. I didn't have anything else to say, and I felt like a stand-up comic who has finished his routine but the time isn't up. I finished with the sobbing part in a couple of minutes. Then I let David lead me away while I went on to silent weeping and wiping my eyes with my sleeve. We walked down the porch steps, across the lawn and through the bushes into the wild scrub above the dunes. We stopped there as if we had come to look at the view. After a while I was dry-eyed again, but I still couldn't talk. And it seemed as reasonable as anything else to keep on walking, down through the dunes on a trail of wooden planks laid end to end, until we came to the last rise before the flat sand and the water. I sat down and drew my knees up. David lay down on his side. He didn't touch me.

He told me some of the story of Mrs. Carroll's death and the reaches of Phidias's plan. Though he told it badly, in all the wrong order, it was some time before I could ask questions calmly and *put* it in order. What they had done scared me, and what they wanted to do now stupefied me. But I see that I really didn't raise any objection. I assumed Madeleine would tell Phidias no, and we would be right on schedule at American Airlines for flight 41. Meanwhile, the pain I was in had to do with David, because I knew how much I missed him now, and I remained at some remove from both the drama David had been through and the one he and Phidias were proposing. In a way, the plan had a curious charm. It also meant that I would not have to leave David right away. Just by hearing him out, I let myself be brought in on the secret. And for me, a secret is such a seductive place.

On Tuesday morning, Phidias had gone back up to the dairy just after dawn. He hitched a donkey to a donkey cart and made a slow and ancient progress back to the house. He called up to David in the tower. Together, they carried a plain pine coffin out of the wine cellar where it was stored and brought it up through the house to Mrs. Carroll's bedroom. Phidias had dressed her. It only took a moment to move her from the bed into the coffin, but David was feeling green and shaky in the knees. He was told to sit down. Phidias put the cover on, not even glancing at Mrs. Carroll, and as he drove in the nails all around it, he told David how happy she was to foil her ceremonious children. She had saved her death for herself, he said.

It was noon before they were on their way into the woods, walking on opposite sides of the cart, swatting the donkey. By now David had stopped thinking about death, or at least it didn't upset him when he thought about *this* death. Phidias had completed during the night the first flood of his own grief and then had committed the shape of it to memory and had put it aside whole, to take up again when the work was done. "The coffin in the cellar made her feel safe," Phidias said, and it came to seem that day like a good-luck charm to David, part of a passage so in touch with the lay of the land above the sea that death seemed incidental to it.

Mrs. Carroll was a southern girl who married a rock-face New England man of property, a reader of books and a dealer in ideas. She never took to the weather, but she had chosen to lie in a scrubby hill field deep in the middle of her land whose beauty left her mute as it changed its slight colors from month to month. She liked the conceit of a homemade coffin too. It signified to her that her final act would pose a stark and lawless version of the human question, a journey to the earth like a lost scene out of Faulkner. Phidias appreciated the lady rather than the conceit, and thus he brought to the event a heart kept innocent in homage to her. Nothing he said was a way of saying something else. His gestures were never self-conscious. "Well," he said as they brought the cart out of the woods and the donkey stopped, unwilling to walk in the sun, "didn't she pick the perfect place to hide? This is the place," he continued, spreading his arms to indicate the breadth of it, "where we first came to be alone. Thirty, thirty-five years ago. We used to ride up here on horseback. She decided to come here for good at the end of the winter. 'No one will ever think to look for me there,' she said."

Phidias talked about the near past and the far past without regard for the fear of lost time. The very thing David wanted to learn. So when they arrived in the shelter of low bushes in the center of the field and started to prepare the ground, David began to talk about himself. They were not pressed for time. Phidias had already made two trips out here during the spring and had dug down three feet. Mrs. Carroll had wanted some assurance that it could be done, that the soil didn't end on a plate of granite six inches below the surface. "Go dig me half a grave, Phidias," she said, "and find out if it's all skin and bones." But the land was deep enough to hold her. So they worked their way down. Phidias loosened the earth with a pick while David shoveled.

He told Phidias he was gay, then talked about Neil for a while, but he found that he had to go back to the years he spent with me to find the real beginning. I don't know how Madeleine's name came up so soon. But when David talks about the past, he does another nervous thing people do on television. He tells you everything. He backgrounds the relationships and draws little maps of the scenery and gives résumés of all the major characters. Phidias, who had so many plans to make that day, stayed one step ahead of the burial scene. He knew he needed an actress, and Madeleine was the only actress he had ever known. When he learned that David had a connection to her, however circuitous, he listened closely to discover how likely it was that David and I would do something together. He figured he could take care of Madeleine himself, once he had succeeded in getting her onto the property. This is my reconstruction of what was going on. David's reconstruction was at some points so naive that I realized he didn't know about Madeleine and Mrs. Carroll at all. In David's view, Madeleine had merely been a famous houseguest there a generation ago. She was taking a break from the rigors of her fame. By the same token, Phidias and Mrs. Carroll were a pair out of D. H. Lawrence, the rude farmer and the lilac duchess. Phidias seemed much less rustic to me.

The problem was this: Mrs. Carroll, who persisted all year in predicting that this was to be her final summer, had been working on a will with Mr. Farley for several weeks. She had never revealed a southern passion for testaments before. She had lived for years following Mr. Carroll's lead, dividing her assets equally between John and Cicely and little Tony. She was an indifferent mother who developed a working disdain for the children only in the last years. But there were no *King Lear* scenes to speak of, no threats of disinheritance and no petulant bequests. They were all rich already, and Mrs. Carroll had come to understand they would bulldoze her land and make subdivisions of it before she was quite cold. So she took the land away. The new will turned the estate over to the public, subject to a hundred controls. And a group of trustees that the will created was empowered to tenant the house with high-minded sorts, the Audubon Society, say, or the Sierra Club. One catch. She hadn't signed it yet.

Mr. Farley was appointed to arrive before the middle of July, just as the sun was beginning to warm the waters off Block Island, where he would soon undergo his summer vacation — taking a second sweet sherry before dinner and frying his fish in a pan. Mr. Farley, a conservationist in all things, had to applaud Mrs. Carroll's impulse to keep the land wild. But he was troubled by her contention that her children were neither as faithful nor as pure of heart as a single tree seen from her bedroom window, though she thought them a good deal more witless. Family conservation was Mr. Farley's business. Between the two, he was more concerned about the waste of Tony Carroll than he was about the elm and chestnut groves a buyer might uproot. Mrs. Carroll had expected a fight from

Mr. Farley, a plea to reconsider. But she planned to wield her pen like a sword and have done with it. Mr. Farley, she knew, was a man who lived by saying he had done what he could.

Apparently, Phidias thought it would be simple. He and David finished burying Mrs. Carroll in the late afternoon, and he didn't even pause at the grave when it was done. They trekked back up into the woods. Phidias let David lead the donkey on ahead, and for a while he followed a few paces behind, his head bent. But he caught up with David before they came in sight of the house again. When they were home, sitting over a drink in the library, David was made to understand that the issue of the will had become a crisis. They had very little time to see what they could do. How ingenuously he said it I don't know, but Phidias said that Madeleine would have to do nothing more than impersonate Mrs. Carroll for an hour or two. Mrs. Carroll had been notoriously moody with Mr. Farley, so Phidias figured that the tone could be sullen and the script limited. What they needed was a convincingly alive Beth Carroll, propped up with pillows and of impeccably sound mind, and a round of signatures for all of Mr. Farley's dotted lines.

David had to think about it. That was all right, Phidias said. They would talk about it again on Friday. Madeleine would not even be in Boston until then, and Phidias had work to do meanwhile in the milk business. Tactically, that is the most clever thing Phidias did, to leave David alone for three days. When David said he had to think about something, he meant that he needed some psychic space in which he could stop thinking altogether. As soon as Phidias left, David repaired to the tower, rolled half a dozen joints, and spent the next several hours watching the sun go down, mooning like a princess in a fairy tale. He dragged out of bed at noon on Wednesday and took two aspirins and a Valium on his way to the shower, washing them down with an Alka Seltzer. He ate standing in front of the open refrigerator. In the library, he curled up and read *National Geographic,* cover to cover. When he went out in the afternoon, he found the gardener sleeping under the pear tree in the field behind the house. They had sex there. Not one word passed between them.

"When I came here," David said to me, "I stopped being anxious for the first time since I left Miami. This house was all I needed. It was as if I was getting the house ready to be really lived in again. Mrs. Carroll had pulled back into her bedroom. The rest of the place didn't exist anymore until I came. Then it became my project. But all this week, I don't know, I couldn't seem to make contact with the house. I dropped things. I broke the table next to my bed. You know?"

David lay stretched out on his back, his arms crossed over his face as he rambled on. His shirt had ridden up out of his shorts, and some of his bare stomach was exposed, the navel and the line of hair reaching from it down into his groin. I had let go of my knees and sat next to him more loosely. He and Phidias were defrauding everyone but me, I thought. That left me to take care of them, I suppose. No, I said to myself, you leave it alone. People have to take care of themselves. Anywhere else, I could have made that injunction stick. But I knew that belly better than my own, so all my cautions about people and what they ought to do rolled off me like water. People don't have to do *anything,* I thought. That they do do anything instead of following rules is why we are here, David and I. There weren't going to be any rules, I knew, as long as we stayed within the borders of Mrs. Carroll's curious country, protected as it was from the world by a line of cows and the lull of pasture. It would all depend on how long we stayed.

"I guess so," I said. "The house was practically yours for over a month. Then suddenly Phidias asks you to make decisions, as if it really *were* yours, and you fall apart. You feel like you've run up a bill in a fancy hotel, and you can't pay it."

He uncovered his eyes and looked at me.

"It's the way I used to fall in love."

"Oh? Tell me how." I knew already, but he needed the chance to show me what he could do with the past.

"After I left you, I used to fall in love every couple of weeks. I'd meet someone in a bar, and they'd be the love of my life the next morning. No one liked it. And whenever anyone stuck around and tried to love me back, I ran away."

"It's called being gay," I said.

"Is it what you do?"

"No. I fall in love every couple of decades. And I don't run away."

"Like I did from you," he said, a little more impatient than before. "Is everything we say going to end up punishing me for leaving you?"

"Not everything. But if I were you and I wanted to avoid talking about what happened to us, I wouldn't bring up loving and running away at all. I'd talk about the goddam weather first."

"But Rick, I'm trying to tell you that I *know* some things about myself now."

"Okay." Very, very neutral. Hostile, really.

"Please don't treat me like the enemy," he said. He leaned up on one elbow and put his other hand on my forearm and squeezed it. I had had my share of that kind of squeezing that afternoon and was beginning to find it patronizing.

"All right," I said. A wind had come up, and a bank of clouds. The blue of the sea was a shade harder. It would be gray before long.

"Tell me about Madeleine Cosquer," he said.

"You talked at lunch as if you were writing the biography. We'll change the subject if you want, but you know more about her than I do."

"I mean how do you know her?"

"I met her in France. When I was twenty-eight."

During this moment we changed positions. I mean that I was lying with my hands behind my head, and David was sitting cross-legged next to me, his elbow propped on his knee. "Tell me about it," he was going to say. Then, for the first time, I would be able to do my one number that didn't have anything to do with him or any other man. I thought so well of my meeting with Madeleine and had gone over it so often in my mind that I'm sure I could have recited it in my sleep. Ever since, in fact, the details have clustered this way and that and then floated up in my dreams. But I had never *told* it as a story, and now I had the ideal audience. Madeleine, who reminisced with me now and then about the beginning of our friendship, thought my version of it unusually valentined and soft-headed, at least for me. David was going to love it.

"Tell me about it."

"I spent that summer in the south of France. I was living on a boat with a thin little man who didn't want anything from me except to make his thin little friends jealous. I used to lie around naked on the deck and read books on self-improvement. Yoga and vitamins and foot massage. Everyone sighed a lot at me."

"You sound like me."

"Do I? But you keep doing it, David. I'd rather work the toilets in the Boston Public Library than lie in the sun anymore. I'm all cured."

"I know. You're a mystic now. Get to the part about Madeleine."

We were being a little whorish with each other now. It was the way we had always played when we had a good time, and it had its roots at the very beginning, on the Georgia-to-Boston run in the Chevy. We would talk like hookers and tease each other. It made us feel very much alike.

"Well," I said, "you get to a day at the end of August when the sun is just too damned low in the sky. You're as tan as you're going to get anyway. So they took me ashore in the launch, and I headed inland. I took a train as far as Burgundy, and then I hitched rides through the wine country. A trucker picked me up one morning in Beaune, and since he didn't have to get to Dijon until the afternoon, we stopped at the vineyards along the way and drank their samples. When he let me off on the road north of Dijon, I was cross-eyed. Wine gives me a headache."

"Do you have a headache now?" he asked, brushing the back of his hand across my forehead.

"I'm on the downhill side of it."

"Good." With a little throb in his voice. It deepened when he made love, getting husky and close.

"So I walked up into this hill town and took a room in the little hotel. I had a view of the Romanesque church and the clay-roofed houses, but I drew the draperies and slept all afternoon. When I came down to the terrace for dinner, Madeleine was the only other person eating. They sat me down as far away from her as they could, but I saw who she was. She was wearing a white linen suit and a man's straw hat."

"What year?"

"Nineteen fifty-eight. I told you, I was twenty-eight."

"*No Passport*. MGM. She was fifty."

"Fifty-six. She had finished that piece of shit in the spring. So she said to me, 'Come on over to my table. I have the view.' So I did."

"What did you talk about?"

"I don't remember. The town, I think. The hotel was supposed to close for the month of August, and they were keeping it open just for her. For the accidental tourist too, but it was the sort of hotel whose clientele would *know* it closed in August. There must have been six or eight people working there. The whole kitchen was kept open, just to cook for her."

"I like that about her," he said, grinning. "She always does what she wants."

What he was assuming about her was the myth of luxury. She was wildly rich, he was thinking, so rich she could keep a whole hotel open on a whim. He was missing the whole point of the story, though of course it is partly Madeleine's doing that there is a myth at all. Money, her clothes always say, is no object. But I remember falling in love with Madeleine that summer because she knew she was broke again and not getting any younger, and still she was hoping and making plans. She had settled down in this picture-book country inn to regather her forces and plot her next campaign. In the afternoon, she sat at the same table on the terrace drinking Perrier, writing letters to her agent. "I know more about the business than he does," she would say to me. "I have to give him ideas." You could have called it sad, like an old matinee idol fishing for a cameo. You could have almost called it a bit of *Sunset Boulevard*. But Madeleine was the beloved queen of a medieval town that summer, and she glided through it as fittingly, as much suspended in time, as the lady of the manor in a thousand-flowers tapestry. And in the course of those letters, she also came up with the idea of a nightclub act and thus began her second career. Within a year she was an international event again, the cabaret star in the sequined gowns. So it wasn't sad at all really. But it wasn't what David thought either, champagne and sturgeon roe and five-dollar tips. You can't confuse the thirties with the fifties.

"You don't understand, David. This was her hometown. To these people she was like Joan of Arc or something. She came home to rest, and they took care of her."

"I thought she came from Paris."

"That's Piaf. Madeleine is the other one."

"You're being snotty."

"I know. I just want to make sure you like her for the right reasons. But I shouldn't do it. She can take care of herself."

"Look," he said, pointing up at the house. I came up on one elbow to see, and for the first time saw the beauty of it. It fronted the sea in several moods, its porch open to the beach and its tower reaching up to look out the whole coast. It had been built a hundred years ago, when people took the sea air without much leaving the house, and it was as vast as the industry that ran a Victorian family. A music room and a sewing room, a central hall large enough to exhibit machinery, and a reception room as big as a parlor, just for callers. Rooms with no purpose were part of the given, like the battery of servants and the reasoning that reasoned that the family was to come here only from the Fourth of July until Labor Day. And yet, for all that, it looked like the opposite of a place to live; there was something poignant about it, something as quiet and washed clean as a ship in full sail. It was shingled with a million shingles, gray and beige and streaked, and was at last the color of the sand or the scorched, late-summer grass. Its trim was the dark green of the forest, a mile of it in strips and cornices, shutters and stairs. A doll's idea of a house.

"You'd recognize her a mile away, wouldn't you?" David said. As he said it, I finally saw what I was meant to see. Madeleine and Phidias came into focus. They were talking together on the high terrace that was set into the roof at the opposite end of the house from the tower. It seemed like an architectural afterthought, this airy perch, the nineteenth-century version of the spare and bony widow's walks that topped the captains' houses in the old harbors. It was out of place here because no one would have gone to sea out of this balloon-waisted banker's house. And no one would have gone up for a Gothic hour of scanning the sea's far edge for a sail. But David was right. Though the figure was tiny from where we sat above the beach, it was clearly Madeleine Cosquer. You knew it from the hands on the hips and the throwing back of the head as she paced on the battlements. Phidias sat on the railing, his back to us, in much the same way as he had sat on the porch railing three floors below when he joined us after lunch. Madeleine was doing the talking, and she looked mad.

I turned back to David. "I don't think your plan is going over very big," I said.

"It isn't my plan."

"What *is* your plan?"

He bent down to kiss me. I turned my head away into the grass, but he kissed me anyway, patting his lips on my temple, moving down my face until he nuzzled the tight cords in my neck and stroked them with his tongue. Very close to my ear, I heard him say in a voice so low I couldn't catch the tone, "I don't have one, Rick." And as my face came away from the grass and I began to hold him, I believed that this was as much of the truth as he knew. I held his head close with one hand and gripped his shoulders with the other. We held still while I gave up. Those who have no plans are so unlike those who plot. I am a plotter, and I know. A plan is wrong-headed to them because it seems untrue to the life of the present, which for them just unfolds and unfolds. For me, a plan is at least something for nothing to go according to. What are we going to do now? I thought. Of course I knew that what we were going to do *right* now was make love, one way or another, but I couldn't imagine what we were going to *do* about it. How do you get out of it alive? I wanted to know, because I hadn't the last time.

We were on our sides, facing each other. I felt his body all along me, but I couldn't answer it or move against it yet. I just clung there. We kissed deeply, though, drinking each other in. The taste of his mouth was so familiar and so undimini.hed by the years that I kissed him with a gasp and a sob fighting in my throat. I know I think too much. I always have. But it hovered in my head that we were very, very old right now, and we held each other lovingly, but the passion and sex were something we had left behind in the past. We seemed to be recalling something sweet and very distant. It did not make me unhappy that it had come to this.

"Rick," he said, breathing the words into my mouth, "why don't we go up to the tower?"

What did I know about the tower?

"Is that where you keep your lovers captive?" I said lightly. "Your life is like a folktale, David."

"Don't say that," he said, his face going grave, an ache in his eyes. "I want us to go to bed, and I want it to be real. I don't have any fantasies anymore. I promise. Just make love to me."

Perhaps because I had lived the last minute in my head, I wasn't aware until then that his cock had stiffened against me and rode between us, pulsing against my belly. I pulled away a bit, far enough so that I couldn't feel it any longer.

"David, I can't. I don't go to bed with the people I meet. That's not what I do now."

"I don't understand." And he didn't, of course. Beds are David's life raft. They are his ballast. He can sleep until noon if he wants, and he props himself up on pillows to read in the late afternoon. If there is a telephone on the bedside table as well, he is fixed for the day.

"I've gotten sex down to a science," I said, lamely trying to be light again. "I suck people off in the baths, and I jerk them off at dirty movies. When I go to the library, I don't bother to take my library card. You don't need it in the john."

"If you don't want to go to bed with me, why am I in your arms again?"

"Because I love you. And I wanted to make love a little. But this is far enough." He stared at me as if he didn't believe a word. "That's the plan anyway," I said, reaching for the joke.

"I know what it is," he said. "You're afraid you can't get it up." I took in a breath to tell him no, and he put his hand across my mouth. "No, darling, listen. I'm not trying to test you. You don't have to fuck me." Oh stop, I thought, stop with the "darling." Don't call me things. "I told you, I know some things about myself now. Either way is all right with me. Let me fuck you."

I can't. There is more than one way, I see, of being forty-five. The usual fear of starting to die has long begun. The fear at forty that nothing would change between there and the grave has given place to the darker, insomniac fear that change is all there is and you can't stop it. You have found a new way of being alone, and the trick is that you can't talk about it, even with those who have crossed the line with you. Everyone wants to forget it, so leave them alone. It is one of the things that sells stiff drinks in a gay bar. But you see that you are forty-five in this way too, when the young outsex you. I come from a time when you fucked or you got fucked, you didn't do both. But the boys I meet go back and forth. A bullet of amyl nitrate swings from a chain around their necks, and nothing the flesh is weak enough to want appalls them. I envy them, I know, but it doesn't seem fair. Being gay, you are unmanned to begin with as you shy away from the brute straight world and the one thing men are. You finally succeed in believing that a man can be this and not just that. And see, you come to find out that you haven't gotten it quite right. Some people's houses are all doors.

"I can't."

"You'll see. Come on up to the tower. From my bed you can see everything." He sprang up and stood above me smiling, humming with energy. "Don't worry. You're going to like it here."

"In a day or two I hope to have forgotten that it ever existed."

"No, you don't. Come on."

"David," I said, "what do you want from me?" It's my own fault. I lay there and let him caper around me, and my voice came out full of melancholy humor. I should have shouted and shaken him and pushed him off the dune. I was mad enough. He had decided I was feeling what he wanted me to feel, and he steamrollered right over me. And yet he was so unencumbered by time that I held it in, just so that I could watch him. He was electric, and now he was laughing at me.

"Nothing," he said, grinning and playful. "I don't know what this *means*. Why don't we figure that out later? You can give a sermon on it. Up there," he said, pointing again to the roof terrace. Instinctively I followed the thrust of his arm again and saw that Phidias was alone there now. He leaned on his elbows on the balustrade, looking out to sea. "You can tell it to the tide and the wind. But right now why don't we go for a swim? And then go up to my room and take a shower."

"No. You go. I'll watch you."

He has always loved to be watched. He pulled the T-shirt over his head and shook his head loose from it. He dropped his cutoffs and kicked them off. As he put his fingertips into the waistband of his briefs, he looked down at me and smiled a smile I might have mistaken for Madeleine's — knowing and disbelieving at once — if I had come upon it by surprise while turning a corner. He slipped them off and stood free, and there I was again, back at square one. Leaping twice like a deer, he reached the flat sand and began to run toward the water. He is not a runner, but there is something more physical, more beautiful even, in the heavier step with which he moves, the breaks in his rhythm. He splashed in. He threw himself forward in a marvelous surface dive, slapping the water and taking off.

As soon as he began to swim, I stood up and started to jog along the boards to the house. I don't know what I expected. I didn't really think that Madeleine and I could make a clean getaway. But I wanted the rest of the afternoon to be played out with Madeleine beside me, and then he would not be able to get me alone again. Can I possibly still have thought we were talking about nothing more than a Sunday afternoon? I ran the other way, away from the sea, and was panting after a moment and holding the stitch in my side. If he catches up with me, I thought as I slowed to a wheezing uphill walk, I will start crying again, and then he will lead me back to the beach to comfort me, and the sex will start all over. I can't. And I hate him because he doesn't believe me.

When I reached the line of bushes that separated the sea's land from the clipped front lawn, I heard him call my name from far away. I turned, and he waved and began to swim in. He had a long way to go. Good. I stepped through the bushes, and there was Madeleine, standing on the porch at the top of the steps, leaning against a pillar. I could not for the moment recall what scene this reminded me of. We were about fifty feet apart. It is a tribute to the control she has over her instrument that when she called out to me, the words reached my ear just above a whisper.

"Let's do it," she said.

So I was the only one not asked to commit a crime. I was being invited along, I thought, to keep them company. And I had the getaway car if they needed to make a fast break. But I can only guess, since they had all gone crazy, what they wanted me for. I knew differently. I had been running away from it all afternoon, and the stabbing in my side bore witness to the shape I was in, but someone had to take care of them. Look where they had gotten to since lunch, one in the sea and one on the roof. Someone had to put this thing together.

"Madeleine," I shouted, "how long is this going to take?"

"Just the summer," she whispered back.

4

"FOR ONE THING," Madeleine said, "she couldn't stand to have an animal around."

"Don't make things up about her, Madeleine. You're trying to make her more interesting, and she's interesting enough."

Madeleine shook her head at Phidias, stood up from the table where they had been having coffee, and walked over to the stove. I was steaming clams for chowder, and next to me on the cutting board were mounds of potatoes and onions and mushrooms, sliced for the next step. Madeleine took up a handful of raw mushrooms and popped them into her mouth like grapes or peanuts. She turned back to him and gestured as she spoke, a fat white mushroom between her fingers as she waved her hand. She usually made me nervous in the kitchen, feigning interest badly, for the sake of the moment trying to convince you that she kept a file of recipe cards in her purse. Worse, she would try to help if the food seemed peasant enough to her. Some things evoked the rough and pungent kitchen of her youth, and it delighted her to have a hand in, touching the pulse of things as her mothers and aunts must have done. But in fact, she didn't cook because she didn't eat. She never wasted a wish on food. And I and my soup were safe today because she was taken up by her argument with Phidias, coloring in the portrait of Mrs. Carroll.

"You can't expect to know everything, Phidias. I've seen her. We'd walk along the streets in Boston, and she would mutter and glare if we went by someone with a dog."

"Dogs and cats," he said, nodding agreement, as if he had finally put the muddle in some order. "You said animals."

"You know what I meant," she said, as if dogs and cats were all the animals there were. And though she was talking to a farmer.

"Tell me about your daughter," Phidias said, inviting her to practice.

"You can't say anything about Cicely anymore," Madeleine said, and I was hard put to say how the voice had aged. The spaces between the words were not as equal as they might have been. The breath was thinner. "I did not bring up my children to be boring. I've said to her, 'Why don't you have a nervous breakdown, like Tony.' "

"That's not fair. Tony has never been in a hospital. Not for anything. He's never even had a cold." He could not quite add a name at the end of any sentence. He couldn't call her Madeleine, because she wasn't. With my back turned to the stove, I was ready to believe Madeleine wasn't in the room at all. But he could hardly call her Beth.

"Well, he's not *boring* anyway. Except for sex. Cicely keeps a calendar, and she fills it up tight, to the last hour. If you threw *that* away, she'd have a nervous breakdown. She doesn't talk to me."

"Why?"

"Because I don't like children. *She* says. The point is, I don't like *her* children. They're about as lively as stuffed animals. I don't like animals either," she said, coming out of the voice as seamlessly as she had entered it. The insistence about the animals sounded deliciously witty in her own voice, and she had returned to us as if out of a time warp. To prove she was really she again, she laughed her one-syllable laugh.

"Hey Rick," she said, and I turned around, "how was I?"

"You'll have to ask Phidias, Madeleine. I never heard the original."

"Well?" she said to Phidias, throwing open her hands, smoking him out.

"Better. Madeleine, I just realized you don't have any French accent when you do it. How do you hide it?"

"Phidias, I haven't had a French accent for twenty-five years. I just slur a little, and people hear French. They hear it because they want to hear it."

She does not speak cynically about what it is people want from her, but she is a realist who has studied the phenomenon of herself and come up with some answers. I have watched her annual Boston concert for thirteen years. I am convinced every time, in spite of knowing at first hand that even she has not been able to hold back *all* the changes, that I am seeing a woman arrested in full flower. You could say, and it would be true, that the myth has taken over; but at the same time you can't deny the craft and the rigorously studied effects. Madeleine pooh-poohs it. She once said to me that it works because her fans are looking at her through the blur of their own teary eyes. But I have seen her spend a whole afternoon on the stage directing the lighting men, getting the spots right for the love songs. She wants it to *work*, and the worker in her is as tireless and unpressured as the women who bake the bread and hang out white washing in the hill town north of Dijon. So the French accent is another trick she plays, and at the same time it isn't. If you told people that Madeleine Cosquer didn't have a French accent, it would make as much sense as to say de Gaulle had a button nose.

"He says I'm *better*," she said to me. "He's a bastard to work with. All I have to do is perform for a half-hour for a lawyer who has the sense of humor of a tree, and *he* thinks," pointing over her shoulder with her thumb, "that I have to know when Beth Carroll got her first teeth and who took her first confession."

"She wasn't a Roman," Phidias said. "Just the husband and the children. She wasn't anything."

"He's like a museum, right?" she said to me, but there was in the remark a sense of admiration that he knew so much.

I looked over at Phidias where he sat at the table. "Is it going to work?" I asked him. I had been asking him that for ten days, but I had become so used to the unreality of living there that the urgency had gone out of the question. Of course it was going to work. Madeleine did not get bad reviews.

"Sure it will," he said, as if success had never been an issue. Then: "Like I told you, Rick. It *has* to work." And suddenly he had made it sound dicey again. I was never satisfied by his assurances. He trusted that some form of Providence would see us through, as it always had. He seemed to assume that if you stated the goal often enough and gave yourself to it, you landed bull's-eye on the target, your parachute billowing down around you. But wait, I wanted to say, what about Mrs. Carroll's goal? "I just want to get through this summer," she had said to David. "I'll cheat the bloody winter and go in September." What about that? Things don't *have* to work, I thought. It is my experience that they practically *never* do. But I didn't say anything because I didn't want to be caught talking down the dead.

He drank the last of his pale, heavily doctored coffee. Half sweet cream and three sugars. It tasted like pudding. He stood up and walked to the swing door leading into the dining room.

"I'm going up to look through another stack of her papers," he said to Madeleine. "Come when you want."

"I'm going to run a cold bath and sit in it and do isometrics. I may act like I'm eighty-two, but I feel like a hundred."

"You don't look it," he said, wryly but on cue.

"So they tell me."

He left, and she hung back to watch me fill the chowder in. But I wasn't going to give her the satisfaction of making a mess. I turned the flame down low and walked over to where she stood by the door, propelling her into the dining room and in the direction of her bath.

"He's the least simple farmer I've ever met," I said as we walked across the wine-dark rug, the glint of polished wood shining in the still and curtained room. "And the least Greek Greek."

"He's always been something of an overseer here. I don't think he's ever spent much time with the cows. That's what the sons are for. Isn't that Greek enough?"

"I guess so. Was Mr. Carroll here when you were here before?"

"In a way." She shrugged, as if all this were too petty to explain. "He was in Boston most of the time. Once the children were born, he and Beth stayed out of each other's way."

"Was it sad?"

"For whom?" she asked as we passed into the lighter air of the hall. We stopped at the foot of the main stairs.

"I don't know." I wasn't certain what it was that jarred me. I didn't, for instance, care who slept with whom in 1945. "Was Phidias as free then as he is now? To come and go in the house, I mean."

"Not so much," she said, looking away to think for a moment. The wide mahogany banister started at the ground floor as a kind of pedestal, and on it was a marble nude of a young girl on tiptoe, reaching into the air to capture some fuzzy Victorian abstraction. Madeleine touched the girl's heels with her fingertips and followed the arch of the foot and rested her hand there. As she turned back to me, she seemed to be holding the girl up on her toes. "You're really very proper, Rick, aren't you? You want the masters and the servants to know their places. That's a very bourgeois notion of aristocracy." When she said "bourgeois," her French seemed a thousand years old. "I met Phidias in Paris, when he and Beth had been traveling together for seven months. They had a chauffeur and a lady's maid with them. The servants rode in the front seat. Phidias rode in back."

"And then they met you."

"It was a big car. There was room in the backseat for the three of us. But it's the sex you want to know about, is it?"

"Madeleine, don't browbeat me."

"He's a very lovely man, Rick. I think it upsets you that he bosses me around. I like it. It reminds me of making a picture, and he knows it. Beth and I were very temporary. He and Beth were together the way people are in storybooks. It never crossed their minds to be sorry they were married to other people. They liked stealing time to be together. Do you understand?"

"A little. I'm just being jealous."

"Of him and me," she said, exasperated. "Be jealous of him and Beth, like I am. They had a destiny."

"What does *that* mean? You're talking movie talk."

She lowered her eyelids and shrugged her shoulders. She brought her hand away from the feet of the statue, and the girl stayed on tiptoe, all by herself.

"They understood the time they had," Madeleine said. "There was something inevitable about them. In the war, you could see how daily life — just getting up again in the morning — killed people. Not them. The day-to-day run of things didn't make them crazy. It made them laugh."

She didn't expect an answer, perhaps didn't even care after a certain point whether or not I was listening. She didn't address the remark about movie talk, and she hadn't stopped talking it either. But the past may be a place where you have to talk that

way. In any case, she had made me see that it was not my place
to censor it. One talks as best one can, her shrug seemed to
indicate. You take a risk. You say things that words are not
about, things that are the opposite of words. She had looked
away from me while she spoke, as if to bring them into better
focus for herself. Now she looked me in the eye again.

"You know, she and I were lovers during all that time, from
the day we met. But it was the two of them I needed to be
with."

"Okay, Madeleine, I'll take a closer look at him," I said.
"The green-eyed monster's dead."

"We'll be done with it day after tomorrow," she said, referring to Mr. Farley by the time he took. "Then it will be a
vacation." She turned and began to climb the stairs. "I'm glad
I have more confidence in my work than you do," she said
without looking back, teasing me with it.

"You haven't made a picture in ten years," I called after
her.

"It's like riding a bicycle."

She went on up, and I stood there next to the girl on tiptoe.
At the top of the stairs, Madeleine turned and smiled.

"You know," she said, "that's a very funny way to make
chowder. You're doing it all backwards. If you wait until I'm
done, I'll come down and help you." And she walked away
toward her room, savoring the joke. The last thing I heard was
the laugh, "Ha!" like the toot of a boat. It hung in the air of
the hall for a moment and then disappeared. But not before it
got to *me*, and it was me laughing back that finished it off.

We're going to make it, I thought. I can't believe it, but we
are. We have to.

We had not eaten on the front porch since the afternoon we
had arrived. But the rusting, wrought iron table and chairs
were there still, and they seemed so solid to me that I had

taken them over. I agree with Goethe that every view pales after fifteen minutes, though I am inclined to be restive even sooner than that. Five minutes is about my limit. It is true too that I have stared at a beautiful man in a park or on an airplane for an hour at a time without flinching, but that is not the same thing as a view that is just a landscape. The beauty in nature seems willful to me. So it wasn't the dunes and the cold summer ocean that drew me there at different times of day. I think it was this: that I was not convinced that the house was ours until we had passed the inquisition of Mr. Farley. It may be, I thought, that I will not be able to take care of them after all, but someone has got to remain uninvolved. I did not permit myself in those first days to be anything more than a caller, and it is significant to me now that I spent so much time at the table where I had first paid the call, not yet caught up in anything. The house belonged to nobody yet, and I responded to the limbo it was in by sitting outside.

It was Thursday morning, the third of July, and Mr. Farley had an appointment with Mrs. Carroll at two o'clock. She had made a point of not inviting him to lunch, it seemed. Madeleine was upstairs by herself, making up. At breakfast in the kitchen, she had told Phidias and David and me to meet at noon in the courtyard next to the library. Her plan, I guessed, was to appear on the balcony outside the bedroom doors, when it would be in full sun. We would catch our first glimpse of her from below and at a distance. I could hardly blame Madeleine for counting on the advantage of an operatic entrance, but she was not going to be given so much latitude with Farley. He was coming to see Beth Carroll up close and in bed, the same as always. However, we all agreed on high noon and synchronized our watches. Then we went off in all directions, and I came out on the porch.

As it happened, Madeleine and I were able to flee at once that first afternoon. There was packing to do in Boston before we settled in at Mrs. Carroll's. She did not press me about David on the ride back, and she said nothing more about Phidias's plan than to make sure that David had explained it well enough. "Well enough," I said. When we had reached the highway again and found ourselves caught in the crawl of Sunday traffic coming back from Cape Cod, she asked me to pull over and put up the top. No, I said. Why not? I don't want to. And then she lit into me, and we had the proper argument about the turn things had taken as we crawled back into the neat and gridded city.

It appealed to her sense of risk. It was like singing "Now Is All We Need" at the front lines, the shells popping in the distance. In the car, at least, she had not been full of the high-flown purpose she had since developed. I don't think for a minute that she saw herself as playing a part in the destiny of Phidias and Beth Carroll. She wanted to do it, she said, for the fun of it. She had been turning down movie offers for so long, letting half-finished screenplays pile up beside her bed, that people had ceased to ask. She didn't feel finished or, worse, passed by; but she did miss the work. "I want to get my hands dirty again," she said. The old Dijon mustard-maker, doing up a small batch of the old recipe. I might have asked, "What fun is it going to be for *me?*" except I knew. I hadn't risked a nickel in years. For the wrong reason. I had convinced myself that it gave me no pleasure, and I had once known better. For fifteen years, I had cruised the bars and had risked falling in love, daring to go so far and no further, getting out alive. Whatever the specter of David and me might have in store for us, I could feel that first day the lilt in my head that hazardous living induces. There is no outer manifestation of this feeling, unless it is Madeleine's half-smile. I was half smiling myself.

But perhaps it is best not to attach my shifting and parroty motives to her. I was scared to my bones about David, and at

the same time I was thrilled and merry about the caper. I
didn't want to explore that paradox too closely, for fear that
the answer was Madeleine's own, that I wanted the pain back.
But now that I thought of it, I just wanted to *do* something, to
do *something*. I don't work, and I don't see people much, and I
don't have the patience to sit down with a book. I don't even
go to the movies anymore. I just run a lot of little errands. I sat
in the car, going home, a thousand years after Madeleine had
warned me about the pain, and yelled at her about fraud and
shallow graves. She hit the dashboard with her fist and told me
I talked like a skinny Anglican spinster. She had said from the
porch, "Let's do it." Okay, I must have thought, as long as
there is something for me to *do*. And not just taking care of
them. I would do that anyway. But as I shouted about the law
and made prophecies, I realized I was going to ride shotgun in
this caper. The devil's advocate or, since I had been living
clean, the angels'. "Wait a minute," someone ought to say,
"while we think this over." And they wait because he forces
them to, and he does use the time to think, and at last he can
tell them what it all means.

Madeleine put in a call first to Aldo, her money manager in
Beverly Hills. She had found a quiet place for the summer, she
told him, and asked him to pack her a couple of suitcases and
air-freight them east. "You hate quiet places," he said, but she
ignored him and started her list. She rattled it off like a pilot
talking to mission control. Madeleine admits that her mind is a
memory bank of the clothes she has worn, both those she has
owned and those she has only worn in passing, in films. They
say that Isadora Duncan, writing her memoirs, wrote in a large
hand on scraps of paper that were thrown about the room as
she reached for a fresh sheet. Every few days, a secretary
picked them all up and put them in order. If Madeleine were to
write hers, the pages would be stacked and pinned like sales
slips, all method and no madness. These memoirs of hers

would read like the paragraphs about the bride's clothes in wedding announcements. She paced about my living room, the phone in one hand and the receiver cradled between her shoulder and her tilted head. They would have given her a job buying and selling on the commodities market.

"Now listen, Aldo," she said, "for the Geoffrey Beene I have to have the gold chain with the sapphire clasp. That's in the safe. And my gray sunglasses. In the top left drawer of the vanity. Then a scarf. Send a lot of scarves in the coral range. No reds. I don't have any shoes that are right. Go to Gucci and charge me some boots. Ask for Helene, and tell her they're for the Geoffrey Beene. She'll know."

I had never met Aldo, and I was not clear about how busy a millionaire in the computer software business was. I had always assumed that he did a little work on Madeleine's taxes and spent some time on the phone every now and then, ironing out the terms of a concert contract. It was a very different thing entirely to think that she could order him about like the upstairs maid. In the past, when I had asked her for details about her financial wiz, she dismissed the question with "Aldo? Aldo's just an old queen who's been looking all his life for a pet movie star. It's considered a very respectable relationship in LA. I couldn't go on without him." Now, as I listened to her pack a suitcase over the telephone, I thought: Madeleine, don't you dare take advantage of him. Or me, I added, glowering to myself. Fortunately for us all, I thought grandly, I am coming down to Mrs. Carroll's to raise these questions of ethics. I pictured us walking in pairs like the monks in an abbey, the air heady with ripening as the scent wafted in out of the orchards. And we would idle the afternoon away in a field above the sea while we did a Plato dialogue.

I didn't hear the end of Madeleine's call. As I looked around at the disarray of my apartment, I found myself saying good-bye. I'm not coming back, I thought, half in panic, half shoot-

ing the moon. I don't know where I'm going after Mrs. Carroll's, but it won't be here. I didn't breathe a word of this to
Madeleine, hoping it would go away. We packed our bags and
went to sleep. Madeleine slept in my room, and I lay awake on
the swaybacked blue-velvet sofa and tried to guess what was
wrong with me. I felt like Huck Finn, rough-and-tumble, and I
knew as sure as I was lying there that it would pass in a day or
two. I would be sliding down the banister or chasing David on
the shore when, *pow!*, I would have the existential equivalent
of a cardiac arrest. So turn back. That is what the prudent, big-
eyed animals say in fairy tales, and the hero pats their heads
and passes on. The last thing I thought before I went to sleep
was: What am I going to do with my plants?

I took them. And my tank of tarnished fish, who tenaciously
lived on, despite my indifference. There were three of them,
and they were seven years old, which probably adds up to
untold decades on the fish scale. David had brought them
home one winsome afternoon and called them Matthew,
Mark, Luke, and John. The fourth one died shortly after he
left, perhaps out of grief. I didn't know which one it was when
I flushed him down the toilet, though David always averred he
could tell them apart. I called the three survivors Blind, Deaf,
and Dumb.

There wasn't much else I needed that I couldn't fit into a
duffel bag and a wicker picnic hamper. I had never owned a
suitcase since I had left my father's house. I think I always
expected to flee Boston, and I always wanted to be free to take
with me nothing more than the clothes I wore. A suitcase, by
tying me down to changes of underwear and a coat and tie,
disturbed my sexy picture of Rick on the road, out to make his
fortune. Well, it is an academic question, since I never did go
until now, and now I was taking a carful of goldfish and
asparagus fern. But it goes to show you that you might as well
scrap all the resolutions you make in your twenties. "I refuse

to own a suitcase because it will order me around" is a dumb idea. Once, on an evening train to New York, I jerked off a bodybuilder I met when we tried to pass each other in the aisle. We sat in the back of the coach with a raincoat draped over our laps. Later he told me he was a nurse in a geriatrics ward. He was really rather delicate, like other muscle queens I've known, and he told me he was going no further than his sixtieth birthday. That, he figured, was his body's limit. He had gotten a doctor friend to agree to put a bubble of air into his blood and "needle him out," as he put it. But I know he won't do it. Things sound so noble when you're young and morbid.

I stayed in an antic mood, my pulses racing, as we made our second trip out of Boston. When Madeleine told me that Aldo had decided to bring the suitcases himself and take a vacation too, I was too far gone to be able to stop him.

"Why didn't you tell me as soon as you hung up the phone?"

"Because you seemed to be having a vision," she said. "I didn't want to spoil it."

"But Madeleine, where is this going to stop? You know, you can't invite the *Variety* critic to watch this performance."

"I have to have Aldo around. I'm glad he suggested it. Besides, you ought to meet him. He's so gay he'll make you blush. It's very bracing."

We had expected him for days. I had a horror, as I sat today on the porch steps looking out to sea, that he was going to breeze in on the heels of Mr. Farley. And he would barge in and storm her bedroom just as Madeleine's hand had taken up the pen and started to sign. But otherwise, I was afflicted with considerably fewer horrors than gripped me on a regular cloudy day in Boston. Madeleine and I had had an edgy talk here and there, as we had on Tuesday in the hall, but they always ended in sunlight. Phidias and I were still sizing each other up and spoke in shorthand. Mostly, I was on my own and free to wander. Since the house was not open territory yet,

I roamed outside, on the beach and in the dunes and fields, and came back to rest on the porch. At meals, I was more and more quiet and felt like I was floating.

"He's become a yogi," Madeleine said one night at dinner. "His body temperature has dropped to forty, and his blood doesn't move at all."

"I don't think so," David said playfully. "I think he's becoming a creature of the wildwood. He used to want to fill in the sea with cement, and now he looks as if he might go off and be a sailor. I bet he could live on roots and berries if he had to. He has burrs in his hair."

David. Somehow, David had pulled in his horns. He came down to my room from the tower in the middle of the first night and sat on the edge of my bed in the dark. "What do you want?" I asked, and he said "Nothing." He stayed there, I think, until I fell asleep and made no move to touch me. It was a major change in tactics from the old days, when he would try to counter my bad moods with his hands in my pants, not seeming to realize that the sex would be bad and the after-image snarling and gloom. With David, loving never lost its aura as a cure, however much I might finish up staring at the ceiling. Besides, he was blessed with a capacity not to see sex as good or bad. Its primary feature for him was its way of turning everything else erotic. We both were always wanton, but the difference was this when we came together to live: I did it every day for fifteen years in order to put it behind me every day, and he thought about it the whole day through and didn't need to do it much at all. He loved to jerk himself off and would lie in bed for an hour bringing himself up to it. He once compared it to a man rowing in a single shell on a river clear as glass. When I did it, I felt stunned and alone and knew I had made a mess. So it probably turned him on just to sit on the edge of the bed. He knew he had made a mistake to smother and attack me on Sunday afternoon. He also could see that I had arrived back at Mrs. Carroll's in a euphoric state — "wide open to the cosmos," he called it in himself — and he wanted to keep in touch, however marginally. If he kept his hands to himself, I was willing to let him.

On the morning after the second night, I awoke to find that he had fallen asleep next to me, still in his clothes. On the fifth morning, I saw he had taken his clothes off and crept in under the covers. I was brushing my teeth on the seventh night, Sunday, a week to the day we fell into this, when his face appeared in the shaving mirror above the sink. He leaned there in the bathroom doorway.

"Why don't you come on up to the tower tonight?"

I ducked and spit a mouthful of foam into the sink. When I stood up, I didn't turn around but held his eyes in the mirror instead.

"I thought I turned down that offer."

"I thought I'd make it again. Now that you're such a beachcomber, I think you'll fall in love with the view. It's like living in a lighthouse."

"Does it warn the ships at sea that there is danger here?"

"They already know," he said. "They avoid us like the plague. I'm glad, though, because if a ship docked here, you might ship out on it."

And he turned and left. Wait, I nearly said, I haven't answered your question. Yes, I'll come up to the tower, but please tell me when you started to sound so world-weary and stripped of illusion. You sound too old. I saw that he was not going to twist my arm now either, but neither was he going to pretend it was a good idea to go on this way. He accused me in the neutral tone of his voice. Still, he was trying to show me that I could hate the boy who left me five years ago without losing the time I had with the man who had just appeared and disappeared in my mirror. More than he wanted us making love again, he wanted to have it out about the past. A week ago, he wanted to make love first. So I had won, if you could call it that.

I had not yet been in the tower. When I came up the stairs into David's darkened room, I saw him in the light of the midsummer moon. He was facing me on the bed, the sheet drawn up only as far as his hips, and he was honey-colored against the pearl white of his linen. I came up close to the bed and looked down at him as I undid the belt of my robe and let it fall to the floor behind me. I thought he was asleep because in the past he had always fallen asleep instantly, but as I pulled back the sheet, I caught a glint of moonlight in his eye.

"Are you awake?" I said.

"I was just waiting to see if you'd come. You know, you haven't even looked out the windows."

And as if it had been a command, I stood up and went to the windows. It was the old story of the moon on the sea. It had never broken my heart and had never made it feel like a valentine either. But here there was something in the distance and the height together that caught at me. I walked from window to window around the room and was monarch of all I surveyed. I took the measure of the beach I combed in daylight, where I ran and swam and threw rocks in the water, and it seemed only inches long in the scheme of things — the bay in which the house lay harbored and the set of points and inlets that zigzagged to the south. Even when I am wide open to the cosmos, I don't seek it in the scheme of things. I make do with the heft of a rock or a dive into icy water from my own staked-out bit of shore. David thought I would like to be both king and beachcomber, since I could have it both ways just by feeling free with the tower stairs. I wondered if they wouldn't cancel each other out.

"It does make me feel a little like Rapunzel," I said. "But you're right, it's ravishing. Tell me what everything is out there. As the crow flies, where is the world?"

I walked over to the bed again, and he was fast asleep. It felt
like a slap in the face. I sat down and reconstructed what we
had been setting down as rules. If I had succeeded, it was in
forcing him to be confounded by the distance that channeled
between us. But he had agreed by agreeing that it could be
seen that way, not that it *was* that way. Damn him. I believed
that there was only one gospel interpretation of what had
broken us before, and the crime and the punishment were
rooted in David's illusions. He thought not. So he had turned
the problem over to me, as if to say "*You* think of something."
He knew I couldn't, of course. He slept like a baby and left me
sentry over the whole luminous curve of the planet. I wish I
could say that I stood watch until the sun bleached out the
moon and brought on the sober blue of the sea. But I curled
my body around him and buried my face in his salty hair. I
stroked the flat of his stomach. I was not aware of the windows
again until I woke to the full dazzle of the morning sun. I lay
on my back, my cock as stiff as the needle on a sundial. The
tower room was as hot as a furnace, and David had gotten up
and left, I didn't know when.

As things stood on July third, then (and they didn't stand
still), I was sharing a bed with my long-lost lover in an eagle's
nest, but we had left the loving out of it so far. I walked the
beach and took the sun and ended up with my head in my
hands at the iron table on the front porch. Phidias and Madeleine huddled from breakfast until dinner over the project. I
had wondered aloud to Madeleine what went on among the
cows and whether Phidias's farm wife complained, that he
should spend so much time on the coast. "I don't know," she
said, giving me a look. "Why don't you go ask them?" David
had abandoned his polishing and stayed outside, but he must
have found his own windless inlet because we never crossed
paths. He was tanned so dark that it seemed a pity to clothe

him. His skin sheathed him like an animal's coat, and he walked on the pads of his feet like a light-footed Indian.

Curiously, it was the gardener and not David who was prodding me about sex. There was only so much gardening that needed to be done in the front yard, since the hedges fronting the sea were meant to grow wild, and David watered the window boxes on the porch rail. The lawn needed mowing no more than once a week. And yet he made an appearance every day. As I sat in a mild trance at the table or on the steps, I would hear the clippers or the chink of a hoe farther along the porch. Then he would come into view, looking as if he were studying the condition of the shrubbery that lined the porch. He would stand there intently and strike poses. He took his T-shirt out of his back pocket and rubbed the sweat away from his bare chest, or he put a hand to his groin and rubbed himself as if absentmindedly. He was a little too chunky and slow in his limbs for my taste. Still, when he held the rake upright in one hand and leaned his elbow to rest on the bar of it, it threw his steamy body into a pose full of lust and abandon. I was meant to make the first move. He would only give me a perfunctory nod as he passed the porch. My return nod was almost imperceptible. There had been no progress.

It never rains but it pours. That day, as I shook with the jitters about the imminent showdown with Mr. Farley, the gardener gave another turn to the screw. He came across the lawn, his hands in his pockets. He looked down meditatively at the grass and stopped here and there to kick at it with one foot, as if he were measuring the spring in it. He passed very near to me and stooped down at the foot of the porch steps. He worked at the dirt with his hands until he was able to bring up a handful of it. He held it to his face and sniffed at it. Then he turned.

"This soil is too sour for good grass," he said. His eyes were wide, dark, and impudent.

"Really? How can you tell?"

"Like this," he said. He brought his hand to his mouth and took a bite of the earth. Without wincing, he worked it around in his cheeks and seemed to savor it, as if he were tasting wine. Crumbs of dirt clung to his lips. Then he turned his head to the side and spat hard, wiped his mouth, and spat again. "It *tastes* sour. Sweet soil tastes sweet. Try it," he said and held out his hand. When he grinned, two of his front teeth were covered with a thin mud.

"No thanks," I said. "I'll take your word for it." And I saw him look over my shoulder at something behind me. Then the screen door to the front hall slammed, like thunder following lightning, and I heard David's voice as he walked up.

"It's noon, Rick," he said.

The gardener had stopped grinning, and he must have felt the grit in his teeth, because he put a finger in his mouth and wiped it away. He flung the other hand to the side and down, throwing the dirt to the ground again. He had been kneeling on one knee below me, and now he stood up and slapped his hands twice on the sides of his jeans to dust them off. All of this only took a moment, but David and I seemed to wait for a long time while the gardener made the first slow moves. At last he nodded, his eyes flashing first at me and then at David. He hooked his thumbs in the beltline of his jeans and sauntered away across the lawn.

"Did I interrupt something?" David asked.

"You sure did," I said, turning to him. He sat down on one of the wrought iron chairs, but just on the edge of it, in a kind of crouch. "But I'm *not* sure what we were in the middle of, so I forgive you."

"Are you and he," he said, hovering over the verb for a moment, "getting it on?"

"Um, no," I said, but I realized in the low key of his question that I had stumbled onto the two of *them*. If the gardener had been my type, I would have felt a brief erotic thrill at these two men locking bodies in the underbrush. As it was, it made me sad to think of David, fucked and fucked over, going after something that went nowhere. I seethed with protective feelings for a moment, but I swallowed them. "He's a punk, right?"

"I guess so, but we don't make any demands on each other."

"I'll bet," I said.

"Don't tell me what to do, Rick."

"Okay," I said, and I stood up. "Let's go, or we'll be late for the curtain." I jogged down the porch steps fast and turned at the bottom to wait for him. He stayed there, still crouching, and there was no expression on his face at all. "David, I'm sorry. It's none of my business."

"Yes it is," he said. "But I won't let you make snap judgments. There are a lot of things I want from you, but one of them is not the Ten Commandments." He came down the stairs and paused on the last step, so that he still stood a foot above me. "I keep telling you. There are no rules."

"You sound like a lapsed Catholic." We fell into step and walked to the end of the house. If this was an example of a Moral Dialogue, I didn't like the topic much. And we made a funny pair of monks.

"I'm a lapsed adolescent is what I am," he said.

He looked easy again as we came around the corner of the library and into the courtyard. Phidias was there already, sitting on the low stone wall that rimmed the basin of the fountain. I had never seen him sit still before. Even now he was throwing a black rubber ball against the library wall. The ball did a double bounce, on the flagstones and then against the shingles of the house, and he caught it and let it go in an instant. I knew it was unlikely that he would be at some peasant task, whittling or mending a sweater, and I had not quite forgiven him for not being a farsighted, squint-eyed Greek fisherman. He was not strong in his old age. He had not been

weathered into something lean, and there was instead a soften-
ing of his angles and a delicacy about his postures that refined
and civilized him. It would have been easier to live carelessly
from day to summer day if he had been a man in full possession of his youth and a wrestler's timing. With a hero as our
leader, I would have risked myself with a soldier's abandon in
a battle. In truth, I expect I would have been more spurred by
the thought of a sailor slipping off his uniform in the captain's
cabin while the hairy captain lay in his bunk and smoked his
pipe and waited to mount the fair, slim boy. In the worst way,
I wanted a brute man at that moment to be in charge.

Instead, I thought, we are just two fairies and an old farmer.
It shames me that anxiety sends me into stereotypes, but there
you are. In a crisis, I am not so sure what a man is and what a
man would do. Seen less harshly, we were still an odd group,
David and Phidias and I. We were gathered in the court like an
unlikely collection of cousins awaiting the reading of a will.
We all knew Mr. Farley was coming at two o'clock, and it was
all talked to death. Phidias continued to throw the ball. David
took off his shirt and sat facing the sun at the bottom of the
spiral stairs going up to Madeleine's little theater. I stared into
the bilge, green as a grasshopper, that lay in the bottom of the
fountain basin. The statue here was of a sea boy riding a dolphin, and the water was meant to stream out of the dolphin's
mouth. I caught myself wishing we could fix it.

"Have we made any plans for the Fourth?" David called
out. "We have to do *something*."

"I think we'd better get through the third first," I said.

"When the children were small," Phidias said, catching up
his ball, "we had fireworks down on the beach."

The silence that followed the bouncing of the ball thickened,
and instinctively we all turned our attention to the balcony
above us. Just to make some noise, I was going to ask what
time it was. Suddenly, from behind us, the key turned in the

french doors of the library. "We've been caught," I thought angrily, turning to face the music, expecting to see Mr. Farley and a squad of police detectives. But the doors swung in, and a bent old woman stepped onto the threshold. I had never met her, remember, so I was not spooked in quite the way that David and Phidias must have been.

"It's my own damn fault," she said in the bird's voice, fixing me with her eyes, and I would have sworn that they too were not Madeleine's, were more blurred and less blue. "I spend too much time in bed, and I don't know my own kitchen anymore. Where's David?"

"Here," David said, his voice a little ashen. He came forward and stood next to me.

"The butler's pantry is so clean, it looks like an exhibit. But I can't find the fingerbowls." She shrugged, for a moment like Madeleine. "We will have to eat lunch second class."

"Where are we having lunch?" Phidias asked quietly.

"Guess," she said. She held on to the doorknob, partly to hold herself up and partly, it seemed, to let it be known that this was *her* house and she still had a grip on it.

"The library?" David asked.

"No."

"Your room," Phidias said.

"No."

"The front porch," I said. I had known all along, I realized.

"Rick," she said, "you are a classic case of still waters. Yes, the front porch. I had a dear friend who loved to eat there. We will drink a toast to her, I think. I permit myself a glass of claret once a day, because it clears the kidneys."

She reached behind the door and took up a heavy cane, making a motion with it to let us pass. David and I walked in, and when Phidias reached her, she took his arm and set off across the room, very shaky in the legs. Beth Carroll was tiny and clean and breakable. Her hair was still thick, and she had pulled it back and pinned it willy-nilly in a bun. She wore a waistless, dark green dress that Madeleine would not have let her housekeeper wear.

"Where are my jewels?" she said to Phidias as they reached the door to the hall, her tone suggesting that he might have sold them on the black market.

"I'll show you later," he said. "They're in a hollow panel in the wall behind the bed."

"I thought I would wear my cameos," she said. "Do I have cameos?"

"Yes," he said. "You remember. We found them in Venice."

And then they were out of hearing, making for the front door. David and I hung back.

"I thought she was bedridden," I said.

"I thought she was dead." He was beginning to enjoy this in a new way. "No, she used to get up every couple of days and make a tour. Otherwise, she only went back and forth to the bathroom."

"Is it going to work?" I asked.

"Yes, yes it is," he said impatiently. "It's worked already. Come on."

So we came out onto the porch to show we had come full circle. Madeleine and Phidias sat across the wrought iron table from one another, and David and I went to the remaining chairs. I was facing the water. Lunch was simple, a salad and fruit, but it seemed infinitely more magical because David and I had just left this place, and the table was empty. I pictured Madeleine listening at the front door until we went away, then rushing out and setting up the meal. And then I realized that everything was falling into place much easier than that. It just *happened* that David and I rounded the corner of the house as she stepped out onto the porch with her tray. We were in luck. The old woman was fretted with time, but the ocean air had pinked her cheeks. None of the lines that scored her face were worry lines.

"Give us a toast, Rick," she said, lifting her glass of claret.

"To your dear friend," I said.

5

IF THERE HAD BEEN such a thing as a four-piece suit, Madeleine told me later, Donald Farley would have worn it. I disagreed. From what I saw of him, what little, I figured he wouldn't have worn it unless his grandfathers down to the eighth generation had worn it. He did not just look like he had come over on the Mayflower. He looked like he did it every summer. There must have been places set for Indians at his Thanksgiving dinner. It must have killed him not to be a judge, with the Mayflower Farley's discretion in the use of a stake and an armload of faggots, but he wasn't wasting his time crying over it either. He judged everything, and he found it wanting. It is said of certain primitive tribes that they have a hundred different words for the fish that is the staple of their diet. Fish-caught-on-a-snowy-Monday. Fish-cooked-hard. Bigfish. Donald Farley had as many different ways of saying private property.

He was about sixty-five, and he had been narrowing his eyelids for so long that they had permanently fixed in an expression of contempt. He must have expected David to be dressed in livery. I thought even David was pushing things by remaining in his cut-off jeans when he answered the door. But all he said was "I put on a shirt, didn't I?" He had been biding his time waiting for a private confrontation with Mr. Farley ever since the day Mrs. Carroll had hired him. Though he had never met him, David knew his man. Given as Mr. Farley was to the ideal of the four-piece suit, he wanted the underling who opened the door to take his hat and wish him good day and announce him. A beach bum opened the door. If possible, Mr. Farley's eyes narrowed further until they were mere slits. It was a wonder that he could see at all.

"Does Mrs. Carroll let you go around like that?"

"Like what?" David said.

"Not dressed. You know, all you do is *work* here," he said coldly. The point he was trying to make, I think, was that David had no right to set the tone of things, either by his clothes or by his surly tongue.

"So do you," David said, and walked past Mr. Farley onto the porch, down the steps, and away.

"Young man!" Mr. Farley shouted after him, and the phrase was an accusation when he said it. He couldn't remember David's name, and David kept on walking down to the beach. From where I was witnessing this scene, peering through a crack in the library doors, I couldn't see Farley until he strode across the hall to the stairs. He was the avenging angel. He might have had a hydrogen bomb in his briefcase. As he took the stairs two at a time, I suppressed a whee of laughter and danced a bit like a boxer.

When he walked into Madeleine's room, she said, he was a furious, disoriented man. He looked as if he'd just found out that Farley had been deleted from the firm's name. He was too shaken to look very closely at the details of his wizened client. She had gained the advantage without even trying.

"Beth," he said, "something is going to have to be done about that boy."

"What I plan to do, Farley," she said, "is double his salary.

I have been poisoned and starved for twelve years, and my house was falling apart when he arrived. What could I expect? That old couple was sweet, but they practically needed a nurse."

"I mean it, Beth. You don't look at all well. I'm sure he isn't feeding you right. He looks dirty."

"I'm not *trying* to look good. I'm trying to *feel* good. I told you, all I want to do is get through the summer."

He knew she didn't care how it looked to anyone on the outside, but he told her anyway. He said it looked like she had given up the little bit of reputation she had won back by finally getting old and slowing down. He did not mention Phidias by name, nor anyone else, but then he had no memory for names he had not known since prep school and his first boyish sails off Block Island. He meant Phidias, though, when he spoke of the tarnishing of the Carrolls. It is one thing to dally with a servant, to have a tumble in the bushes now and then, and quite another to drive your husband out of the house with it. Madeleine got the impression that Beth and Phidias, in spite of their penchant for secret night meetings, were a matter of public outrage in Mr. Farley's set. Mr. Farley didn't *say* as much, but Madeleine had a second sight for reading between lines.

And it could only mean, she figured as she sat propped up in Beth Carroll's bed, that *Mr.* Carroll had talked. He must have slumped in a leather chair at his Boston club and whined around his cigar about his wife's infidelities. Madeleine did not have the stomach for the tears of a grief-stricken cuckold. Now, Mr. Farley was telling her, she was allowing her house to be overrun by an unmannered, arrogant, lower-class boy. It didn't look *right*. Madeleine bit her lip in anger and took a good look at the family lawyer. She gathered that Mr. Carroll must have been cut out of the same cloth.

"Tell me," she said, "do you mean unclean-dirty or sexy-dirty?"

"What are you talking about?"

"David. You said he was dirty."

"Oh, him. I don't make the distinction between one kind of dirt and another."

"Well, that's very revealing, Farley," she said. "How did you come by your children? Immaculate Conception?"

"I know what you think of me, Beth," he said, snapping open the latches of his briefcase to indicate that they were moving on. "But someone has to tell you what's right. Besides, I owe it to my friendship with Arthur Carroll."

He had not been asked to sit down, and he had not done so. As he turned his attention to the documents in his briefcase, he rested it on the end of the bed. He slipped out a folder and handed it over to her. She opened it and pretended to read at it but was aware that he was now in a position to watch her closely. She had lost the advantage of the tension and sharp tongues, so she turned to the next diversion. She softened her voice and told him to bring a chair over close to the bed from the bay window. No, closer still, she said, so that he ended up sitting right next to her at the head of the bed and no longer had her in his line of sight. If he had turned his head and looked right at her, he would have had a close-up. But Madeleine risked that. She thought he would be too modest and discreet to look a lady in the eye from only a foot away. And she knew it was time to trigger his legal dream of order and get him absorbed in the business of the will.

She wanted it read aloud to her as she followed it along. She let him know subliminally that she needed him after all, that in spite of what they thought of one another, she was an old enfeebled woman, and he was a gentleman who would not let a lady down. As she lapsed into frailty and deferred to him, she made him understand that his reference to her husband had found its mark. In fact, Madeleine had found the remark about Arthur Carroll so cheap and underhand that she determined to give Farley an extra bruise or two before he left. But it seemed prudent to lull him into a false security right now. She made purring and clucking sounds as he read through his accurate clauses. He became almost sprightly. She hadn't said anything out loud about needing him, and she certainly hadn't apologized. But there was a pitch to her attentiveness that must have made him feel that his moral posturing had been successful. Thus, from somewhere deep in the filing cabinet, the meat locker of his heart, he felt a little glow of good feeling for Beth Carroll. She couldn't be half so bad as she seemed if she listened to him so well.

He'd probably never seen a movie. That may be harsh, because I bet he would have loved World War II movies, where men are men and prove it when they throw themselves on hand grenades to save the platoon. But Madeleine's movies surely could never have been his cup of tea, and so he missed the clue he might have had to this performance in Mrs. Carroll's room. In 1934, Madeleine made her first film in Hollywood, *Off-Season*, and in it she seduced a good man and broke up a good marriage for the first time in English. She is sitting at the races with an improbable group of fussy snobs when Joel McCrea sits down beside her. He is supposed to be finding a job, except he isn't. She's rich. She tells him she doesn't understand a thing. If only he could explain about the betting and the odds. So he launches into a monologue as he tries to watch the race (because he has his carfare and lunch money riding on this), and Madeleine just purrs and chuckles and says, "Aha." Before the race is over, he is smitten, and he is drinking deep of Madeleine's eyes when his horse comes in, paying nine for two.

So Madeleine could change the course of events without talking, particularly when her course of events was different from the one her partner was pursuing. She didn't have to listen very sharply to Mr. Farley's explanation. She knew what the will said. Phidias had coached her so thoroughly in the minutiae of it that she only had to make sure that Farley hadn't slipped in anything new. For the first time, she thought about Beth Carroll's love for this land that had depressed her for three seasons of the year. It seemed to Madeleine, listening to the plan that would leave the coast to its own erosion, the forest to its terms and cycles, that Beth Carroll had been true to the ancient Carrolls and their first sight of an unowned country. Madeleine wore the other woman as a mask that afternoon, but she had learned so much about Beth's late relationship to her estate that she felt proprietary herself. Beth had loved the land for the land's sake, not for her own. As she had told David in the spring, she found the place glacial and brutalizing. But trees cannot take care of themselves. Therefore, Beth had made it her final business to protect the trees' interests.

Madeleine had an immigrant's pride in material things, and she resorted to her own range of words when she spoke of her private property. The Acadia ruby, which she had owned from 1940 until 1946, was still hers in some fundamental way. She had worn it during the war concerts and been photographed wearing it around her neck with everyone from Mrs. Roosevelt to Gandhi. But because she had been poor and philosophical before she was rich and frivolous, she also had an immigrant's love for virgin soil. It did not seem a paradox to her that she could want luxurious things of her own and at the same time want things to be free of the ties of possession and ownership. The same sort of contradiction appeared to move her when she was in love in a film. *Let me have it but let it be free.* No such paradoxes clouded Mr. Farley's world, and Madeleine fumed at how little he understood the fierce spirit of Beth Carroll.

When he looked up from the document, calmed by the precision of his own voice, he glimpsed the rush of tears that had come to Madeleine's eyes. But he misread them. She had been moved to mourn the woman she played, but she was too much in control of the performance to let go. She let the tears sting and kept them in. She turned them into rage at Arthur Carroll and Donald Farley and waited to pick a fight. Mr. Farley thought she was getting weepy about the shadow of death that the will threw on her kingdom. He was a fount of experience in these matters. Dryly, ever so dryly, he had patted the hands of those who made their testaments and saw therein how time is a stream and it flows away. He had a whole *Bartlett's* at his fingertips about inheritance and continuity. Now, he must have thought, was the time to bring up Mrs. Carroll's poor, dispossessed children. He walked right into it.

"Sign it and it's done, Beth," he said, "but I wouldn't be a good lawyer" — and God only knew that he *was*, Madeleine could hear him thinking — "if I didn't mention the children. You simply can't do this without telling them. It takes all the nobility away from your gift to the people. If you don't let the children take part in it too, they will think you have done this just to punish them."

"I can think of three reasons why we shouldn't tell them."

"Why?"

"John, Cicely, and Tony," Madeleine said, reciting the names like a list of the damned.

"You know you care about them more than that." Mr. Farley appealed to reason again and again, like the waves of the sea combing in and beating on the shore. But the tide was going out.

"I just want to make sure they don't challenge this will. Or, if they do, that they don't win. I told you," she said, so cold-blooded that he couldn't look at her, "I would rather have three of the pine trees in my woods for children than *my* children. Now go open the doors to my balcony and call up my witnesses."

"You're not yourself today, Beth," he said, standing up and moving across the room.

"Oh yes I am," she said, feeling more like herself every minute, whichever self she was. There was a thread of consciousness between Madeleine and Beth that she had been aware of from the moment they met in Paris, and Madeleine had reached the dramatic peak in her performance where she was dancing on that thread like a tightrope. Madeleine's high-wire act.

I don't know what Mr. Farley expected when he opened the doors and came out onto the balcony. Calling up the witnesses seems like such a biblical thing to do, but then I think he was too taken aback by Madeleine's railing about the children to have thought about it. In any case, there we were, Phidias and David and I, lounging in the courtyard in much the same way as we had at noon, like people in a waiting room. Mr. Farley seemed surprised that we were all together and ready to sign. He probably had an inkling that Mrs. Carroll had planned her moves as much as he had planned his, and he must have begun already to throw up his hands and think he had done what he could.

We started to climb the spiral stairs in a line, and Mr. Farley went back inside, keeping as much distance as he could from us, the lower orders.

"Who's the third one?" he asked Madeleine.

"You mean Rick? He's David's friend."

"Does he do anything around here?"

"He's David's friend."

When we came into the room, David and Phidias walked just ahead of me. Their postures made clear that they knew their rights and weren't going to be cowed by the old class instincts. They did it for different reasons, but it was touching to see how the swagger of the one echoed the other, like a grandfather and his serious grandson. I shrank back like a coal miner in the owner's parlor, fearful of smudging the rug, and I would have nervously fingered my hatband if I'd had a hat. I was partly compensating for the other two. But I was also making a meek last stand of reluctance about the counterfeit, shrinking from the G-men Mr. Farley might still have stationed out on the stair landing. I looked over at Madeleine. Her eyes blazed out of the mask, and she beckoned us to her side. She called out our three names as if they were the antidote to John, Cicely, and Tony.

Mr. Farley drew his sixty-dollar fountain pen out of his inside jacket pocket, where he had kept it for forty years and where it would stay until the undertaker pinched it. Madeleine signed, with a deliberating air, "Elizabeth Lucey Carroll." Then the pen made the rounds, and each of us stepped up to the bed and leaned over and witnessed the crime, our eyes wide open. Mr. Farley stood away from us at the bay window, looking out to sea as if he were soothed by its pedigree. I noticed that Madeleine whispered something into Phidias's ear as he bent forward and wrote. The same with David. So when I crouched like a wrestler beside her and smelled the long-bedded inertia of old age, I was paying more attention to what she might say than I was to my name as I wrote it down. But I wrote it out in full, including my middle initial, which I never used or said or even saw anymore. What she said to me was "Try to back out of it now and we've got the evidence to hang you."

Gallows humor is a sure way to jinx a delicate operation, and I gave her a stone-faced look as I left her side. But she was right that the deed was done, and my anxiety and holding back were beginning to be out of place. Our four names stood, a list of felons and a cast of characters, and we appeared to be home free. I handed over Mr. Farley's pen to him. He glared at me as if my chunky hand might have flattened its precision point. I have not seen my North Shore, stock-manipulating father in years, but I had a sudden sense that he must be aging in much this way, drying out like a winter bouquet of pods and grasses. Utterly sexless, and yet still possessed of the smugness of a man whose first power is carnal. I was the last of us, then, to hate Mr. Farley, but I brought to the experience now the purity of a late convert. He already had a curdled image of both David and Phidias. I wanted that bastard to remember me, too.

As I joined David and Phidias and we three walked through the open doors and onto the balcony, I wished hard for the sort of meeting David had had downstairs. I turned and pulled the doors closed behind us, and I could see that we had shaken him. Though he believed himself superior to all of us, we were still three to one. The mineowner can count on his aloofness to carry him through, that and his Persian rugs and his horsehair sofa, when a delegation of heavy-limbed miners troops in. But when they tramp out again, even if he has outtalked them as usual, he must feel a little jolted by the force that is pent up in them. His cups must rattle some in the china closet, and the gas light flicker. Or so it seemed to me, who felt in that moment a sentimental musketeer feeling about my two mates. Really, Mr. Farley looked a little scared as he stood there and twiddled his pen. He looked as if he didn't know what pocket it went in.

I pulled the doors to, and I laughed coarsely as I waited my turn to go down the stairs. I laughed long and hollowly enough for it to carry as far as the two of them in the bedroom, meaning for it to make Mr. Farley feel that he was wearing the emperor's new clothes. The silked and powdered duke pees in his brocades when he can feel the coachman and the butch footmen snicker at him. I had never been in a class war before, never on the smutty side anyway, and I liked it. I was a real rake. You'd never have known that an hour before I saw us shamed and standing in a row in the prisoner's dock.

We regrouped at the fountain and nodding knowingly at

one another like saboteurs, bombs planted, checking in for the
countdown. I told them in a low voice what Madeleine whispered to me because I wanted to know what she whispered to
them. Phidias would have shared his without any pressure.
"She said she had an irresistible urge to write her own name,"
he said, "but she couldn't remember it." He beamed at David
and me as if to say, "See what a professional job we did, she
and I." And when we turned to David, I couldn't tell if he was
disappointed that his secret was lifeless by comparison, or dis-
concerted because he had to spill it. As it happened, the moment suddenly took a different shape, and he was let off. We
were only allowed to go so far before the next change intervened. But I was getting used to it. We heard the rattle of the
key in the library doors again. What now, I thought, though I
must have had Aldo in the back of my mind, because I didn't
hear the police in every noise anymore.

When I saw him, my first thought was: "He's *my* age." I had
always thought he was an older man, but it may be that I
always thought of myself as a younger man than I was. Yet he
was an old forty-five. He was fat and soft and balding, one of
those Californians whose skin is pasty and untanned so that
you wonder why he bothers to live there. His clothes were very
pricey, but wrinkled and awry because his body didn't hold
them up. His cloudless face and his manic charm indicated that
he knew all about it but had somehow lost control. He wanted
you to know that you had to forgive him for it. He had forgiven himself.

"Mary," he said with a sigh of irony, "there isn't a soul at
the front desk. How the fuck am I supposed to check in?"

I think the three of us had the same thought, that this one
was Madeleine's affair. Meanwhile, he had to be hidden until
Mr. Farley had taken his leave. I stepped forward and greeted
him, reluctant though I was to give up the initimacy of the
rabble. I would see them all later, but there was something

especially pungent about the moments just after the caper that I had to let go. I took Aldo by one fleshy arm and guided him through the house toward the kitchen.

"So you're Rick," he said.

"I guess we've heard a lot about each other," I said, feeling giddy as we crossed the hall into the safety of the dining room.

"Really?" he said. "I would have thought we hadn't heard a thing. She's said your name enough, but it's blood from a stone to get any hard information."

"Well, I guess I know more about you." And I did, though not much. I was glad Madeleine had confided more to me than to him, but I knew too that she wouldn't gossip and never told more than she had to. Because I lived far away, I think she had given me the clues and filled in the background that she kept from people whom she saw all the time. During our several days in France, when she was what she now called "between careers," she had talked over with me her time in films so that she could get at the narrative thread. She said then that it was unusual for her to be free with details. Since then, I have gotten only fragments here and there, but I am very good at the narrative thread of Madeleine's life and so can piece them in.

"Really?" he said again. It was his favorite word. "Do you know the *kinky* things about me?"

"No. I know you've been taking care of her finances."

We had come into the kitchen and now faced each other across the counter. Aldo played with a crock full of wooden spoons as if he were arranging flowers.

"Such as they are, my dear. She's broke."

"Again? Why?"

"Ask her. She's a one-woman welfare state. She gives cash to every broken-down bit player she ever worked with. If only she weren't so European. She feels she has to *earn* it first. I'd give her Japan if she'd take it."

"Do you own it?"

"In a manner of speaking. It's all to do with transistors and diodes and things. I don't understand it. I just sign the checks. She did tell you I was rich, didn't she?"

"Yes," I said.

"Oh good. It's so much less complicated when people know already. You're very good-looking."

"Thank you."

"Is that boy out in the yard yours?"

"No," I said, bristling. "I don't own anyone."

"So he *is* yours," Aldo said wistfully. "Well, mother will find some other mischief to get into. Don't worry about me, I can always amuse myself. It looks like the rest of you are going to be in jail anyway." He took a wooden spoon out of the crock and put it against his lips, as if he were about to lick chocolate off it. Then he waved it like a baton. "Jails are *very* kinky. But really, don't you think it's a little extreme?"

There were clothes everywhere. When David and I brought up the last of the luggage to Madeleine's room, she and Aldo had already opened four suitcases. One lay open on Mrs. Carroll's bed, another on the chaise in the bay window. Aldo was making room in the closets, bunching up the dead woman's clothes to one side. He had emptied drawers in the high dresser, the low dresser and the vanity, and I don't know what he did with the things he cleared out. Then he had gone into every bedroom on the second floor and ransacked the closets for coat hangers. Now he stood in the middle of the room, clutching a bundle of wooden hangers in his arms, deciding what next to throw into disarray.

"Don't worry," he said to me as I let down onto the floor a canvas and leather sack of boots and shoes, "I know where everything goes. I can tell you're a worrier. But I can put everything back where it was in five minutes if I have to. Tell him, Madeleine."

"Aldo is very visual," Madeleine said absently. She was standing at the bed, holding up a long linen skirt and examining it closely for wrinkles. She was wearing a peach-colored dressing gown, yards and yards of chiffon that must have taken up the whole of one suitcase itself. Her head was wrapped in a towel.

She had come out onto the landing after Mr. Farley left and, still in Mrs. Carroll's reedy voice, demanded an hour entirely to herself. When Aldo and I appeared in the downstairs hall, she sighed in her own voice. "Oh Christ, Aldo, I thought you'd never get here," she said. "Find me something to wear, will you?" Then she went away to take off her makeup and bathe.

Aldo paced around the downstairs waiting, the peach chiffon over his arm. He groaned about the austerity of Mrs. Carroll's oaken furniture. He flipped through her records in the library and said he'd never heard of any of them, giving you the impression that he owned all the records you ought to have heard of. "So you can't listen to music," he said. "What do you do? Talk? God help you." He said he didn't even need to ask, he knew we were without television. He said it as if we were without running water or indoor plumbing. I shook my head no, and I stood around listening to him and felt few-worded and unflappable like Gary Cooper. By comparison anyway. He never stopped talking. He made you think something terrible might happen if he did stop. And yet he was not one of those people who makes everyone as nervous as he is. All the nervous energy in a room flowed into him. He looked like he would register on a Geiger counter.

At last he was so edgy that he said we were going up, whether she was ready or not. He strode into her room, and I heard her squawk briefly from the bathtub. But the chiffon must have melted her because he came back and called down the stairs that I could start unloading the car. I had never volunteered to do it, but I didn't care until I reached the car in the back drive and found it piled with luggage like a first-class stateroom. I bellowed to David in the tower, and he came down.

Just now he entered Madeleine's room behind me, a fat garment bag slung over his shoulder like a sail.

"David, you're an angel," Aldo said. "And see, I've made a place for it right here in the closet. This is just for *dressy* things." David walked by him into the closet and hung up the bag. Aldo filled the doorway and said in a smutty voice, "We can meet here whenever you like, and we can play in the dark."

"No thanks," David said. "I'm not into closets." He squeezed by Aldo and took a long look at Madeleine as she drew one thing and then another out of the suitcase on the bed. He would have loved to sit cross-legged on the pillows and talk with her about her clothes. But he couldn't get his bearings on the situation. He looked at me and said, "If you need me, I'll be outside. I'm going swimming."

"I think that boy's in love with me," Aldo said when David had closed the door. He grinned at me. "You'd better watch out, Rick. I'm a terrible home-wrecker."

"Don't worry," I said. "We're all homeless here."

"Aldo," Madeleine said, holding out silk blouses in each hand. He went over and took them from her. "Go easy on David. Don't swallow him up."

Madeleine surprised me. I hadn't thought she was paying attention. It was difficult to say what was wrong anyway, since David had answered every one of Aldo's antic lines breezily enough. I thought I was the only one who noticed. David had never gotten on with the dizziest gay men, the reckless, boy-hungry types with their hysterics, their vamp's humor, and their greeting-card sentiments. I found Aldo's Ping-Pong conversation endearing as it shuttled back and forth between air-headed chatter and seamy innuendo. David seemed threatened by it. Once, when he was young and perfect, he must have sensed a nonstop sexual hunger in a man like Aldo, and he feared attack. He should know by now that they are harmless men, and they shock and act wildly camp because they don't get much action. Besides, Aldo was more complex than the queens in bars who drink too much and try to appear gay in the older, sadder sense of the word. I would have to remind David, I thought, that there were no rules. The queen's way was in its own way delicious and brave.

"He can take care of himself," Aldo said, folding the blouses on top of the dresser.

"Of course he can," Madeleine said, as if that were self-evident. "But he's not as jaded as you are."

"I'm not jaded. I still like simple pleasures. Salted nuts and cocoa. Clean sheets —"

"You have a bad case of reality, Aldo, and he doesn't."

"Don't let David put a spell on you, Madeleine," I said, walking over to the bay window. The late afternoon sun was hot and shining in, and I could feel sweat between my shoulder blades. "Remember the Desert Inn. He's been around, and he's gotten what he's wanted since he was a boy."

"If I didn't know you better," she said, sitting down on the bed and adjusting her turban, "I'd swear you were jealous of his youth."

"I'm not. I just don't want us to labor under the illusion that David is innocent."

"I didn't say he was innocent. I said he wasn't jaded."

"Like me," Aldo said, laying the blouses in a drawer.

No I'm not, I thought. Not jealous and not like Aldo either. In fact, I thought I was doing beautifully, keeping cool and free of jealousy during the onslaught of Aldo. I wanted to talk to Madeleine about the scene with Mr. Farley. We had had a brief laugh over it when I brought the first of the suitcases up. She did a cruelly apt imitation of him reading his Latinate legal prose. But I wanted every pause and every shade of irony, and she wanted to unpack. Phidias had been so pleased with things that he didn't even wait for Farley to leave. He went home to the dairy, David told me, to supervise the afternoon milking as usual. David, too, seemed to think it was all behind us and, having won his round with the lawyer, didn't think twice about Madeleine's. Only I needed to know. The lone musketeer. But the mood had altered utterly with Aldo's arrival, and so I went along, trying not to pout and get left behind. I stood in the bay and looked down onto the dunes, and I saw David in his shorts, trotting along the planks toward the beach.

"Don't be cross, Rick," she said, and I turned back, not realizing we were still in conversation. "We agree in principle. He hasn't been hurt so badly yet, and we both want to protect him so that he won't. It's dumb of both of us, but there you are."

"In a way he *is* pretty innocent," I said.

"You keep saying that. It's not a word I attach much favor to. You know what he asked me yesterday?"

He had reached the beach. He slipped off his shorts and ran naked to the south, toward the cove where I spent my afternoons. My chest tightened. I turned away from him and watched Madeleine dry her hair with the towel. I noticed that she was still wearing the cameo earrings.

"What?"

"Who, if I had my choice of anyone, would I have liked to know. 'You mean since Adam and Eve?' I asked. No. He meant the twentieth century."

"David has no past," I said. "He doesn't understand that there have been other centuries."

"Carole Lombard," Aldo said. "That's who I should have known. We were both Virgos."

"Who did you say, Madeleine?"

"Well, that's it, I couldn't think of anyone," she said. She stopped toweling her hair, and she shook her head and let the hair fall. It was blond again. "I mean, I've met everybody as it is, and I don't go out of my way to meet them a second time. I said it would have been nice to meet Freud because I knew Jung a little bit. I would have liked to compare the effect on the two of them. But really, it's not the same as *knowing* them." She shrugged like a movie star. "I don't know anyone at all."

It was the glamorous, offhand answer David must have been looking for, full of small confessions. And I think it is probably true that Madeleine didn't care about the names on her dance card. But I suspected what the question reminded her of.

"I know who you didn't say," I said.

"Charles A. Lindbergh?"

"Right."

Madeleine once admitted to me that she survived her fame by putting on the Madeleine mask in public, particularly when she crossed paths with someone famous. She had told me long ago that the only star she met before she took on the press herself was Lindbergh, in Paris when she was twenty-three. She had not been so impressed as the French at large about his flight, since she had little patience with technology in any incarnation. He was all tarted up in a leather flyer's jacket and a white scarf. It was at a party on a boat in the Seine. She had spent half a year's wages to take the train to Paris and buy a dress. "It was a fabulous dress," she said. "Black crepe, with white silk gardenias sewn on at the shoulder, and then a shower of white petals down the front." And Lindbergh had looked right through her. He asked her a dumb question and then turned to talk to yet another reporter. It was the single occasion where Madeleine had stood with her nose pressed against the glass of the sweetshop. God knows what resolutions she made that evening.

"Who did *he* say?" Aldo asked.

"David? David is so irresistible," she said. "He said *me.* Now is that jaded?"

"Well, it's a very complicated bit of seduction," I said, as precisely as I could.

"I think it's darling," Aldo said, and he walked back into the deepest closet and for the moment disappeared.

"Wasn't today marvelous?" she asked me. "Weren't we *all* marvelous?"

"Yes. But I thought things were going to stand still for a while." I opened my hand in the direction of the shipwreck that littered the room.

"Don't worry, Rick. We're going to settle down now to our summer vacation and get fat and lazy. Aldo is going to last about a week here. He likes you."

"I like him."

"I guess you do. But you don't know what to make of *me.* The point is — I was thinking this in my bath — you've seen too many Madeleine Cosquer concerts and not enough of *me* in these last years. I lounge around your apartment for three days eating my vitamins and unwinding from my singing. Now we have a little time, and that's good." She stood up and walked toward the bathroom, the chiffon sweeping in a wave behind her. She called over her shoulder. "On the other hand, don't expect things to stand still. I have to get dressed. They used to say in Hollywood, 'If you don't get dressed after a bath, you'll start to drink.'"

"Who used to say that?"

She paused at the door. It didn't seem like a question that would stop her. I hadn't expected an answer. She worried her hair with her hand, impatient to look at it in a mirror. It

looked fine, and she looked from where I stood roasting in the
sun very cool and untrampled.

"Some sad little drunken starlet, probably. There's something I have to tell you."

There's something I have to tell you. I think that's what she
said. It didn't sound at all like a cliché when she said it, and it
had the effect of pulling me to attention, as if I had been
drifting away from the critical matter without realizing it. I
don't know whether we say some lines because they are movie
lines that fit our scenes or whether the lines got written into
pictures because people talked that way to begin with. When I
was on the boat cruising in the Mediterranean, a ratty execu-
tive dismissed a heaven-blue bay we anchored in by saying,
"It's the same color as my swimming pool." Because I was the
boat's sunstruck beauty, I got away with snarling back at him:
"Your swimming pool is the same color as *it*. Isn't that what you
mean?" The heightened reality of *There's something I have to
tell you* told me that we were going to zero in and get to the
bottom of things. You hear a remark like that and know you
have dreamed it before and have been waiting for someone to
speak it.

"What?" I said, coming out of the sun and taking hold of
one of the bedposts.

"After you all left, Farley brought up the children again. He
said I ought to let them know what I've done. He thought they
might even understand and support me." And then she got
very logical. She sounded as if I had objected, but I wasn't
even sure yet what we were talking about. "It's all *signed* now.
They can't make me change it back. And they're rich already,
and besides, they care about wild land."

What are you trying to convince me of? I wondered. I heard
Aldo come back out of the clothes, and he must have paused at
the closet door to listen. I couldn't see him. He was on the other
side of the bed and behind me.

"How are you going to tell them?" I asked.

"Well, Farley is going to arrange it. He's their lawyer too, and he'll gather them together in a couple of weeks."

"Will *he* tell them?"

"No."

"They're coming here."

"Yes."

Run, I thought. Get out of here. I wobbled a little as I clung to the bedpost, but my anger was icy clear. I wanted to fling the suitcase off the bed. Then I changed my mind and wanted furiously to pack us up and undo all our evidence. And then I saw that I wasn't going to do anything but talk. Aldo let out a gasp behind me, but it seemed less frightened than thrilled. It filled me with grief just to talk. Before I could tell them what they were doing, they had gone on and done the next thing. They never thought why they did what they did until afterward. Well, I would talk it down their throats then. I had to start talking even louder.

The both of them were waiting for me to speak next. I let them wait.

What made me angry at *myself* was that I thought we could handle it. In my mind I was racing from door to door, from window to skylight, and I found them all secure. I knew, because I had been so drunk with it, that we had made it through the afternoon without a hitch. I also knew that Phidias wasn't well enough informed about the Carroll children, and I had been anxious about a visit or a phone call out of the blue. I didn't believe that anyone was ever *that* estranged. So it was a problem that was bound to come up, and Madeleine had merely precipitated the moment. We could handle it. But still she had no right to do it.

"I suppose Aldo and I will get a pair on the aisle," I said. "But excuse me if I don't wait in the rain at the stage door. I've seen too many Madeleine Cosquer concerts as it is."

I had thought I was going to yell. I wonder what I do with my anger when I become a bitch. I can wound like a sharpshooter with that vodka tone in my voice, and then I'm still angry when I finish. I talk to find out what I want to say, but I don't always get a chance to say it once I find out. Because I've talked too much.

"What do you think I'm looking for?" she asked me, and I could hear her daring me to say it out straight.

"You want your name in lights, isn't that it? You want lots of cruddy newspaper copy, and you want to be fabulous."

"She *is* fabulous, honey," Aldo said, the vodka on the rocks.

"I figured that's what you thought," she said. It was unlike her to be so quiet. We were supposed to be fighting. She touched her hair again, and she looked tired. I was sorry I was getting rough, and angry all over again for being sorry. "Some days I do want that. It's a terrible thing, but you can never be fabulous enough." She smiled, so it was hard to say how she meant it. "You'll think I'm crazy, but I'm bothered about the children. I'd feel better knowing what's going on between them and their mother. Phidias is pigheaded about it."

"Nothing is going on between them," I said. "She's dead."

She made a little gesture of impatience, as if I were being factitious.

"A will is one thing, Madeleine. You can't change the relationships with the children."

"I don't know," she said uncertainly. "That's what I want to talk to you about on our vacation. The rest is crap, I agree with you. You *know* I agree with you. That's why I don't have any friends in LA."

"You have me," Aldo said.

"Aldo darling, I don't mean you. I mean movie stars. You two are going to have to let me go now and put myself back together," she said, as if the air were all clear. "I'll be fabulous again in about an hour and a half."

She slipped through the bathroom door in the same way as she would have parted a curtain. I looked at Aldo, but he was already busy again with the suitcase on the bed.

"She doesn't really believe they'd put her in jail," I said.

"They wouldn't," he said, lifting a nightgown out.

6

ONE THING YOU HAVE TO SAY about David, he's not ornery about his privacy. I walked along the planks, trying to think nothing at all about the implications of what Madeleine had just admitted. What I had to do was find David. He would be brooding about some specific thing, or he would be contemplating the currents and the drift of the water he sat at the edge of. But he would be glad to share it, such as it was. He wouldn't intrude on what I was thinking or trying not to think about. There was that to be said about there being no rules. I could go to him now and sit and draw in the sand next to him, and he would not have to know why I was doing it again after all these years. In my ten days here, I had not once thought: "I have to find David." But I had to now.

I slow-motioned down the last dune, my bare feet going in over my ankles, and reached the flat of the beach. Right away I saw David's frayed and faded shorts on the sand. I stopped to take off my shirt and dropped it in the same place, thinking it was as good a place as any. I'm not pretending that I didn't remember David had no clothes on, but until then it didn't mean anything to *me*. Seen from the upstairs window, he had

gone along here like a figure in a film. An erotic film, if you
like. I don't mean to say that I wasn't turned on at the sight of
him. Still, suspended as I was upstairs between Madeleine and
Aldo, I couldn't include an erection, so it hadn't even begun. It
was just an involuntary ripple counter to the movement of the
stream. But now that I was here and making a still life out of
our things, I felt my desire at an even greater distance. The
course of the past did not trigger me. It boxed me in.

Of course I recalled the horseman and the beachboy on Sea
Island. They played out their scene in close-ups whenever my
memory went their way. But the sea itself did not always set
the scene going in my head, nor even a naked boy, though
there weren't so many of those after David left. To this day, I
don't think I've seen a horse since I rode into David's inlet. Or
a deer. What usually brought me back to Sea Island was any
slowing down of time. I am waiting in line at the Stop and
Shop, two days' puny food in my grocery cart, and around me
people stand by their prize marketing, food heaped high. They
appear to expect life to be boring, and so they don't seem very
bored. It is only another line at the Stop and Shop to them. To
me, time puts on the brakes, and the flashbacks begin. You can
cut out of your life the sea and the sensuous boys and the
horses, so as to keep you from going back. But if time itself
was once erotic, time itself will make you remember.

So it happens too when I am a little drunk or when I wake
up in the middle of the night and can't get back to sleep. And
yet the memory of sex with David is not sad, though I know
that these slow times I am talking about are blank and
freighted with rainy weather. It never hurts me to remember
my wrestling and dazzling with David in bed. I wanted him
and had him again and again, and the certainty that it could
keep happening was itself enough to make me moan for him,
come up to him when he was reading on my blue sofa and put
my mouth in his hair and handle him all over. What scalded

me about Sea Island and gave it the effect of stilling me and not arousing me was that it broke time down into David and no-David. I used to feel all through my fifteen years of one-nighters like a pickpocket. I am getting away with it, I would think as I walked home to my own bed at two or three A.M. after a good fuck. When David left, all that time before him became the time without him. And the time after him was the same except I knew it even as it passed, and I could no longer give myself up to the wild hour that began in a bar and ended in bed. I couldn't get away with it.

I thought of Sea Island as I followed the shots of David's footsteps in the sand where he had been running. But it made me want to cry, not fuck. I knew I could no longer see the house behind me if I turned around. The dunes tapered away here, and the rugged, gray-grassed, rocky fields came all the way down to the beach, ending at a break above the sand. In some places, the two kinds of landscape met neatly, and I could sit down in the sand and lean back and lay my head on the slope of the field. Sometimes the field ended in a crumbling cliff, with a six- or eight-foot drop to the sand, and I had the habit of resting in the shade when the sun was still high and hot above the pine forest at four or five in the afternoon.

But Mrs. Carroll's beach was most arresting for its two natural windbreaks. From a point deep in the woods, two stone ridges came fanning out into the open fields and down to the sea, stopping only at the high-water line. The earth had heaved in a quake or been sent up by glacial ice. At the shore the two ridges were perhaps a hundred yards apart, and they were ten feet high, with boulders littered at the foot of each. They were too far apart to turn the beach between them into a cove, but they cut that beach off from the rest of the shoreline. The architect of the Carroll estate, moved to improve nature wherever he could, hadn't passed them by. On top of the nearer ridge, he spun a gingerbread summerhouse, though it was so far away from the main house and so hard to get to that it was more of an ornament than a resting place. He built the boathouse against the inner curve of the farther ridge. The old dock, what was left of it, jutted out from there into the open water.

No one had ever bothered me on the boathouse beach, and no one except me ever went so far. It was a ten-minute walk from the house. When David went swimming, he sprinted the shortest distance between two points and dove in just below the house where he had swum that first day, when I tried to flee him. We could see the summerhouse from the tower room and, beyond it, the end of the dock in the water. But the beach lay hidden behind the promontory and could not be seen, even from the top of the house. I couldn't help feeling that the architect sited it that way, to keep the best way to the water secret, like the center of a maze. I had pointed it out to David from the tower last night or the night before, hoping I think that he would tell me in turn where he spent his afternoons. He didn't. But at least he had come to my beach today. I realized, as I walked toward the shadow of the plum and gray rocks, the lichen-covered granite crowned by the white wooden railings and cornices of the circular summerhouse, that I wanted to hear him thank me for it. He was going to love it here, and I believed it was a gift I could give with no strings attached. Except a thank-you.

I knew where he would be. If he had been dressed, of course, he would have been sitting in the summerhouse by now, having swum and explored the boathouse already, climbing up to the airy perch to take the long view. The naked sprinter in him was a different matter. After the run from the house, he would dive into the surf to cool down, then stand for a bit like the Sea Island statue, lost to the sea lights, dispossessed. I have seen him stand like that at my living-room window after a shower, looking down at the traffic on Commonwealth Avenue. If you had only watched him take the stance in a cramped apartment, still you would have known that he learned to do it while standing in the ocean. But I knew he would be out of the water now and lying on a flat rock that had split off the near ridge and slumped into the sand, the smooth side tilted to the afternoon sun.

I orchestrate these things down to the specific rock, until the image in my head is watertight. I leave no room for chance. I wonder if I do it to prove that things don't go my way. If sex was the farthest thing from my mind, why did I walk around the water end of the cliff face convinced I would discover him dozing face up on my own favorite rock? I said I wanted only to *find* him. But I plotted it out in such detail that it seems to me I refused to look for him at all. Or I looked for him to be me, to take over my place for himself and in doing so make it truly mine. I was engineering it in such a way that I would hardly recognize him if I stumbled on him. I hardly did.

I came around onto the beach suddenly. It flashed through my mind that he had abandoned the rock I had given him because the wrestlers were tumbling over it. I even registered that the wrestlers were David and the gardener before I saw they were making love. David straddled one end of the rock, hunched over onto his arms, his head down so I couldn't see his face. The gardener stood behind him and fucked him. He moved slowly in and out, and the muscles in his arms and chest stood out as he gripped David by the hips. His head was tilted, his eyes closed. Except for the genital connection, they both seemed detached, each centered wholly in himself. I had nothing to do with the slowing down of time here. But I felt it too, as if I were moving underwater now. I stared at them without a thought in my head, and nothing in their rhythm changed during a moment so long that I knew the world on the other side of the ridge went on for years while we stayed still. David was swaying his hips, and he rested his forehead on the rock. The gardener did thrusts and releases. They moved together like a single creature breathing in its sleep.

They were no more than twenty feet away from me, but I would have had to shout for them to hear me because the further rhythm of the waves bathed the afternoon in white noise. I suppose I could have jumped back out of sight, since I had only come a step or two onto the beach, but it didn't occur to me that I didn't belong. I believed so firmly that I was expected here that I assumed this was what I was expected to see. The gardener became aware of me first. He opened his eyes and then opened them wide, and he stopped moving. His face was streaked with sweat, and his stomach muscles relaxed as he began to catch his breath. David continued to rock his ass back and forth, almost lazily, but the movement seemed idiotic all of a sudden. Someone ought to tell him, I thought, because it is no longer the appropriate response to the situation for him to be lost in passion. Now that we are all here, I thought, what are we supposed to do? It seemed that David should come back out of his head and tell us.

But the gardener had an idea. His mouth opened as he breathed faster, and his whole face went slack as he pumped hard into David. I heard David gasp at the first thrust, and his head snapped up from the rock as if he were surfacing for air. The shock in his eyes as he looked at me happened in response to the gardener's shudder, but it deepened when he recognized me. He held my eyes, and I wondered, watching the sorrow pass through him, if I looked as sad as he. Since there were no rules, I knew I had no right to get in the way with my pain and tears, no matter how his making love might touch me. I had no say in the matter. I had given it up for ten days now with every refusal to take him in my arms. So I tried to look as unconcerned as possible, but of course I couldn't stop looking at them. The gardener was riding close to the crest, and David could no longer steady his eyes on me. He had to give over his whole body to the storm he had helped to start.

"Bring me off," the gardener called to him roughly, "bring me off." He leaned over now and took hold of David around the chest. David seemed to dance underneath him, swinging the two of them this way and that. Though he was pinned to the rock by the weight of the other, David moved as if he were swimming. The gardener, who had seemed throughout to control them both, had now become a mere rider. He raised his head and leered at me, but the final spasm overtook him. He grunted and gritted his teeth and buried his face in David's neck. David froze, and the gardener quivered again and again until he appeared to faint. Then they lay there quietly for a moment. It was only a moment, but I was not measuring it by the clock. I felt I was getting older with every breath I took.

As the gardener lifted himself from David's body, he gave me the defiant look I had seen on his face when he chewed the dirt. I had the eerie sense that he was thinking he was one step closer to fucking me. David rolled over onto his back and said something to him, and the gardener looked at David and laughed dryly, then turned to the litter of his work clothes. David, his hands behind his head, watched him dress with what was no doubt the same appraising eye with which he considered him on the evening Mrs. Carroll died. I sat against a boulder and watched David watch him. I found myself blistering with rage at the gardener, but I was feeling as mild and blurred about David as if the intervening scene had not intruded between my dream of him sprawled on the rock and the way he lay now. I was hurting, of course. But the pain of distance and jealousy was so immediate, so much like the ache of simple longing for him that had so far eluded me, that I welcomed it.

The gardener dressed with his back to us. When he had

pulled on his T-shirt, he turned before he took a leap to the cliff and clambered up and away. I didn't expect him to say good-bye to David because I knew the manners of the event were not in that direction. I thought they might exchange a ritual smirk. But he didn't look at David at all. Instead he glanced at me again, and he seemed to be both cocky about what he had just completed and daring me to do something I didn't understand. He looked willing to go further than I knew, as if he had just swallowed the dirt he rolled around in his mouth. Then he was off.

David did not immediately turn to me, because he first took note of the gardener's scramble up the steep slope of the ridge. When he was entirely gone, David flopped over on his stomach again and propped his chin on one hand. I could tell that his mood was playful, and that the shock of my arrival seemed more crazy to him than dark. I knew he was going to wait until I spoke first, in case I should be arch or censuring. If I *had* been, I think he would have laughed in my face, and then I might have run for good. But that is easy enough to say now. I had never run away before until I ran here to Mrs. Carroll's. As I said, between us two David was the runner. What I felt was that I had to know what *he* thought about all this. For the first time, I was not afraid that he would be wrong.

"Did I interrupt something?" I said, coming forward.

"Not really. Did you know I'd be here?"

"Yes. Did you know I was coming?"

"No," he said a little more sharply, as if to warn me not to play rough. "I've thought about it ever since you told me, and I wanted to see it without you first. Would you believe I met John here by accident?"

"No," I said, "but you don't have to come up with a good story."

"All right. He and I agreed to meet here at four-thirty. I knew I'd need it after this afternoon."

"David," I said gently, "you don't have to tell me the truth either."

"I know I don't have to, Rick," he said, more gently still. "It isn't even the truth. It's just the facts. They're not the same until I understand them better."

"Does he put you in a philosophical mood?"

"No. I do it all by myself."

"Have you seen the boathouse?"

"Yes," he said. "I have something to show you now. I'd like to take a swim first and wash him off me, but I'm afraid you'll run off."

"You don't have anything to worry about, David. I never do the same thing twice anymore. Shall I go with you?"

He shook his head yes, and his eyes shone. I sat on the end of my flat rock, where he had just been lounging, and took off my boots. David shivered in front of me, bursting to get in the water. "Let's go, let's go," he said to urge me on. Then, as I unbuckled my belt, he broke into a run to the sea. "I can't wait," he shouted back at me. But I was right behind him, and I plowed through the surf and jumped over the first low waves until I couldn't clear them and fell with a heavy slap. I swam straight out and didn't look to see where I was until my arms hurt. David had not come in very far. He bobbed and floated and then slipped beneath the surface and swam a little underwater. I always tore through the water as if I were in a race. David, because the sea was his natural element, let himself go with the drift.

But now he was standing up in the shallows and beckoning me in. "I have something to *show* you," he called. I headed back to him with a slower, broader stroke, and I moved to the rhythm of David's remark as it played against Madeleine's remark. *There's something I have to tell you. I have something to show you.* The one and then the other, they flashed in my head like the two sides of a spinning coin.

Though I had muffled and hidden the pain I felt about David and the gardener and talked lightly about it instead, I thought I had gained something in the bargain. David always said that his whorish sex, the little pornographic scenes like the one just aborted, didn't *mean* anything. He called it his private life, and he swore he wasn't out to anger me or hurt me. Swimming in, I began to feel what it would mean not to care if it was directed at me or not. Or not to care if David got hurt *unless* he got hurt. Luckily for him, it would mean I could no longer accuse him of leaving me. More to the point, I might have to accept that all my moralities might only apply to me. I was free whether I liked it or not.

But I am way ahead of myself. In the water, I was not so analytic — and if nothing else, the experience goes to show that I ought to spend more time in the water. It was just this: for the first time I saw David as a separate man from me and wasn't sad that it was so. There had never been anything I could do about it, but that hadn't prevented me from raging and getting seared with despair in the past. I saw what David meant, that days like today were crazy instead of dark. I didn't agree, of course. And yet I knew he was not wrong. For some reason, the contradiction seemed like a marvelous turn of events. My hand struck bottom, and suddenly I was whirling in the shallows myself. It did not occur to me to say, "Wait a minute, we have to talk about this." I *couldn't* wait.

I stood up, and the water streamed down my body. My cock had shrunk in the cold to the size of a peanut. My eyes cleared of salt, and I could see that David was loping on up the beach toward the sandy cliff. "Wait," I shouted, and he was near enough to hear me because he cried, "I can't." I laughed at the thought of a chase and knew, as I ran out of the water, that I could catch him easily. He was only fifty or sixty feet away, gliding along on the balls of his feet. But I took his pace without thinking, or thinking only that I would like it to be something of a chase. The sun was in my eyes, but it didn't seem hot because it was drying me off.

At the cliffs, David climbed easily up to the field, and I thought the route he took over the rocks was natural until I was on top of it. But I could see there was a set of stairs cut into the cliff here, though it was now fallen into ruins. The frost had wrecked the right angles of the steps, and the flagstones were tipped in all directions. But I made my way, once grabbing hold of the wall of earth beside me and coming away with a fistful of clay and pebbles. When I reached the top, the field spread out ahead of me for a hundred yards before it stopped short at the pines. The land was all scrub and hard grass, but I could see that I was on a path now as well. David continued toward the trees. He was moving toward the point, deep in the trees, where the two ridges converged. As I started after him, moving up the buckled path, I felt the symmetry of the place all around me. Down on the boathouse beach, the world was somewhere else because of the power of the two walls that set the beach apart from the world. As the ridges came together on the hill field, they made it seem as if there *were* no other world but the one toward which they were now converging.

David reached the woods, for a moment hovered at the edge of the dark, and then was swallowed up. In the same moment, I ran into the long shadow thrown by the pines and felt myself slow down. Hot as the day was, there was a chill breeze blowing out of there. Or if there couldn't have been a breeze, then it was my being naked that made me go cautiously. "David," I shouted when I got to the trees.

"I'm here," I heard him say matter-of-factly. And since his voice sounded close and the path went on into the trees, the light gravel half-buried in pine needles, I couldn't sustain the dread and so jogged on in. The air was a dense dark green. The sun appeared in patches and sometimes in pools, and I did not have my usual reaction to woods, which was to imagine them in a dreary rain, no matter what the weather was. I wondered how many other places on the estate were marked by these restless and curious sketches of order. Why gravel a path through the woods? People either make a path all by themselves, by the way they go, or they don't.

And then it stopped. I was surrounded by a blur of under-brush, and again I called "David," convinced there was nothing to worry about.

"Over *here*," he called back, more insistent than before. His voice came from the left, and I sidled that way and saw a splash of light and took two great steps through the bushes to reach it. "Here," he said again. I looked up and saw him on the spine of the ridge. It sloped up here at a sharp angle to the forest floor and was covered with moss. David stood in the sun and beckoned me to follow, but he meant that I should follow on the ground as he maneuvered his way along the ridge ten or twelve feet above me. I watched him lose and gain his balance a dozen times. He moved like a tightrope walker. I padded on the warm bed of pine needles under my feet, once again letting him strike the pace as he tested his footing and then darted ahead a few steps at a time.

I had not seen him naked for so long and unbroken an interval in five years. As I was walking now at my ease, there was ample time for me to see him in a hundred different attitudes that brought to the surface the range of the past. In the tower room, in the bathroom, on the beach below the house, I caught mere glimpses of his body. At first I turned from them in sorrow at what was broken in me when I lost him. As the days passed, I should have admitted that the pain was gone, though I clung to it enough to say only that it had changed. I had begun to freeze like a deer when I came upon him in the nude, if he stepped out of the shower and shook his wet head like a dog or if he stretched at the closet door in the morning,

deciding among his shirts, while I lay in bed behind him. I took
in the simple beauty of him at those times. There was something abstract about it, like the running figure in the film that I
saw from Madeleine's window. I insisted, as if I might have to
prove it in Farley's court, that my feelings were not *sexual*.
This new pain had to do with brief and perfect beauty. I swore
to myself that I was aching as I would ache about a rose poised
in its midmost hour. This was a high-flown pain, and I was as
faithful to it as Keats.

Naked myself now, and on a fragrant carpet of pine, I didn't
any longer know what I had to prove. The pain was not there,
and with it had gone the double-crossed reasoning that said
pain made me real. I would be so glad, I thought, if this wall
went on forever. My neck throbbed from looking up at David,
but it had the sweet simplicity of localized pain. A week earlier, I would have supposed we had earned this moment without rules or borders by living through the day we had just lived
through. But I thought it took away from the newness and the
merriment of a naked forest walk to see it as a reward. If we
were survivors, it was not today we were surviving. You would
have had to come up with a myth or a fairy tale to compare
David to as he led me along. He was not, in this brief journey,
compelled to mirror any action from the other life we had left
behind. Nothing in the tower and nothing in the past had any
force here.

He stopped and looked down at me, his legs wide apart as
he stood on two stones. He was grinning, I thought, because he
seemed to understand how lewd he must look from where I
was standing. "Well," he said happily, "we're here."

"Where?" I wanted to know, and said so, since it seemed to
me there *was* no "here." We had been where we were from the
moment we ran out of the sea. He shook his head at me gently.
He could see now, I think, that it was he and not the landscape

who had caught my eye and given it a lighted path out of the cave I lived in.

"You know what you look like?" he asked ironically, and because I didn't, he told me. "From up here, you look like you've been struck dumb by a vision. If I put a rag around your loins, you could pass for a saint waiting for the sky to open."

"You always said I was a mystic."

"Mystics aren't hunky like you," he said, and he reached out and pulled in the branch of a maple tree that grew at his height. He snapped off a leaf and put the stem in his mouth. "Aren't they all skin and bones? They have big Adam's apples and red eyes."

"I don't know. I think they look like you and me, except when they're being mystical."

"Do they get turned on when they get turned on?"

Without thinking, I reached for my genitals. My cock had swelled and lifted until it thrust out at a right angle from me, but I didn't know it until I gripped it around and felt a leap of delight. I was surprised, because I usually knew what it was doing. I usually *told* it what to do.

"I don't think so," I said. "I think they leave the body far behind."

"Well, I don't want to be a mystic until I'm old, then. They see the forest all right, but they lose track of the trees. Let's not be mystics." He had been chewing the leaf stem all the while, and now he took it in his hand and dropped it. It floated down, and I caught it with one hand while the other now cupped my balls.

"Rick, *look!*" he said, as if he couldn't seem to get my attention. I felt the feather touch of the leaf and looked up, and he was pointing off to my right. I turned, thinking I would see an animal or a seabird, some cousin of the deer who had long ago eluded me at Sea Island. There was water a stone's throw away. I could see now that we had arrived at the angle from which the two ridges sprang toward the sea. This high up in the woods, the hill just seemed to unfold, to open on a hinge like a box or a book. The pool in the crook of the two ridges was faced by steep, sheer walls of rock that went straight up and down and looked as if cut by a jeweler. The pool was twenty feet across. I walked over to it, out of the sun, and I could feel David walking above me. At the edge, I saw that its banks were all solid rock. I couldn't place the natural force, what sort of tempest or ice age had scooped it so perfectly out of bedrock.

"What is it?" I asked.

"It's a quarry," David said. "They hauled granite here, but then they hit a spring, and it filled up, so they went somewhere else."

"How do you know?"

"I figured it out."

It was deep, and it looked cold. I stared down at myself in the water and then saw David reflected from the top of the wall, higher than he had been, perhaps twelve feet. When he jumped, I saw him suspended for an instant like a dancer in the blue surface of the pool. He knifed in, feet first, and I felt the explosion of it in the water that broke on me. Darts of cold hit me on the legs and belly, and my muscles clenched. Then there was just time to see the pool's surface flashing in a million pieces before he shot up in the center and again took over the scene. He swam in a couple of strokes to the edge where I was standing, then heaved himself out and came to his feet in front of me. He hugged his shoulders, smiling through chattering teeth. I put my arms around him and shivered at the coolness of him.

"You know what?" he asked, his voice as clear as a boy's in the aftermath of his leap.

"What?"

"You're all covered with salt, and I'm all clean."

I kissed his cold and dripping hair. As I ran my tongue along the side of his neck and across his cheek, I licked the water from him. His open mouth met mine, and the heat of it smacked like whiskey. I held him around the shoulders and didn't move, as if too much motion would awaken us and dissolve us like a dream. But David's hands whirled between us. He stroked the hair on my chest with his open palms and then squeezed my nipples between his fingers until they throbbed. We were both already hard. He took our two cocks in his right hand and kneaded them. With his other hand, he massaged the small of my back, at last trailing one finger lightly along the crack of my ass.

I brought my own hands up to cradle his head. Our tongues came apart as I drew his head back and looked into his face. Spit glistened around his mouth, and his eyes were shut. The thought flashed once in my mind that I would love to go over and over with him the approach to this moment. In the tower. He would tell me everything he thought and wanted from the instant the gardener came inside him. The head of my cock tingled in David's grasp at the mere idea. But I knew I was, as David kept trying to tell me, *here*. I could have come in seconds, just as we stood by the water, but I figured we had a way to go yet.

"What do you want to do?"

"Lie down," he said.

"And do what?"

"You mean, which of the acts of darkness do we perform? I don't care. I want you to stop thinking about it. We don't have to *do* a fucking *thing*."

He took my hand and brought me to the ground with him. We stretched in the pine needles, side by side, and he studied my face. It was a stepping backward from the brink, I suppose, to hold off both the fiercer pleasure of coming and the declarations that welled up in my throat like tears. Our hands grazed one another's skin more slowly. We drew back from the center, and yet the pressure in my groin did not diminish. It gathered to a greater spasm as we groped like sleepers with our hands and held each other's open eyes like hypnotists. What do you see, I used to wonder long ago when David stared at me. I didn't think to ask now. I saw the same thing he did.

When we finally moved, it was as if we both assented silently to the same desire. He turned me over onto my back. He leaned over and took the tip of my cock between his lips, his tongue vibrating against the opening. I began to roll my hips to the rhythm of it as he straddled me and braced himself on his hands and knees. He rocked back and forth as he sucked. His genitals brushed across my face, and before I took him in my mouth, I let my tongue play loosely against him, lapping at his balls and burying my face in the swirl of hair on his thighs and in his groin. We fed like animals, furiously. We gauged each other, closer and closer to bursting, working for the shared instant. He was riding deep into my throat when he began to come, and at the same time he seemed to swallow me entirely. I spilled over in a great rush that about broke me in half, while my mouth filled with jet after jet of David's heat. The stream ran out of me, and then, wed to a perfect cycle, it streamed in again.

He collapsed on top of me, and the grip of his legs loosened at my head. But we both held each other in our mouths, breathing through the nose until we were soft. Then he drew back his mouth and let my limp cock fall back between my legs. He folded his arms across my abdomen, laying his head on them as if he were going to take a nap. I stared up at the sky through David's thighs. Now how do we get out of it, I thought. I didn't think it all that anxiously, and part of me thought it gleefully. By this point in the past, after all, I would have had my daily dose of post-coital *tristesse* — "PCT," David came to call it, since he had occasion to observe it so often. Instead I was getting giddy, and I wasn't sorry to be pinned down on the piny earth. I might have floated off otherwise. Get out of it, Rick, I dared myself.

"Are you having a mystical experience?" David asked from my waist.

"No. I have not left the body far behind."

"How are you?"

"Thirsty," I said. "I just took in a lot of seawater."

He lifted off me and leaned in a crouch over the edge of the pool. He scooped up water and splashed his face, then bent way over and drank at the surface. Though he was only an arm's length away from me, he was still as beautiful as the boy who lived in the film shot from the upstairs window. That said something about beauty, if not about me. As he swung around, I saw that his cheeks were bulging with a gulp of water. He held his face above mine. I opened my mouth. The water drizzled down all over my lips and teeth, and I held my tongue out to catch what I could.

"Yum yum."

"Don't mention it," he said, and he didn't move. His face was still only inches from mine.

"David, what did Madeleine whisper to you?"

"She said you'd be horny once you'd signed your name." He smiled and kissed me lightly on the lips. "She said I'd better be ready."

7

THERE IS A TIME in midsummer when every day seems more what you mean by summer, when to wake up to the sun is a relief because it proves it is not just in your head. This hasn't anything to do with the light, which has after all peaked weeks before. But different people reckon their summers by different certainties. Mrs. Carroll was such a broken-hearted type, for instance, that she said it was all downhill after June twenty-first. She said the winter had not unlocked her bones before the longest day was past, and so there was a sting that the year never lost. For me it all comes true in the middle of July. It is not possible for it to be too hot for my taste, and when the humidity pressure-cooks the city, I like it even more. The people I don't understand in New England are the ones who complain about winter and summer both, about the cold and the heat. I don't understand what they want.

But I think the weather is all right in Boston. I like July best of all, but I don't need it all year long. David says he does. He is all right from the Fourth of July until Labor Day, and thus he thought he would have been a happy Carroll child at the turn of the century, in and out of the water all day while his nanny sat guard in her puffed uniform next to a pile of white linen towels. The sea upset him the rest of the time, chill with winter coming or winter going. He and Mrs. Carroll had pinpointed it about their differences one night over claret and Gitanes. David told me all this about the weather as if I had never heard him talk about it before, when in fact I remembered whole days in Boston when he talked about nothing else. He used to brood and piss until we had a fight.

"Do we have to talk about the weather?" I asked him now. "I know the winter brings you down, but why don't you just enjoy today?"

I was a regular little Pollyanna. We were lying side by side, covered with oil, on the high roof terrace where Phidias had first argued out the plan with Madeleine. The oil was called Tahiti Gold, and Aldo, who had bought it on a South Seas trip last winter, swore by it. He said it would turn us the color of chocolate in no time.

"It isn't just the *weather*," David said pettishly. "It's a theory I'm coming up with about how you're born with specific climate needs. It's genetic or something."

"You're way ahead of your time, David. Most of us are still struggling with astrology."

"Nietzsche," he said, rolling out the name like a college kid, "says we all have to Mediterraneanize ourselves."

"Where does he say that?"

"I don't know. Someone told it to me on the beach in Miami."

"I don't think Nietzsche was talking about Miami. Or the beach." I squinted over at him, but he lay face up without moving, a slice of cucumber on either eyelid. Another of Aldo's sun tips. "I think the weather is just an excuse. It's something people talk about when the television isn't on."

"The thing is, Rick," he said, leveling his voice, "whenever you ask me what have I done since I left you, I know you're really asking why did I leave."

"I am?"

"Yes. And I know you don't believe me that I left because of the weather, but I did. When I finally decided, I didn't even think about you."

I sat up and faced away from the sun and out to the sea through the dark green railing. Is *that* what we're talking about, I thought. How bizarre of him, to suppose it would comfort me to learn that I didn't come into it at all when he ran from me. He was right about one thing, though. All I cared about now was why he went, because I didn't want it to happen again. I would let the past be all my fault if only he could convince me exactly what it was, so I could change it.

"No," I said, "I don't believe you."

"That's why I'm *telling* you. When you hear the whole theory, you'll understand." Then, without a pause, because gay men sitting in the sun never talk about anything for long, he said: "We have to buy some stuff for our lips. Aldo says it's lip cancer that everyone gets in Palm Springs. Skin cancer is just a scare."

"David, if we're going to talk, do you think you could take the garnish off your eyes?"

He peeled off the cucumbers and looked up at me, squinting only a little in the sun, as if nothing in him, not even his naked eyes, shrank from it. I didn't mind our changing subjects. And really, I had lied about the weather. There wasn't anything we didn't have to talk about.

"Aldo was telling me about the Shalimar gardens," he said. "He says the air is so wet it's like swimming, but nobody minds because they wear silk. Maybe that's where I should live."

"It doesn't matter where you live. Tell me about Neil Macdonald."

It is difficult for me now, as summer draws to a close, to recapture the scatter-shot quality of mid-July, but I swear that every conversation David and I fell into went all over the place. It is more difficult still to describe the mood I was in. They were two weeks of shipboard romance that had the advantage of not confining us to a ship's artificial routines. It was instinctive in me to cast about for a way not to lose him again, and the process brought me inevitably back to the past and its question of what went wrong. But I say shipboard romance because something in me knew it was doomed. It would end when we had arrived at our destination, wherever it was. That is how I assumed we were defining the freedom which let us be lovers again. No rules meant no future. And so we were very free to talk. There was no reason not to say everything, since we would soon enough be on our way. My mood was such that the more I talked, the more I thought I would get somewhere when the lull of July was over and we had split. I wasn't going back to Boston, no matter what.

I sound so sure. But the tone in which I harbor no illusions is just my Sam Spade act. Since I walked into it this time with my eyes wide open, I had to tell myself it wasn't going to last. More important, I had to promise not to get hurt when it happened. It was a mood that hit me like the memory of an errand I hadn't done, where I might have to lie to gain time. It shivered through me that day on the roof terrace when David said, "I know you're really asking why did I leave." Don't count on anything, I said to myself.

I am reluctant, I see, to say that I was happy as well. Because the gods are perverse, I don't favor talking and knocking on wood at the same time. It gets their attention. And I think that if I just say I was happy and leave it at that, I will look slow-witted and unsubtle. I will seem to deserve the complexity that rains down on me for being so simple. I am afraid, if I say it, that people will ask me why and I won't know. But all right,

I was happy. I was a lover again, for one thing. I woke up in the morning twitching with desire. David and I climbed all over each other, still only half-awake, as if this morning passion were another level of our dreams. By nightfall on a given day we spoke about love as if we knew the whole truth about it at last. And we did not get locked into roles. His first entrance into me cracked like a gunshot, but the pain was dazed by a wave of pleasure. From that moment, the baton passed back and forth between us like relay runners on a racecourse, and we were the equal lovers we wanted to be.

"Neil worked in a bar when I met him," David said tentatively, not sure what I was after. "He had a string of sugar daddies starting when he was eighteen, but they always threw him out because he got into trouble."

"What kind of trouble?"

"Street trash. He brought home people who mugged him and robbed his daddies' apartments. They don't like it when their Chinese bronzes are ripped off, no matter how pretty you are. Why do you want to know about this?"

I stood up and stretched. I felt a buzz in my head from so much sun, and I wanted to swim. I had no clothes on, and it occurs to me now that I took off my clothes in mid-July at the slightest provocation. David was wearing a pair of black racing trunks. He could have gone naked on the roof terrace too, but then he wouldn't have had a white line to measure his tan by.

"I don't. I want to know about the *two* of you."

"Oh that," he said, flipping over onto his stomach, to even out the color. "I was in love with him because he was a bastard. I tried to take care of him, and he treated me like shit. So what's new?"

"Was he good in bed?"

"You mean, is that why I put up with him? No. As a matter of fact, he couldn't get it up most of the time. I think I stayed because it was like a job. Do you know that I've never had a job longer than a year?"

"I've never had a job at all," I said.

"You don't need one. You have money. I *mean* it, Rick. I've never had Blue Cross, and I'm not on a pension plan or anything, and I have about a hundred dollars in the bank in Florida."

He was suddenly tense, but I don't think he even knew himself what he was trying to say. I realized that I couldn't give him a word of advice about the business of being secure. Partly, I think, he was articulating the panicky moment in gay life when you see that you have given over your youth to the body and that the body is going to be less and less a negotiable asset. David had always worked until he had enough money to get by or move on. It used to make him feel terrific. His string of one-horse jobs gave him the air of a man who could go on indefinitely being part troubleshooter and part Peter Pan. And though he loved Gucci shoes and Turnbull & Asser shirts when he got them, in fact he seemed to get by on a change of Levi's and T-shirts and tennis shoes. He went on as if I had spoken aloud, the pout still rising in his voice.

"Everything I own fits in two suitcases. I don't even have a TV. I bet even hobos have TVs."

"Some people would say you're lucky."

"Some people," he said, turning onto his back again and reaching for his cucumbers, "are full of shit. Some people do it with chickens."

We talked all over the place in those two weeks, coming back by turns to things we couldn't solve by talking. We made glancing blows at bewildering issues and then abandoned them in a sentence or two, and yet I think we came nearer to telling the truth than we did in the old days, when we worked by overkill and beat things into the ground. During all that time, I don't remember a single day when it rained. My memory of midsummer is lush with noon colors and the peak of the sun. But it is not as if I had nothing else on my mind. I was determined to undermine Madeleine's children's hour, and I began by grilling Phidias. I assumed he would be on my side. Knowing Mrs. Carroll's children as well as he did, he would be more convincing to Madeleine that it wouldn't work. But he seemed not to take it in. Watching for him from the tower, I went down one morning and intercepted him as he walked down the road from the dairy to make his daily inspection of the house. I remember we stood talking under an apple tree, because I kept looking up to see how far along the apples were.

"I don't think we have to worry about it," he said. "Did you put those canvas chairs out on the lawn like I told you to?"

"She can't pull it off, Phidias. People *know* what their mother looks like."

"I don't know who put them in the cellar, but whoever it was doesn't know mildew," he said, radiating the assurance of a man who knew mildew and therefore much more. "You don't understand, Rick. *Christmas* is when they come here to do their business."

"But Farley's going to call them."

He sighed. The self-evident nature of things inhabited his unworried face like a summer home. I saw now that he was going to tell me what he knew. I had already decided that he kept things from us only because he thought we had already figured them out. I tried to let him know as artfully as I could where in the story I got lost. It was best to have it out front that I for one didn't know mildew.

"It's this way," he said. "Last year Cicely told Beth it was her last Christmas, so *she* won't come. John is sailing in the Chesapeake, like he does every summer. I don't think either of them would come up here for Beth's *funeral* unless she had the courtesy to die at Christmas. Farley won't be able to find Tony."

"Why?" Tony, I knew, was the nervous one.

"He teaches school, and in the summer he runs away." Somehow he didn't have the same grasp of Tony as he did of the others, and consequently it was more difficult to detest him. I wondered if Mrs. Carroll had made the same distinction. Also, it struck me that Tony was gay, though I didn't know why I thought so. "He sent Beth a card from North Africa just before she died."

"But what happens," I persisted, jittery about the idea as I brushed away the facts, "if he does get through and they do all come?"

"What happens happens," he said, slipping into a farmer's logic as if he were taking a rest. He seemed to have lost interest. He drew a red checked handkerchief out of his pocket and wiped the heat from the back of his neck. "David's a good boy," he added after a moment, but he seemed to expect no reply to the notion. It was a comment that began and ended with his own thoughts, and it appeared to surface as briefly as his mention of the canvas chairs. So I went on.

"Another thing, Phidias. What are we going to do about Mrs. Carroll? She's legally still alive now. How does she die?"

"That's all figured out." He took up his pace along the road toward the house, and I fell in beside him.

"How?"

"I'll take care of it. She disappears at the end of the summer, like she's always said." It was clearly meant as the final word on the matter for the time being. "The reason I mention David is that he wants to go to work. He's good at taking care of people, so I think he'll come up with something, only he's scared. What you have to do," and he slapped the back of my hand with his own as we walked along, "is make sure he doesn't make do with taking care of you."

Everyone, I thought, is going to start getting involved in David and me because we are the lovers, and no one can seem to leave lovers alone. It seems inappropriately Romeo-and-Juliet of me to have responded so defensively, since Phidias and Madeleine and Aldo were not out to part us or poison us or use us. But I did not want to be the object of their enlightenment, no matter how well-meaning they were. I wasn't going to let David get trapped. Phidias seemed not to understand that I had spent a few years looking out for David's best interests. Of course, it could be argued that I had botched the job. But who had given Phidias the cause for concern? If he could come up with the scenario he just came up with, then someone was telling tales out of school about the past. David, I thought. Had David thought I needed taking care of when we were young and foolish? I thought I took care of *him*.

"David is free, and so am I," I said tartly.

He shrugged as if to say that freedom might not be the issue. David could *freely* choose me over his future, after all, and still be making a mistake. Well, maybe, but if he were free, then it would be his own bad mistake and not my fault. And besides, he wasn't heading in that direction because this time we were different. I cast a sidelong look at the rumpled farmer who could make me go through such contortions and justifications. He looked like nothing more than a practical man, possessed of a good head for numbers and an intuition about the properties of pipes and wires. Since I believed that men infatuated with method — carpenters and captains and makers of systems — made wonderful lovers and nothing more, I thought over again what it was in Phidias that Mrs. Carroll needed. I could explain them as an affair of passion, the hot-blooded lady in the tower and the big-shouldered farmer, and get them into focus when they were young. I could see them spending money in Paris. Even on this estate they made sense, exchanging significant looks in front of dry-lipped Mr. Carroll. But it was more than that.

Phidias was not just the shell of a heavy lover. I was beginning to see that he was the real moralist among us. He decided what had to be done and did it. A moral act was an act, pure and simple. He never said as much, but then he also seemed to feel that talking too much could rob the act of its moral clarity. I pictured Mrs. Carroll loving him for that, with no bullshit between them. It made me wonder about Madeleine's remark about their destiny. I couldn't believe it when she first said it because it was drowned out by the Hollywood swell of violins. But if destiny did operate in the human air that breezed about us, and if lovers could be touched by it, then perhaps it attached to those few who went ahead and did what they thought had to be done.

It threw me into a silence as we walked along. I savored Phidias and Mrs. Carroll as having no regrets, and I envied them. I found myself paying him the compliment I usually saved for Madeleine alone: he didn't seem old at all. He was asking me not to let David just happen to me. If David and I wanted it, then we had to know what we had to do and then do it. Destiny had no commerce, it seemed, with those who listed their options again and again and combed the past for clues that made the future easy. Begin by not letting David take care of you, I thought, and then you will see what you have to do next. I had a picture of the two of them laughing, Mrs. Carroll in a white satin dressing gown with a white fox collar and Phidias in work clothes, unbuttoning his shirt. Then laughing in a three-star restaurant on the Left Bank while the waiter flamed their steaks. The rides with Madeleine in the Pierce-Arrow. It was heady stuff, these visions of the moral life.

My not talking seemed to bring us closer together as we neared the house. I imitated his style, affecting my own rhythm in the face of the sweet, self-evident shine of life, or at least I *walked* that way, swinging my hands and crunching my boots heavily on the gravel. I am a notorious parrot when I want to be liked. It is the last of my youthful wiles, and it always works with candid, open-eyed people. They'll nail you in a minute if they catch you in a lie or an evasion, but they get all tender and expansive if they see themselves in you. Especially if you are younger than they are, and then they see themselves in their own youth. Some such fury of tacit understanding was operating between Phidias and me. He began to talk again, but more mildly.

"You first knew Madeleine," he said, "in France. So did I. It's the best place to meet her first."

"Well, it's the *only* place where I met her first, but I see what you mean. I met her in Burgundy, though, and you met her in Paris. There's a difference."

"Is there? How did the village people treat her?"

"Like a goddess."

"In Paris too. It's because it's a Catholic country. Beth and I were introduced to her at a party, and Beth asked her where she was staying. 'The Ritz,' she said, and she acted confused, as if you had asked her what day of the week it was. There was a story about her and the Ritz that everybody knew but us."

He stopped talking abruptly. We had come as far as the house, and Phidias headed around to the front lawn. I went along and waited for the story. When he saw the canvas chairs all in a row as if they were on a ship's deck, he beamed at them. I was storing up points all over the place. We stood there side by side looking off at the water, and he went on.

"After she did her first tour in the front lines, she came back to Paris, and the French navy gave her the royal suite at the Ritz. They were using it as a war room, but they moved all their charts across the hall so she could have the view of the square. It turned out the Ritz was the only hotel that had hot water, so she invited all the entertainers who were in Paris to come over and take baths in her room. They never saw so many stars going in and out of one room. One right after another."

"Who?" I asked. His attention had drifted back to the canvas chairs.

"How would I know? Madeleine said they used enough towels to dry off a tugboat."

He walked over to the chairs and peered closely at the fabric. Leave it to him not to know the names of the stars in his own story.

"It's a wonderful story," I said. "She never told me."

"Like I said, it's something you're supposed to know already." He turned back to me. "When she got there, she opened the closet and found a set of new uniforms from all the Allied powers. They had been done up for her by a tailor in Savile Row and sent over secretly on an RAF plane. I don't think she ever found out who ordered them. They say it was de Gaulle who put in a call to Churchill, but you don't know what to believe when it's about Madeleine, right?"

"Right," I said, and we smiled at each other.

"I know about it because she and Beth spent a whole winter afternoon at the Ritz unpacking the uniforms out of a trunk and trying them on. The war was over then, and she had no use for them. It was too much trouble to take them back to the States. She was sick with a virus. But that afternoon, she and Beth were like two girls in their grandmother's attic. You should have seen them."

I could see them. And I could see him as well, sitting by in an overstuffed chair, drawing on a fancy cigar or picking at some little dainty from room service. Cheerful and pampered while the women played dress-up. Was he really so super-humanly mild, I wondered. Madeleine had given me the impression that he was simply not exercised about the liaison between Madeleine and Beth, but I had found it hard to believe. He had to have been offended or threatened or jealous, I thought. Yet the story of the women in drag at the Ritz evoked something so mellow about the drunken days in Europe after

the war. People recovered their senses like gleeful children in a
toy shop who want this and then this, on and on. In his memories of the time, Phidias did not come through as a man who
questioned his virility or raised his prerogative as Beth's true
lover. If he did not strike me as a man who could be turned on
by the opulence of the two women making love, he seemed as
if he might at least have gone along with the luxury of it all,
wherever it took them.

And of course there was the possibility that he believed in
the destiny business between him and Beth Carroll. If so, it
would have been as Greek of him as he could get. Perhaps she
was free to follow out her scandalous romances because, as he
saw it, the stones and the sea recognized nothing but his love
for her and hers for him. Well, no. When I looked at him with
the sapphire sea behind him, I felt the force of something
simpler cutting through my embroidery. What happens happens. It was just midsummer carrying me away that made me
flirt with the notion of fate. It was my experience that people
did not actually *feel* such operatic quivers in the soul. Except
in some of Madeleine's films.

When he asked me about my own time with Madeleine, the
week we spent touring in Burgundy when I was twenty-eight, I
talked haltingly about the vineyards and the medieval towns. I
gave him a wearying, fuzzy travelogue instead of a lovely
Madeleine story, because I couldn't think of one. It came out
as if it were the single dullest week of Madeleine's life. He
didn't seem to mind, and he made a point of saying we must
talk again. But we didn't have a chance to during those still
and cloudless weeks. Or we talked nearly every day, but it had
to do with canvas chairs and the like. Not that I wasn't happy
to be the labor force in housekeeping matters, and it was sane-
making to know that he would come by every morning armed
with a chore or two. But we didn't soon again get into the
moral laws. I was on my own.

"You don't have a good memory, Rick, because you think too much." That was the last thing he said to me that day. I didn't think he was being entirely fair. After all, I had remembered about the canvas chairs.

I thought I was the only one concerned about the children, and it made me twice as queasy, because I don't like children. The Carrolls' bottomless well of guilt and fixed positions increasingly left me with the feeling that I was holding the bucket. I thought I had to keep bringing it up, to make them see we were on a collision course with big trouble. But it didn't seem to me that I was able to get anyone's attention when I talked about it. Then David reported a scene that I had missed, where for a moment it came up again about why we were doing what we were doing. It was the sort of talk I loved. I would have known just what to say, and I was fuming, blaming each of them in turn for leaving me out. But as David told me what was said, I saw how it wouldn't have happened if I was there. They got to it by accident, and it lasted only an instant. I would have pushed too hard, and no one would have had the space to figure it out for himself.

How it came about was that Madeleine asked Phidias for pictures of the children, because she couldn't find any in the drawers or on the shelves in Mrs. Carroll's room. So one day, late in the afternoon, they met in the attic. Aldo came with Madeleine because he was in the middle of a sentence at the time and refused to yield the floor. And David met Phidias going up the front stairs and tagged along. It wasn't *planned*, David insisted. I don't know where I was. Digging down to China in the sand or something. Filling my pockets with water-washed stones and bits of glass.

It was hot as an oven in the attic, and they began by not talking at all. Even Aldo. They got right down to it, each of them turning to a sea chest or a stack of cardboard boxes, right away staggered at the brute accumulation of it all. Because the

Carrolls had dwindled so by the time of our tenancy — coming to life only by turns in Phidias's stories, insubstantial phantoms in this solid, solid house — the memorial detail in the attic gave overwhelming focus to the patterns of the Carrolls' summer lives. It wasn't just the heat in the attic that hastened them along. They were spooked.

"You won't believe it," Aldo said, "because you can't believe it. You know what these are?" He held up a deck of stiff white cards. "Menus for dinner parties. Hand-lettered. There must have been one at every plate." He began to read from the top one. " '*Terrine de grives.*' And the wine is Pommard, nineteen thirty. What's '*grive*'?"

"Thrush," Madeleine said.

"That's the first course. Why would anyone want to do that to a thrush?"

"Here's a box of tennis medals," David said from the shadows. "They're all silver."

"Why did she save all this junk anyway?" Madeleine asked with some distaste.

"Because there was the attic to put it in, probably," Phidias said, full of his customary lack of irony in these matters.

"Not good enough," Madeleine said, shaking her head. David said that he knew, when he heard her, that she had no attic herself. For her, it was a bad compromise between what you couldn't live without and what you couldn't help but lose. "You have to have some idea what you're liable to *do*, so you know what to keep and what to get rid of. The point is, you don't *need* old props. You buy new ones." She was slapping her way through a foot-high pile of *Playbills*. "And you don't need clues to the past, either, if you remember what's important."

"You're such a consumer, Madeleine," Aldo said. "Just find the photographs. If we don't get out of here in thirty seconds,

I'm going to be pressure-cooked. I'm not supposed to sweat this much. Extremes aren't good for me."

"Here they are." Phidias drew the photograph albums, one by one, out of a carpetbag. They were uniformly bound in brown suede, stamped on the front with the summers in question — 1933–1936, 1937–1939, 1940–1946. They kept a photographer in residence, Phidias explained, for a few days in the middle of August. The estate went into production like a summer stock company when the photographer arrived. The servants set picture-perfect tables and sported starched whites. The children were dressed and undressed and arranged in holiday tableaux. Even the cows were summoned into service, dotted about rustically in the background.

Madeleine sat down next to Phidias on the lid of a cedar chest, and they began to look through the earliest of the albums, turning the pages over slowly until Phidias found the children. David and Aldo hunched behind them and craned to get a view.

"John and Cicely on their ponies," Phidias said, pointing them out in the midst of a sunny little group of maids and governesses dancing attendance.

"It says they're ten and thirteen," Madeleine said. "Cicely looks about thirty-five."

"Maybe it's the ponies that are ten and thirteen," Aldo said. "Can we please get out of this heat?"

"Where's Tony?" David asked.

"Not born yet," Phidias said.

"Find him." This last from Madeleine. She knew enough already about the lost tribe of the children to know that Tony had grown up to be the loner. They were all three so unforgiving of their mother that their tantrums and accusations didn't distinguish them from each other. But Tony had ended up with no one and, from all reports, hated the very air he breathed. If

Madeleine's secret plan — the one she swore was a figment of my imagination — was to settle accounts with the children and tie it up nicely before Mrs. Carroll passed on, I'll bet it was the fragments about Tony that started her mind racing with scenes out of O'Neill. In 1945, when Madeleine came to stay for the autumn, the children had already gone back to Boston for the winter with their father. But she must have had some feeling for who they were, even then. And as Phidias turned to that very summer in the third volume, Madeleine must have looked to see how the children fared in the days when their mother was away in Europe with her lovers.

"Here he is," Phidias said, pointing at a little boy swinging on a rope in the woods, holding tight with both hands. "He's the one who loved to pose for the photographer."

"I have to get out of here," Aldo said. He did look, David said, as if he might pass out. He headed for the stairs and, starting down, turned for a parting shot. He was wet quite through. "Why do you suppose you're all doing this?" he asked moistly.

Madeleine looked up and cocked her head. She said very quietly: "This?"

"You know what I mean. This summer. This whole masquerade."

It got *awfully* quiet. David didn't know which of them was the appropriate one to answer. The answer itself was as simple as ever, as far as he was concerned — they were doing it for Mrs. Carroll. David thought Phidias should be given the chance to say it, and then he wondered if he shouldn't step in and do it instead. If *I* had been there, of course, I would have leapt into it headfirst. "He's right," I would have said, "it's run away with us, and we're in danger." As it turned out, Madeleine took the cue. She is always given the best lines, but then she is the most practiced at being on the spot where the best lines fall.

"It's a thriller, Aldo," she said, "and you're doing it too, so
don't try to palm it off on us. We're all doing it for ourselves."
What a way of seeing it. As she got more and more comfortable in Beth Carroll's bed, she got to kill two birds with one
stone. She was taking a break from her own life and at the
same time accomplishing something in someone else's. And so
were we, she was quick to add. Just by sitting out the summer
on the coast, we did a noble deed. The reward for the generous
act was written into the terms of the act itself. It was like doing
a nightclub gig at Monte Carlo, I suppose she would have said,
because of the chance to play all day. Perhaps I should only
speak for myself, but she seemed to know that the rest of us
thought we were lucky if we brought down even *one* bird per
stone in a given season.

As to its being a thriller we were in, with a hum in the
background like the zither in *The Third Man* — well, I didn't
want to take too close a look at that. Between me and Madeleine, it would have been one more argument about conduct-
ing life as if she were directing a film.

"Just testing," Aldo said with a smile. He approved of
people doing nice things for themselves, whatever the cost.
Nice things, he was fond of telling us, cost an arm and a leg.

So the other reasons never got stated out loud, because they
all filed single-file again down the ladderlike attic stairs and
then dispersed. It was no less true, of course, that we were
doing it for Mrs. Carroll and the pines and mossy rocks, for
the love of summer theater and the dead-of-night dreams that
shimmered between Phidias and his lost love. But David said it
was as if all the reasons had been reiterated, crystal clear.
Whatever Madeleine meant, she allowed us each his own ec-
centric notion of the time. Walking down the stairs between
Aldo and Madeleine, David knew that our summer was not
quantifiable like those days of the Carrolls. It wouldn't register
on a camera. As they came into the cool of the upstairs hall,

they all looked delirious at the change in the weather. And they all knew what they were doing.

The five of us almost never found ourselves together in the same room because Phidias had gone back to his old habit of being overseer and spent most of his time up at the farm. The rest of us met in the evening for dinner. Aldo and Madeleine huddled together every afternoon doing business, and it annoyed me that Madeleine was not being treated to the easy vacation she had promised herself after the will was signed. But there was the money to think of. Aldo wanted to set up the concerts for the winter and spring. Credit-card calls went out to London and Paris and Berlin and Las Vegas. Mrs. Carroll's bedroom took on the air of a classy small business like diamonds or Pre-Columbian art. They renegotiated a recording contract. They sketched out an agreement whereby Madeleine could donate certain of the artifacts of her career for tax breaks and put others up for auction.

We drank a toast one night to a fast sale to a private bidder in Los Angeles. Six thousand dollars for the opera gloves with the cigarette burn between two fingers from *The Ambassador's Lady*. She wears them in the scene in the empty ballroom while she waits to find out who wins the duel for her honor, Tyrone Power or Randolph Scott. She sits on the piano bench and holds the cigarette and looks glassy-eyed until she feels the burn. Then she cries out and runs across the room in her hooped dress, calling the Scott character's name over and over. She reaches the doors just in time for Power to catch her in his arms. 1946.

"That's three thousand dollars a glove," David said.

"No," Madeleine said, shaking her head. "Only one of the gloves has the cigarette burn. I figure five thousand for the right hand and a thousand for the left."

It had not sunk in before, what Aldo had confided to me about Madeleine's money problems. When he first spoke of it, we had just finished defrauding Mrs. Carroll's children out of twenty-eight hundred acres of coastal lowlands, enough property to build a suburb on. I wasn't able to take him seriously. Madeleine looked rich and acted rich. She was rich in the same way as she was French, inevitably and for good. As we all clinked our glasses and laughed about the gloves, though, I realized that I was accustomed to taking Madeleine's view of liquid assets. You make a lot of money on a picture or a pair of gloves, and you pay a lot of money for a Dior suit or a first-class passage across the North Atlantic. None of these things seemed to have anything to do with *real* money, what you buy groceries with or what pays the rent. Madeleine was not engaged in keeping the wolf from the door.

But if she was penniless (and I allowed enough room for Aldo's exaggeration to know that she wasn't reduced to eating cat food or taking in boarders), then she should be getting something more steady than glove money. I was grateful to Aldo after all for his afternoon manager's sessions with Madeleine. When I met him the next day in the kitchen, where he was eating right out of the refrigerator, I told him so.

"Aldo, you must have broken the record for opera gloves. You ought to go into the antique business."

"My dear, I already have," he said, waving a drumstick. "I just acquired a pair of slightly used opera gloves."

"*You* bought them?"

"Honey, she has a whore's pride. She won't take money for free. I had to do something."

Aldo was with Madeleine several days later when Farley called about the children. He answered the bedroom phone in the middle of a sentence, assuming it was Lake Tahoe returning his call, and he gave a bug-eyed look at Madeleine when Mr. Farley asked, in his ashen tone, to speak to Mrs. Carroll. Madeleine didn't mind at all. She took up the phone and greeted him as Mrs. Carroll, bracing herself for the second act.

Who, Mr. Farley begged to know, was answering her telephone as if the place were a delicatessen. "That was the undertaker," she told him. "I want my funeral to look like New
Year's Day at the Rose Parade. You're not invited."

Farley had no comment. He was just calling to pass along
information, and it turned out that Phidias had predicted the
outcome accurately. Cicely was not about to come when her
mother called. She had turned over the financial end of her
family life to her brother John. She was fifty-six years old, and
she didn't think she and her mother had any chance of suddenly getting chummy with one another. "She's probably
right," Madeleine said to Farley. "When she was here last
Christmas, she said most people's mothers are dead by the time
they're fifty-six. I told her it was all her fault. I just can't stand
to leave my little cubs behind."

Meanwhile, John was going up and down the Chesapeake in
a sloop. John was a lawyer like Mr. Farley, and they had
presumably agreed that Christmas would be soon enough to
deal with mother. John and Mr. Farley agreed about everything, but they agreed most passionately, until they were
practically hoarse, about the skeleton in the closet that took
the form of Phidias and Mrs. Carroll. All of this came out in
Beth Carroll's diary, which Madeleine had begun to read
piecemeal before going to sleep. It was shelved, several
volumes of it, in the hidden cupboard behind the bed where
the cameos were kept. Madeleine had discovered that Donald
Farley had been something of a father to John Carroll ever
since the day Mr. Carroll fell over onto his desk with a coro-
nary in the middle of a memo. In turn, John was father to
Cicely, even though she was three years older, and to poor
nervous Tony.

"What about Tony?" Madeleine asked.

"The school says he's in Africa," Mr. Farley said.

"I know *that*. Of all of them, you know, he'd come if you got hold of him. He's the only one who'd suspect that I changed the will."

"I think it can wait until Christmas," he said. He exuded good sense and authority. He was giving his judgment.

"It can. I can't," she said, to tease him mostly.

"You aren't sick, are you, Beth? You know, you don't sound like yourself."

"Don't jinx me, Farley. You've talked half of Boston into an early grave with talk like that. Does someone pay you a bounty?"

Hanging up, Mr. Farley seemed to feel she was more herself again. She had always talked tough. Madeleine decided that Beth survived by it. The diary showed how they all got even with her by cutting her out of their lives. But Madeleine could not find any evidence that she cared or fought back. Because the love affair that wrecked their home had been going on so long, none of the children was entirely sure that Phidias wasn't their father. Cicely and John apparently convinced themselves that they were purebred Carrolls, but they never forgave their mother for the doubt. They saw a little Greek in Tony and spooked him about it. Mrs. Carroll wrote it all down in her diary, but she didn't seem to know what to do. She fell into tough talk and dismissed it and so got even with them.

When he was eight, Madeleine read, Tony wandered into a dinner party in his pajamas. His father commanded him to go upstairs. "Do what your father says," Beth said, and Tony asked, "How do I know he's my father?" The eerie thing about the diary entry, Madeleine said, was that she gave no indication of what it made her feel. She wrote down what they had for dinner and who they had for dinner and even ticked off the flowers. Madeleine was furious. She would read Aldo passages while he sat in the bay window and fattened her bank account.

He told her it was none of her business, that nothing could be done about it now. I had won him over to my position. Madeleine said we were scared of our own shadows.

Now it didn't matter because they weren't coming. When Aldo found me on the porch and told me, I swear that the sun came out from behind a cloud. Suddenly the time was free again. I can't pretend that my anxiety about the children had really gotten in the way of my good humor, my lust, or my sense of summer. David and I followed our own course as much as Madeleine and Aldo did when they sat upstairs and made money. "You be the grasshoppers," Madeleine told us, "and we'll be the ants." But we were a little less likely to wind up in jail on Labor Day if the Carroll children kept their distance. Also, Madeleine would not have to go through the indignity of being unmasked. In a way, I was more relieved about that than about jail. I had had such a horror of the scene, the assembled family rising to their feet in shock when the parody of Mrs. Carroll walked into the room. Angry as I was at her for thinking she could get away with it, nevertheless I didn't want Madeleine to be disabused.

"But that's not the best part," Aldo said. "Madeleine has agreed to write her *memoirs*."

"She said she never would."

"Mrs. Carroll's children and Mrs. Carroll's diary have changed her mind."

"How?" I asked. I saw myself taking dictation. Or sitting at a typewriter set up on the porch table, transcribing it off a Dictaphone.

"The children because, now that they're not coming, she has no *drama* to look forward to. There's not enough show business in this burg. And the diary because it's so out of phase with the woman Madeleine knew, so out of touch with the facts. Madeleine wants to do a better job on her own life."

"Is she going to tell the truth?"

"I don't think that's been decided yet. You mean about the ladies in her life, right?"

"I guess so." I wasn't sure what I meant. How was she going to get it all in a book? I liked it the way it was now, some of it legend and the rest documents — films and old recordings, Beaton photographs and *Times* photographs, reviews, interviews. "But does she have to? There isn't any more she needs to say about her life."

"You sound like her," Aldo said. "You forget that there is *money* to be made. Her past is a gold mine." He puffed out his chest and poked his thumb at it. "Trust the fat man."

For the next few days, I tried to get Madeleine to talk about the project, but she was not ready to. "Not yet. Not to you," she said. "Your standards are too high. You want it as good as Proust." I protested, but I couldn't change her mind. Then I let it go because she tricked me, telling me she wanted to spend time with me only if I would help her *forget* about the book she had to write. She announced that she wanted to take walks. So we began to walk in the early morning on the beach and in the late afternoon in the woods. It did not even interfere with my midday sun with David. It meant I was outside all the time. She talked about the past, but not about writing about it, and I was a pushover and preferred it that way. She wore pale linen suits tailored like a man's and a straw boater. She looked like she went to Princeton.

One day at the rock pool between the ridges, she took a leather-bound book out of her bag and began to read aloud. It was Beth Carroll's account of the first days in Paris after Madeleine had come into their lives. Dry lists of restaurants and cafés and parties. Names dropped like so many eggs. Outings to places so famous they can't be described, and when she described them, the prose was as tongue-tied as if she had said, "In Venice there are many canals." The remarks about Madeleine were surprisingly star-struck. "I want to wear Madeleine's beaver wrap," she wrote, "but I am afraid to ask. When she is asleep at night, I put it around my bare shoulders and walk back and forth in front of the bathroom mirror." It didn't sound very tough to me. Madeleine looked up, her mouth thin and sour.

"What the hell is that supposed to mean?"

"It's a kind of shorthand, Madeleine. She probably never meant it to be read."

"Don't be so nice," she said, cutting me off. "She doesn't talk about anyone else that way. She never gets sloppy or stupid, no matter what happens. But *this*" — she rapped the page about herself with the back of her hand — "this is like *Photoplay*. She wasn't *like* that."

"What does Phidias say?" I asked, to change the subject some.

"He refuses to read it. Just as well — she hardly mentions him at all for months at a time. But *here*" — she stared at the book, not able to find the words for how odd she found this particular thing — "she comes off as a brainless southern belle. Her biggest problem is her beaten biscuits. I can't understand it."

"Does it make you wonder what the truth really is?"

"No. I know what the truth is. This little scene with the mirrors may have happened, Rick. She may have done it night after night and modeled everything in my closet. But it isn't the truth about her and me."

"The truth is *everything* about a person, isn't it?" God help me, I sound so sententious. Why, I wondered, are we even having this conversation? I didn't care about this. I didn't trust an abstract opinion, I realized, as far as I could throw a piano.

"Of course not," she said. She was looking down now into the water David had dived into. She seemed in a way to have forgotten the diary itself and to be going back over her own memories. *She* didn't sound sententious. "A love affair only has time for certain things. It doesn't include what you hide in the bathroom."

"Where does the rest go?" We were not getting high marks in logic, I realized, but it seemed worth it to go along for the ride. "All the secrets and the guilty dreams, I mean."

"You save them for before and after your love affairs. Maybe nobody can get it right when they write it down. I could wallpaper that whole house with the crap people wrote about me. But Beth knew me better. I'm *sure*."

"Are you going to try to get it right in your book?" I asked, bringing it up to tease her.

"I'll get *me* right," she said. "I'll probably make a mess of everyone else. Do you want to be in it?"

What a question. But before I could think of a clever, clever thing to say that would keep me from having to answer it, she spoke again.

"Don't move," she said quietly, staring into the water. I was looking at her, and I froze. "Behind me, on the ridge."

I looked up, and it was gone. But I caught the afterimage of a deer, like the glow in the dark after someone has turned out the light. I knew as soon as I saw it that the flag had been dropped to signal the passing of midsummer. A moment of delight thrilled in me, and in a moment it was followed by dread, the same flash of opposites that I get when I'm making love. It is not as if the leaves suddenly yellowed or the wind went cold. Still sunny, still warm, the day circled the clear water of the pool in full green light. But I became aware of the summer air as limited, bounded on either end by — not winter exactly, but more like a diminishing of detail, a drawing back of life to two dimensions. I didn't know which two, but one was time. How much time have I let go by, I thought, without knowing it? I felt a surge of conviction that nothing stands still, not the deer, not the peak of the heat, and certainly not us. If it had been anything but a deer that came and went, I might have given it the benefit of the doubt.

So we had shared a secret of sorts, Madeleine and I, though she only saw it reflected in the pool and I saw the wind that it left behind as it sprang away. But it had the effect of stopping us from talking any more about The Truth and The Past. Madeleine is, she would be the first to admit, such a civilized creature. One can only imagine the most domesticated animals in her vicinity, a pair of chow dogs underfoot, say, in a bedroom full of ancient painted panels and difficult plants. One would have to go further and say that Madeleine couldn't keep animals or greenery at all because they can't take care of themselves. The deer may have fled at the sight of Madeleine, then, because of the aura that clung to her of European squares and Italian gardens. But to me the both of them seemed more alike than they must have seemed to each other, exotic and calm and lordly. Five years before, I would have thought the deer was fleeing *me*. But they move so fast, they seem to move mostly for motion's own sake.

In my heart, I have let the old Sea Island deer go, and I did the same thing now. I didn't smother the image by trying to hold it close, something I always used to do. We hurried home in silence, and the secret made me happy, even though I knew the summer was going to make its way downhill. I was not as surprised as everyone else that things turned upside down again. I wouldn't say that I was braced for disaster. The nimbus of late summer glowing on the land didn't ruin my time with David either. Rather, it seemed to make me squander more at every mating. Those few days following the sighting of the deer were perhaps the most utterly blue in the sky and the sea. I didn't feel sorry for myself. What happens happens. But I did begin to grieve about all of us together, the whole haphazard summer group of us, since I knew we would have to be dispersing soon.

It was after the twentieth of July, and we were having lobsters for dinner. Before Aldo came, we had made do with the little market in town where Mrs. Carroll had ordered her food because they delivered. David would call in a grocery list, and the panel truck would pull up a few hours later. The grocery boy, who was as sexy as the gardener though not as sinister, handed over a carton of food to David or me and traded pleasantries about the ocean. He was a weekend sailor, and he spoke with a certain dumb and simple rapture about his boat. Like all slow-witted people with a passion, he spoke in a language that seemed half religious, half erotic. He drove David crazy. I had a wonderful time when I talked to him, philosophizing with him about the tides and storms and wrecks and runnings aground.

But Aldo had insisted that we were eating like little old ladies, and he had gone off in his car and found a fish market on a crowded harbor to the north of us. So now we had blue-fish and scrod, steamed clams and fresh scallops and oyster stew. Late in the day, Aldo drove away to examine the day's catch while Madeleine and I were off walking. Today he had gone all out and bought lobsters, though they cost about as much a pound as Iranian caviar. He found, far back in the china closet, a set of crazy red plates in a shellfish motif. He fitted us out with giant bibs and nutcrackers. He even convinced Phidias to join us, so we were five at the kitchen table. We worked at our lobsters and made a nice mess.

"We look like the elves in Santa's toyshop," Aldo said.

"I don't really like difficult food," Madeleine said, handing a claw to David to crack for her. "I adore the lobster salad at the Hotel Pierre, but I've never felt the need to know the source."

"There won't *be* lobsters on this coast in fifteen years," Phidias said. "All the beds are going empty."

"It used to give me hives when I was a child," I said.

"But it was all in your head, right?" David said, smiling at me lasciviously.

"It itched all over."

"Did you know that some people are allergic to other people?" Aldo asked. "They wheeze and get all stuffed up and itch and everything."

"It's all in their heads," David said.

"Pardon us, Doctor Freud," Aldo said in a vamp's voice. Then he turned to me. "Maybe you were allergic to yourself."

"No, that's me," Madeleine said. "Write a book about yourself sometime and see how sick of you you get."

"Books aren't expressive enough," Aldo said. "I think I would like to choreograph a dance about myself. A three-act ballet."

"What *you* ought to be," Phidias told him, "is a TV show."

Considering how we loved, we should have been wildly jealous of one another, and we weren't. Somehow we had skipped that phase. Potshots and flesh wounds, yes. Aldo and Phidias still hadn't done time together alone in the same room, and they tended to express a kind of disbelief in each other. David and I did a thirties number sometimes, wisecracking and fast-talking much as Madeleine and Phidias had on the day they met again. Madeleine railed at us all for what we lacked in experience. "Is it because you're men or because you're younger than I that you don't know the difference between getting what you want and wanting what you get?" was a typical speech, and Aldo would beg her, "Stop with the Ethel Barrymore, Madeleine. You are not in church." But there was no discernible heavy artillery on the field. We managed at dinner to keep in motion the guts of the boardinghouse supper and the cachet of the captain's table. For once, perhaps, we were not worried about love. We were so different from one another that none of us posed a threat.

"What *about* the book?" Phidias asked.

"I've done twelve pages about my first year in LA."

"That should work out to about a libel suit per page," I said, swirling a forkful of meat around in a bowl of drawn butter and feeling fine.

"Don't worry, dear," Aldo said. "We'll put the advance in escrow in case any aging stars want to sue her."

"No no, Aldo," Madeleine protested, "it's just the opposite. I'm so upbeat I could scream. I make Hollywood sound positively *rosy*. That can't be how it was."

"Wasn't it supposed to be the fall of the Roman Empire?" asked David, his eyes agleam. You could tell he would have had a lovely time in Rome. "Bathtub gin and heroin and wanton chorus girls and strip poker and riding crops —"

"No David, that was Berlin," Madeleine said. "But I never went out. All those dry hills got on my nerves for a long time. And nobody invited me to parties because I couldn't speak English. Or because I was queer," she added in a sleepy voice.

"Chapter one, Madeleine in exile," I said.

"People had faces then, didn't they?" Phidias asked, and it surprised me, as if it never occurred to me that he went to the movies. Later, I thought it surprised me because it was such a gay line.

"Who said that?" Madeleine demanded.

"Gloria Swanson," said David, ever the earnest archivist.

"Oh, her. *Sunset Boulevard*. I turned down that picture, you know."

"That's what they all say, Madeleine," Aldo said.

And then the doorbell rang. It had only rung once before, when Farley came, and so we all knew what it was except Aldo. "What's that?" he asked, and we answered in a lopsided chorus, "The doorbell." I looked around the table. We all wore expressions that, to differing degrees, seemed to say, "Who can that be?" We looked for a moment like the strangers gathered in a waiting room. The pause was only a second or two, but the talk stopped, and so did the clinking of lobster shells. Phidias broke the silence and said it was one of his sons, which made sense since none of them would have had the temerity to walk right in. He stood up and took off his lobster bib and stopped at the sink to wash before going off to the front door. Hurry, I thought, because what if something's wrong. David and Aldo began to eat again, all unconcerned. Madeleine caught my eye across the table and silently questioned me. What did I think it was? she seemed to ask, but almost playfully, as if we needed a good surprise about now.

"Is it hard to write?" David asked.

"No," she said, "but it's hard to care."

"Bullshit, Madeleine," Aldo said. "What you don't like about it is that you can't pay yourself compliments."

And the three of them were off again while I strained to hear what was going on at the front door. But in vain. There would have had to be screaming for me to hear it so far away. Something like "Fire!" or "Help!" would have carried, but apparently it was none of those. I couldn't at the moment think of a crisis in the milk business that it might be. And of course it was hard to take it seriously that it might be a disaster, because it was Friday night, we were all together, and the enemy was variously on Block Island and in Chesapeake Bay and North Africa.

"Sh," I said. I could hear Phidias coming through the dining room, and then the door swung open. From the look on his face, it was bad but not catastrophic.

"It's Tony," he said.

I knew that's what he was going to say.

"He's in North Africa," I said.

8

OH NO HE WASN'T. He had come home. And in the ensuing confusion, there really wasn't time to get into the fine points of why his plans had changed. Phidias told Madeleine to go up the kitchen stairs and lock herself in Mrs. Carroll's room, and she made him promise to stall off a visit until the following morning. Tony was going to expect to stay in his old room, Phidias said, and that, David and I knew, meant we had to vacate the tower. Aldo cleared off Madeleine's place at the table, but there really wasn't time for us to disappear or negotiate a story that explained who we all were. Phidias said that, as soon as he got his things out of his car, Tony would be on his way in here for a drink. So he drinks, I thought. There was nothing for us to do but sit there and pick through the remains of our lobsters and try to look properly sheepish and brazen by turns. As if we had been caught by the master with our servants' boots on top of his desk while we tried a pipeful of his tweedy tobacco.

As Madeleine opened the maid's door to go up the back stairs, she turned around to give an exit line. As it happened, only I was watching her because Phidias was giving orders, and David and Aldo were bustling to get them done. She spoke in that whisper she could aim like a laser, and no one else heard her as she spoke across the kitchen to me.

"The plot thickens, eh?"

She closed the door behind her, and her footsteps sounded on the steep stairs. She had gotten her way after all, and she loved it. As to the plot thickening, I grinned at the thought that some movie lines were so surreal they had probably never made it into movies. When I think back on it, I see it was the first time all summer that I didn't take my psychic pulse and note what I was feeling. The first time in years, really. As I considered quickly the range of things that could happen in the next day or so, I found myself full of scenes and not full of me. I gauged the other three men in the room as I would have measured my infield in the ninth inning. Or no: as I would have squinted from one to another of the men in my gang before a holdup in broad daylight.

We still had enough lobster to keep us busy, but no one seemed to know what to say. I did. To make us seem casual and self-possessed, I began to spin a yarn about lobsters, something out of my youth I didn't know I remembered. About a lobsterman who wouldn't eat them, who said they were full of slow poison and caused cancer. I talked to him gravely at the town dock when I was a child. "He must be dead now," I said, but it didn't depress me much. When Tony Carroll walked into the room, a half-gallon of Dewar's under his arm, I was talking too much and the others were unnervingly silent, heads bowed to their dinner. We looked like any four dumb workingmen, but I at least looked like their leader.

"Are you mother's nurse?" he asked me.

"You mean David," I said, fingering him as I pointed across the table.

"We don't say nurse," David said neutrally. "She says she doesn't need a nurse."

"That's where mother gets all her power, isn't it, Phidias?" Tony said. "She defines all the words."

Phidias shrugged his shoulders and continued eating, apparently having heard it all before. I saw that Tony Carroll was almost as old as I am, and it disoriented me differently than had the similar recognition about Aldo a few weeks before. I had wrongly assumed Aldo was an Older Gentleman, and I always thought Tony would turn out to be a Boy. Because he was the baby of the family, I suppose. But also, Phidias and Madeleine seemed to talk about him as if he suffered from a very young man's loss of self. The only self that kind has to lose so far is a child's, and they lose it badly and clumsily. If they are gay as well, they lose it again and again until they come out or until they are thirty, whichever happens first. Tony Carroll was an aging baby, and he wasn't aging well. He had a drunk's baggy eyes. His face was curious because in some places it seemed drawn and tight and in others puffy and numb. He wore the sort of nondescript sport jacket and tie that told you he was about to go into a classroom smelling of boys and teach a class in lower mathematics or Latin verbs. And he was gay all right, but you could tell he hated it and kept it to himself. I felt a little leap of rage.

"How was North Africa?" David asked. David, I saw, was the one who was going to be polite. I certainly wasn't.

"Grotesque," he said, putting ice in a glass. He talked as he undid the wrappings on the bottle. Of course, we already had scotch. But people who bring their own liquor do not want to be restrained by other people's fifths and jiggers. "I had the shits in Algiers for four days, and the guide I hired stole my suitcases. There was an airport strike the day I was supposed to leave. I sat in a Quonset hut on the runway drinking rotgut Algerian wine for sixteen hours until I could convince someone to take a bribe and get me out."

"You really make me see it," Aldo said. "I'll bet you teach English."

"That's right." Tony looked at Aldo over the rim of his glass as he took a gulp.

Aldo went on. "You know, you ought to write a letter to the *Times* about it. The travel section on Sunday is full of letters that would make your hair curl. Just write up the facts as if you were telling it at a party. Then people won't go to Algeria anymore, and their economy will get ruined."

"Who are *you?*" Tony asked.

"I'm in antiques."

"What are you doing here?"

"Appraisals. But I can't talk about it. There's a sacred trust between the dealer and his client." He turned to me. "*I* thought Algiers was a real kink. I had to dry out in the Canary Islands for a week before I came home. Algiers makes Vegas look like Kansas City."

Wicked Aldo. If I had been in Tony's place, I probably would have had a small aphasic stroke if Aldo had done a number on me. But, perversely, Tony Carroll seemed to like the rough treatment he was getting from us. It meant, unfortunately, that he thought he could say what *he* wanted, too. I introduced myself as the summer handyman but kept a low profile and talked to Phidias in brief, telegraphic sentences about maintenance problems. Aldo cleaned up the lobster debris and managed to cut and serve a honeydew melon in such a way as to show anyone who might have ideas that the kitchen was his territory. I didn't think he had to fear any competition from Tony, who was so pasty-faced that he seemed to be in the middle, fat-thin stage of alcoholic malnutrition. It is one of my blind spots that I am not nice about drunks. I've been nice to too many, and they throw up all over you.

So David was the only one who would talk to him. Tony sat

down at Madeleine's place and began a story about the house and the past that you knew from the beginning could go on until dawn. David nodded and looked him in the eye and made little noises of encouragement. It annoyed me that he could summon up good manners for the occasion when the occasion was cheap. I knew he could take care of himself, and I wasn't feeling jealous either. But I felt the same way Phidias did when he didn't want David to take care of me because it would hold him back. From what David had told me about Neil Macdonald and before him the primal shrink and before him the soccer player and the TV writer and the antique-car collector, he had finally learned that you can't love someone who does not see the connection between loving and taking care. Neil went so far as to prove to him that some people would rather be taken care of than loved because it's easier to hate the nurses than the lovers. It is the old double bind that goes: how can you love someone as awful as I am? — I hate you for having such awful taste. Drunks have this speech by heart, and they give it from about ten P.M. until they are left alone or fall over.

Well, David had really *learned* that lesson, and I was the exam on which he was getting an A because I *did* see the connection. We were taking care of ourselves and would keep it up if we stayed together. That wasn't the problem here. David had this other habit, the one that let him play as he did with the dean long ago on Sea Island: letting older men particularly but plain men in general have a dose of his piercing interest and his candid, black, questioning eyes. He always said he didn't know he was doing it, and he couldn't seem to understand the difference between cruising and flirting. Cruising is blunt and satanic and carnal. It means, when you stare someone up and down, that you want to go to bed and nothing more. Flirting is too artful and subliminal to interest David much, and it tends to be something you do *instead* of going to bed. Because David favored the one over the other, he didn't believe that a man can practice both. He was teasing Tony and setting out lures and traps.

Tony told his story but lost the thread. "Nothing has ever been as *simple* as the summers on this coast, and I am a man who works at being simple. I used to run away on Labor Day and hide, and my sad father would come and find me. I didn't have the heart to hide very well," he said, pausing to search for the next phrase. But he gave up. "Because he wasn't very bright."

"What I love about it here," David said, "is that the land doesn't have four seasons. It has that many in a day."

He didn't take this sweet-ass cheerful line when he was talking to the rest of us, when he bitched about the narrow summer on this gravelly shore. But when David is flirting, I think he wants to impress his listener most with how sensitive he is. And he gets sensitive in the mawkish manner of naturalists or those same travel writers in the *Times* that Aldo mocked. I put a stop to it. I stood up and wiped my hands on the front of my jeans. I clapped David on the shoulder as if he were my sidekick in a B-western and said we had to go to work. Aldo followed us out of the kitchen, raising his eyes to the ceiling as the door swung shut. We left Tony sitting across from Phidias, his hand around the neck of the Dewar's, and we heard him say in a low voice, "Who *are* all these people?" He didn't have a clue about what it all meant, though the real test of course would be the next day, with the mother-and-son business.

Aldo left us to go give Madeleine a preliminary report, and we didn't say anything until we were safe in the tower. David began to strip the linen off the bed.

"We have to get rid of him fast," I said. "He can have a tender reunion with his ma, and then he's got to leave. Because he wants to turn this place into a Tennessee Williams play."

"He reminds me of so many of my teachers in prep school. They used to seem so smart."

"I'm surprised they weren't in a continuous cold sweat," I said, "with you cockteasing them all the time."

"Is that what's on your mind?" he asked tightly, stuffing the sheets into a pillowcase. Then he flung it into the corner. We were on opposite sides of the bed.

"That, and the sentimental crap about the seaside."

"I was just trying to be nice. You acted like a goddam cowboy."

"Nice is not the plan, David. That washed-out closet case could have us arrested."

He picked a clean, folded sheet out of the laundry basket at his feet and unfurled it between us. It floated down onto the bed, and we began to secure it at the corners.

"Don't you trust Madeleine?" he asked in a tone that can only be described as a dare.

"Of course I do." I did. I was going on the assumption that Madeleine could bring it off. I don't know when I had changed my mind. "But how can she keep it up? This dude is just passing through, I think, and Aldo has made him so nervous I think he'll split. But if he gets to be your pal and teach you a little English and steal your dirty underpants when you're not looking, he may move in for good."

"We'll talk about it later," David said, and he flapped open the top sheet. We moved to the bottom of the bed and tucked it in. The smell of the washed cotton was as sharp as the sea air.

"Should we sleep downstairs in the same room?" he asked.

"Maybe we should each have our own room, and it'll be just like a dorm."

"Cut it, Rick," he said, and the temperature dropped. "If you want to talk about being sentimental, why don't we talk about you and the movies? And if you want to talk flirting, why don't we talk about you and Madeleine?"

There was a pause in my head in which nothing happened, almost as if all the nerves paused at the same time and sent no information to the brain. The only thing I remember from college physics is that Einstein, on the day the general theory of relativity leapt at him out of the void, padded downstairs to breakfast and said to his wife, "I've had a marvelous idea." I could be getting it wrong since, speaking of grades, I got a seventy-eight. But it is also true that Einstein was absolutely the only one who interested me in the whole gray, pinch-printed book. Up in the bathroom shaving, he must have gone through a pause similar to mine. It is not as if I hadn't thought, all by myself, the two things David said, but *I* sure as hell never equated them with the two things I said about David. Could *that* be what I'm like, I wondered in disbelief. Could I be like *David*?

I reached across the bed, put my hand behind his neck, and pulled him down onto the mattress. As I fell on top of him, I thought: I'm not angry, but we have to stop talking now. I tried to pin his shoulders down so that he would be on his stomach and not able to move, but he rolled away, and we wrestled for a long moment in a kind of embrace. Of course I was angry. I couldn't let him know something about me before I knew it about myself. I wanted him to take it back, now that he'd told me, so that I could admit it on my own and he could help me. I bear-hugged and scissored him for telling me so abruptly. We neither of us had wrestled since we were boys, I suppose, and we grappled in a way that was not so different from making love, only it was harder and meaner and somehow shy.

And suddenly I was on top. My knees held him down at the biceps, and I gripped his wrists and sat like a jockey on his chest. He grimaced, and his face went red as he tried to heave me off. That got him nowhere, so he decided to negotiate.

"What do you want, you cocksucker?"

What did I want? He knew as well as I did that I would always be of two minds. In one way, I wanted something new every time I turned around. In another, I wanted the same old thing I always wanted, and it had no name, and the single feature it possessed was that I lacked it.

"What," I asked, "are you going to do at the end of the summer?"

My face was poised above his as if I were bent over my own reflection in still water. But I wasn't going to get away with the question. He bucked and strained and seemed as if he'd kill me if I let him go, which made it hard to want to let him go. Which was too bad, since I didn't like this scene now that it had gone on a bit.

"Hold it, David, hold it. I'm going to get off you now."

"I'll tell you what I'm going to do," he said in a husky whisper, and I stayed where I was until he stopped. "After I shit on you, that is. I'm going to run away with Tony Carroll and live with him in a Quonset hut. I'm going to let him piss in my mouth and handcuff me to his bed and drip candle wax on my naked ass. You don't know what the fuck you want, Rick. Let me up."

"I'm going to, I'm going to. But cool it."

I was hardly the convincing person in this situation to be holding out the olive branch, having thrown down the gauntlet only a minute or two ago. But I hushed him and lifted one knee. By chance he went into a convulsion of fury at the same time, and his wrist broke away from my grip as his arm came free from the mattress. The heel of his hand caught me full at the base of the nose. My head snapped back, and in the first zap of pain I thought my nose had been driven right into my brain. When I looked down at him again, he was wincing up at me as if the pain had struck him, too. And there was blood on his cheek.

One of us has been hurt, I thought, but who? In a moment I knew I was the one, that it was my blood dripping on his face. He turned his head and brought up his sleeve to wipe it away and left a smear. By now his other arm was free. I still straddled him, kneeling on the mattress now, and he was holding me at the waist and telling me quietly to put back my head. I did, and it was then that I saw Tony standing in the doorway.

"Excuse me," he said.

"We were just changing the sheets," David said.

I didn't say anything. I tasted the sweet, syrup red of my own blood in my throat, and I heard it bubble in my nose. I reached up to see if it was broken.

"I just wanted to tell you not to move out," Tony said apologetically, wanting to get this over with. "I've got my gear downstairs in my sister's old room. Phidias should mind his own business."

My nose was in one piece. "Do you need anything?" I asked, a certain phlegm in my voice.

"I bring what I need with me," he said, raising his glass. "Are you all right?"

"Yup."

"Well" — oh how he wanted to stay and chat — "good night." He seemed so embarrassed when he walked away downstairs that I felt embarrassed for him. No one should be that out of place.

"See? He's just lonely," David said.

"What do you mean 'just'?"

"Shut up. You'll start bleeding again."

He pulled me down beside him on the mattress. The moment of rage that had made me fight had passed completely. It receded now on the opposite shore, separated from me by this half-wit injury and the clumsy scene with Tony. I had a sinking feeling that I had to say something about Madeleine and another thing about David and say them in the same sentence. I had come all this way keeping the two ideas apart because I truly thought they *were* apart. David and Madeleine were night and day. But maybe not. I was a washout in algebra too, but what I was looking for was a factor like pi that could change a straight line into a circle.

"What do you want?" he asked again.

"Anything I can get."

"I don't think so. You're not that desperate. *That*," he said, making a motion with his head toward the doorway, "is a desperate man."

"We have to talk about Madeleine," I said.

"Do you really want to go into it now?" It was a warning. We might have to fight an even bloodier fight.

"No. Tomorrow."

"Maybe they'll put us in the same cell," he said, and now he was smiling and gentle, "and we can argue about it for years."

He kissed me lightly, but I couldn't kiss him on the mouth because I felt funny about the rank, steely taste of blood on my breath. So I nuzzled his cheek, but because the blood was still sticky there, I hunched down and kissed his neck. I wondered if there was blood on the sheets.

Just after midnight, Phidias knocked at the french doors to the balcony off the bedroom. Madeleine woke with a start. She was sure it was Tony wanting to come in, and she cursed herself for not turning the lock. If he snaps on the light, she thought, or tiptoes in with a candle, he's going to find a bedraggled and unpowdered French singer where his mother ought to be and raise holy hell. She had set the alarm for eight, though she normally slept in until after ten, to give herself the whole morning to make up. For Christ's sake, she thought, if he has to see her so badly that he needs to wake her up, why doesn't he call her once in a while? When I brought in Madeleine's breakfast the next day and found her whitening her hair at the mirror, she told me that she had almost rasped at the door: "Can't it wait until morning, Tony? An old woman needs her sleep." Then she decided she would just outwait him. He knew his mother was a little deaf.

She was so sure that the knocking was coming from the door to the hall that she nearly screamed when the french doors opened. "It's me," Phidias said in the dark, as if he did it every night, and she sighed with relief. Her head ached. She should never have taken a Valium to get to sleep, she decided, because she would be too groggy now to follow the Greek's train of thought. But she had decided she'd better not have her lights on and so turned in as soon as she came upstairs from the lobsters. Otherwise, she would have been up half the night writing down the winter of 1930 and the shooting of *La Bonbonnière*. (Released in the United States as *Lovesick* the following summer, it played in Manhattan for twenty minutes before it was seized by the police, who burned the only print. No one here has ever seen it, but it made her an overnight star.) On the other hand, she reasoned as she tried to wake up, if she hadn't had the Valium, she *would* have screamed.

Of course, Phidias *was* accustomed to the moonlit entrance to Beth Carroll's bedroom, and Madeleine didn't have the heart to scold him. As he sat on the bed and briefed her about Tony Carroll, in the rose light of the miniature bedside lamp, Madeleine felt certain that the years of midnight meetings were in his mind. Tony's arrival was a crisis that both Madeleine and Phidias were convinced she could handle. There was no need for a strategy session, since they had already been over the details of Beth and Tony a dozen times for Mr. Farley's visit on the third. Phidias wanted an excuse to be there at night.

"I don't think he left until after two," Madeleine told me as

I pulled open the draperies and mixed her coffee and scalded milk. "We went over some things I can't get right in the memoirs, and I read him what I've written. He says I'm jealous of the girl I was, and I said I thought she was a dodo. Then we came downstairs and had a brandy and talked about Beth. The nights are the worst, Rick. Anyone will tell you that. When is my baby boy coming up?"

A little before noon, it turned out. Tony had clearly had a couple of drinks before he walked in, because he was hostile right from the beginning. The rest of us didn't know how to set him up for the meeting, so we decided we should steer clear. David ran into him at about eleven when they passed each other at the door to the second-floor bathroom. David didn't have his shirt on because he had been shaving, and Tony, his face constricted by a searing hangover, had taken a sad look up and down David's bare chest as he shuffled past and closed the door. They hadn't said anything. At eleven-thirty, Tony appeared in the kitchen, dressed and somewhat put together. Aldo was layering a lasagna and tried to be cheerful and talk food talk. He offered Tony breakfast — eggs and pancakes and sausages and grits. He sounded, as he put it, "as down-home as a waitress who can retire on her tips to Daytona Beach before she's fifty." Tony said no and got his bottle out of the pantry, looking suspiciously at the level to see if anyone was nipping it behind his back. We relayed our readings of his mood to one another, and at a quarter to twelve Phidias stuck his head through the french doors one last time and gave Madeleine the word.

For the first few minutes, Tony stood just inside the door and talked from as far away from her as he could get. Madeleine had been concerned, when she originally agreed to take on the children, about the business of kisses and embraces. She told Phidias she was convincing as close up as three feet, but there were bits of putty and tape that would show if anyone got nearer. Nothing to worry about, Phidias said. Kisses had never been much in the Carroll tradition from the Mayflower on down, but the last several Christmases had been marked by a no-man's-land between everybody and everybody else. The policy with Tony was distinctly "hands off." When he walked in, he looked at her and then looked away at the room as if it were a dream he was having against his will. Madeleine told me later that she knew he was gay the moment she set eyes on him.

"I got your card," she said, testing the timbre of the voice. "Why did you go *there?*"

"Why do I go anywhere, Mother?" he asked, as if the question were deliberately aimed.

"Well, I don't know. Didn't you have a good time?"

"That's not the point. The point is, I wrote John and Sis that I did. And I sent chatty little cards to the headmaster and my department chairman and the creature who runs the switchboard at the school. Therefore, I have shown all the powers that be that I am a worldly-wise and self-reliant bachelor. John and Sis will say I'm finding myself. The school will say I'm broadening myself. Thus, they will avert their eyes and let me keep drinking."

"How did Farley get hold of you?" she asked, wondering if he was so transparent because he was accustomed to dealing with adolescents.

"Farley? Why, I didn't send a card to Donald Farley. That *was* naughty, wasn't it? No, he didn't get hold of me. What does he want?"

"I wanted to see you."

"What do *you* want?"

"I wanted to read my will."

And that broke the tension for him at last. He laughed out loud like a cough. Then he came forward to the foot of the bed, and she was surprised at how clumsy and wavering he was. Aldo had always been her image of a ·man at war with his body because he was fat. She came from places where you were thin or else. But Tony seemed less to have given up on his body — as Aldo had, his bread sopping round in the gravy — than never to have caught the drift of it at all. Madeleine had come upon every sort of neurotic at one time or another, and Tony was something else. "Crazy people," she said to me later, when it all came out in detail, "and people who punish themselves are obsessed with their bodies. When they crack up and fall apart, they *study* it. They're like people bent over cutting their toenails — they're hypnotized. But that boy is bodiless. He tries to divert your attention from it. Housewives do that."

"Your *will!*" Tony said scornfully. "How positively Dickensian. Is it to be our last chance to beg for land? I have an idea. Why don't you award the family jewels on a point system? We'll decide who's been the most cruel to you, who's been the most indifferent. It will be like a parlor game."

Madeleine told me she really didn't know what to do. Phidias had promised her it would be like this, but somehow she didn't believe that in the event it would be so sad. She thought there would be in their bickering a certain briskness and a quirky kind of humor. But it was more brutal than she expected. And she was expected to reply in kind. What she had secretly supposed all along was that she could turn this relationship around and let the sun in at last. It was her own damned fault.

"You take to drinking from your father's side of the family," she said. She assumed it was typical of them not to answer each other's questions but instead to go on to the next assault. "It's hereditary, did you know that? They've proved it."

"My father didn't drink."

"Your father didn't drink like *you* do. He just drank enough to feel sorry for himself. It didn't take very much. A double old-fashioned would do it. I don't call a man a drinker because of how *much* he drinks."

"How illuminating. Is the same thing true about sex?"

"What do you mean?" she asked, making an old-lady gesture at the ribbons at the neck of her robe.

"That it doesn't matter how *much* you do it. To be an adulterer, you can make it an everyday thing, or you can sin once in seven years."

"Adulter*ess* is the word you mean, I think. What a churchy word. Have you come home so that we can talk some more about Phidias and me?"

"For once, dear lady, I have not come home to call you a whore." He was wearing a tight grin and holding on to both posts at the foot of the bed. Madeleine was offended by the histrionics because it was just plain bad acting. Madeleine had never been in an American school except once, when she heard a daft man in New York give a lecture about the *tranche de vie* pattern in her films. It had made her queasy to listen, and Tony was doing the same thing.

"I was sitting in a bar in Algiers," he said, "kind of taking sips at a Pernod. I had dysentery, see, and I didn't want to jostle my insides too much. And there was a Britisher there, about fifty, but he talked like a schoolboy about rugger and his old Classics master. And he just *hated* his parents because they went and got divorced when he was fifteen. *Divorced.*" He fairly shrieked the word at her. "Well, I started to brag about *our* family secrets. Lady Chatterley and the milkman, I told him. And I realized something." He smiled a grim little smile, and then the tone lowered. The dramatics fell away. "If John and Sis and I had only had sex lives of our own, we wouldn't have kept up this punishment of you. See, John and his wife do it with their clothes on. Sis lies there like it's someone burning her with cigarettes. And I don't do anything at all. So it's our own fault. I don't forgive you, but it's not your fault."

She didn't *feel* forgiven either, but she was touched by him and (curious for her, who let people alone) wanted to protect him. It struck Madeleine that people do give speeches half the time. But in the last few weeks, she told me, she had not been accustomed to hearing them. As I said, we had all been together here long enough to speak in code, and we had each other's number too well to let anyone spin out a whole speech without a hoot. Her protective instinct sprang from this: it was the first time Madeleine felt that we had replaced the Carrolls as the family in the house.

"You figured all that out in a bar in Algiers?"

"Dysentery is like truth serum. Why don't we have a drink? I bet it's afternoon."

"Do you usually wait until noon?"

He shrugged and turned away. He wasn't guilty about the drink, but he seemed exhausted by his own bile and was signaling for a break. Madeleine picked up the old horn that interconnected the bedroom and the kitchen and asked: "Is anyone there? We want liquor." She told Tony that he might have to go down himself, and then Aldo's voice answered back: "We read your Mayday, Commander. Over and out."

Madeleine had the sense that each of them should go about his own business while they waited. Tony stood at the tall dresser and looked over the silver and porcelain odds and ends. From her bed, Madeleine looked out the bay window and considered mentioning the weather. It was drizzling, and she thought to tell him that it was the first rain in two weeks. Then she thought better of it, because he might hear an unintended irony in the remark, as if she equated his coming with that of the squall line. When she glanced back at him, she was surprised at how intently he examined the terrain of the dresser, as if the totem objects of his mother, her brushes and mirror and flagons, were as real to him as the old woman Madeleine played. The things on the dresser, she thought, must haunt his dreams along with the younger woman his mother used to be. The old woman Mrs. Carroll had become was someone different, and Madeleine knew that her impersonation was successful precisely because old people are somehow all alike to the young and the real mother is always the remembered woman with the clear skin and the long bright hair.

Aldo knocked and came in with a tray and put it down in the bay window and then poured. He had brought the house scotch instead of the Dewar's, and the whole tray was done in crystal, with a decanted half-bottle of Bordeaux for Mrs. Carroll. There was a dish of cold hors d'oeuvres face to face with a dish of hot ones, the food arranged like the petals of a flower. Aldo was very visual. And very observant. He was able to report to us downstairs that the session was in his opinion about half over, that Madeleine's act was still together, and that Tony had at last been civil to him.

"You ought to be a caterer," Tony said when he saw the food.

"I may yet," Aldo said. "I change careers very rapidly so as to keep in step with my karma."

"He's from California," Madeleine interjected.

"I was a tycoon before I was in antiques. I can tell I'm entering a food phase."

"It looks like he's moved in," Tony said when Aldo had gone. "He's gotten a good look at the furniture, and he wants first refusal when the heirs gather."

"You mean when I die," she said, taking the wine glass from him and raising it in a brief toast.

"Well, he'd best not hold his breath. That could take forever."

"It had better not. If I outlive Cicely, she'll come back from the dead and drag me down by force."

"Cicely *will* live forever. She has no vital organs."

This conversation, Madeleine thought, was more like it.

There was a real exhilaration in being antic about death, and some things like Cicely they could laugh about together. As they turned away from what they had come to be and began to talk about the old days, a rhythm was established between them in which the past could be traveled as the present was, as if there were no certain outcome to anything. "What I mean is," Madeleine said later, "it was very impersonal for a while. We could have been remembering the scenes in a film. He would picture something we did at the beach or something I said when I was angry, and we acted as if those things were suspended in time." They were in the eye of the hurricane, where the acts of the past could be seen as having no motives or consequences. The things that had happened were pure phenomena. Every moment was all by itself.

"I haven't forgiven this house either," he said after a while, after they had repeopled it and restored some fragment of its long lost summers.

"For what?" she asked. She never took wine herself because she was from Burgundy and had her fill of it in her youth. But to be true to character, she took a gulp of Mrs. Carroll's wine as if she loved it. She remembered dinners in Paris where Beth Carroll had ordered seventy-five-dollar vintages, and Phidias and Madeleine each left a barely tasted glass while Beth finished the bottle.

"For promising such a wide, virgin world," he said.

"You can't have it both ways, Tony. I thought the world was ever afterwards seamy and corrupt because I was a whore."

"It's hard to explain. This house — and all *this*," he said, gesturing out the bay window at the forest and the sea. "I thought this was like the real world I would live in." He turned and faced her. "I had no plans, you see, to live in the world you and my father and Phidias inhabited. I was so sure that the *places* were clean."

"If they're not, why do you keep traveling?"

"Because I don't know what else to do with the summer. If I'm not on the move, I think too much about my summers here."

"When you're old," she said crisply, tired of his despair, "you'll see there's nothing sad about the past except that it's past."

"I'm a homosexual, you know."

"I know."

It didn't seem abrupt to Madeleine. It didn't even seem like a changing of subjects. He said it as if it might explain the interlocking circles of his angers, give a conscious source for the underwater current in their meeting today. But he was not forgiving himself, either, Madeleine saw. His admission was an acknowledgment of their failure to connect in the past, a nod to priorities long abandoned.

"Why do you suppose we've never talked about it before?" she asked.

"I suppose because there was already quite enough ammunition against you. I didn't need to accuse you of turning me queer, too."

"Did I?" she wondered, not about to be convinced.

"I don't know. I hate it so. It makes me so sick of myself. I've never had the stomach to follow out the guilt and properly assign it." He had drunk down his scotch fast, and he had been holding the empty glass in his hand for some time. It was like a pipe that had gone out.

"Well, it's not *my* fault if sex makes you sick. Sex is the only goddam bonus you get in life. You might as well enjoy it."

"But there is the matter of my taste," he said bitterly. "It runs to little boys."

"How little?"

"Sixteen. Seventeen."

"That's not so little," she said. "But it's just because you're lonely, isn't it? Adolescents would be dreary lovers. So afraid of being funny, and so demonic. But I'm not the one to say. I don't like children."

"I'm not good at it, that's the problem. Being in bed with a man gives me the creeps."

"What gives you the creeps is that you're getting old and haven't had enough. But I'll tell you something. Nobody ever has enough."

Madeleine has never been sentimental in a film, in spite of the tacky scripts and lingering close-ups that snuff out everyone's career in the end. She never seems to be working on unearned emotion. An existential moment occurs in the climactic scene where she appears to realize that things have gone too far, that she is being blown off course and is calling into question the laws about Love that are buried in her like perfect cities. One watches her withdraw, no matter what her lines are or who is holding her or shooting her, to the ancient civilizations where she must have been a virgin queen. Those critics who have never liked her work point to that refusal to play out the scene on its own terms as the key to the fact that she is a movie star and not an actress. Her admirers know that she will give up anything to live on her own terms. What makes the moment superb is that she is the one who goes too far and then must give up the luxury of the sentiment that has gone wrong. You watch her let it go, and you see how fatal it is to be human.

"Nobody ever has enough" must have struck that moment like a clock at noon.

"I don't know what I'm going to do," he said.

"I expect you'll go on drinking."

"Doesn't anything shock you?"

"Winter does," she said. "People don't."

"Someday I must stop trying," he said, suddenly becoming aware of the glass in his hand. She thought he was going to put it down and leave, and she drooped her eyes a quarter-inch to say it was time for her nap. He walked out of the bay window and paused to put the glass on the dresser. That seemed to remind him of something, and he turned to her and smiled.

"There's one other thing," he said.

"What?"

"My mother's dead, isn't she?"

"What?"

"I think you'd better tell me what's going on."

9

"I HATE RAIN," David said.

"So you've mentioned. But it looks like West Texas out there. If you'll permit it just one day, it will make everything green again."

"It doesn't matter. It'll all be dead in a while."

"In about three months. I don't think there's any need to panic yet."

"You don't understand."

I don't understand. When everything else is said and done, that is David's last defense. I remember five years ago when we had reached the last awful weeks, the scorched-earth phase. David had met in the park an out-of-work sociologist — they are all out of work in Boston and thus cruelly horny — and they had sex in the sauna room at the YMCA in the late morning when it was empty. Tuesdays and Thursdays from ten to eleven. I might never have found out about it except that David got gonorrhea in his mouth and in his ass and had to tell me so that we could get treatment. And I remember us waiting to get injections at the VD clinic at the hospital. I had so many crimes to accuse him of, I didn't know where to begin. At the time, his keeping it a secret seemed worse to me than the adultery, whch sounded even to me like a very churchy word. But I didn't understand, David said. It had nothing to do with sex or with me. But then he couldn't really say what it did have to do with.

We were sitting in the library waiting for it to be over upstairs, and David drew the heavy drapes over the windows to shut out the rain. You had the sense with David that he was like a caged animal on a rainy day. Even at the best of times he was not likely to sit and read for very long. When he read, it was all self-improvement, books on isometrics and meditation and the like, or he would undertake a huge systematic work of Jung or Darwin, someone heavy, and put it aside at page fifty and talk about it for two weeks. I sat in the wing chair with my Dickens that I had been losing my place in all summer, and David paced. It was too much for him to suffer both a book-lined room and the rain on the same day.

We made love when we woke in the morning, but there was too much on our minds. Not Tony Carroll, except insofar as he was so grimly gay and thus brought back the self-loathing that attended my own growing up. But I was in turmoil about David and me and how we perceived each other, that each of us seemed to believe he was mastering his life and curing his past while the other was making the same old mistakes. It was not as bald as that, but perhaps it was even worse. It could be that there were more crucial mistakes that each of us had been making all along, and they were masked by the more obvious, self-important bits of chaos that one puts in the way in order to fall over them and bloody one's knees. If it's true, I thought as we lay seized in each other's arms after we were done, listening to it rain, if I do feel in lieu of feelings only a memory along my nerves of the scenes in movies, then I can't love at all. That is much worse than the fiction of freedom that marked my fifteen years in the bars. Worse than the mating dance with

David years ago, in which we vied to see who took care of whom. I don't ever *sound* sentimental. But I recall those purple moments on the screen and go too far and bend reality out of shape to fit them. Unlike Madeleine in the showdown scenes, I don't know when to withdraw or let it go.

"Let's talk about Madeleine," I said.

"I'm sorry about that, Rick," he said, coming over to stand at the back of my chair and look down at me. "There's nothing wrong with you and her."

"I'm not talking about wrong," I said. I could almost feel the heat of his breathing on my head, but I would have had to throw my head all the way back to see him. I felt trapped in my chair by the dark fireplace. Then why don't you just get up, I said to myself. But I didn't. "I know I put her on a pedestal, but it doesn't usually matter because we live so far apart. It only happens a few days a year, when she comes to Boston."

I could feel him shaking his head.

"You have it backwards," he said. "When you're *with* her, you're fine. The two of you play it like Ping-Pong, and then you know where to leave each other alone. You're like two prosperous people who live in a big house and come and go." If Tony would only go, I thought, we would all be like that again. And then I thought it wasn't Tony's fault but the passing of summer, and it pierced me again that David and I were the same. "You and Madeleine both agree that movies and stars are for shit. It's the *rest* of the year that fucks you up. That's when you idolize her and act like a fan club."

"I'm the keeper of her Hall of Fame," I said.

"Usually people like Madeleine do that all by themselves. Have you ever met anyone else?"

"You mean stars?"

"Yes. They either catalog their successes at you, or they arrange it so that someone else does, and they have them on a salary. Madeleine doesn't seem to need it. You and Aldo always accuse her of being a prima donna who has to have applause, but I don't think she cares." When he mentioned Aldo and me in the same breath, he began ruffling my hair with his hand, as if to single me out. The rain had not dampened his little garden of insights. "Maybe she does do a star turn now and then, but I think it's to please the rest of us. She *lets* you and Aldo treat her like a queen."

"You make me and Aldo sound like the seven dwarfs. We're very different," I said, pointlessly enough. "How do you know? Did you meet a lot of stars when you were in LA?"

"Not the kind you mean," he said, finally letting my hair be. "But I met rock stars when I was out at the bars. It's the same trip."

He left me, and I heard him go over to the outside doors and, opening them, bring in the fragrant breeze. There was no sound to the rain, as there had been when we woke up to it, but I knew it was still raining because he would have said so if it was over. Or he would have walked out, but he stood now on the threshold and seethed at the gods. I knew I was angry at him and that it was my way of doing something with the anger I felt at myself. I didn't want to listen to him talk about his rock stars and compare them to anything Madeleine might have felt. Yet I knew I didn't need to protect her. One evening, a week before, David told a story at dinner of being on the set of a pornographic film. He and Madeleine went on amiably about the craftspeople while I sat rigid and hated the implication that there was something in common between his film and hers. I was the one who acted in need of protection. It wasn't David's fault, then or this morning. I didn't know what he was feeling about me, but I didn't blame him, whatever it was.

"I don't like the rain either," I said.

"Oh, I know. You'd probably even say so if I weren't around."

"No, I never have." Get up, I said to myself. Stop hiding out in this goddam chair. So I did. I got up, and I threw down the Dickens and lost my place, and I didn't care, because he wasn't as good as he used to be. I did not, after all, have to finish every book I started. Nobody (alas) was keeping score. "But I don't want to admit that it makes me sad because there's so much of it. You know?"

"Sure. Come look at it."

I walked over and stood next to him. I didn't want to go to bed with him right now, but I would have given anything to start the morning over happy, with a clean and clear-hearted fuck.

"It frightens me," I said, "when I think you feel the same things I do. I don't know why. It's supposed to make me happy. People who meet and fall in love stay up all night *agreeing* with each other, don't they?"

"For the first few nights," he said wryly. "Then they're on their own. The rain looks like it covers the whole ocean, doesn't it? It looks like it's raining everywhere."

He was looking out at it, but I wasn't. I had developed the power not to see it, and besides I was more interested in watching him. Standing next to David in the doorway, loving him as I did, I liked the light wind and the fine mist it blew over us. And he didn't look so stricken either, though I was not ready to tell him so. I believed him that the rain must have thrown him into grief all through his youth and was the perfect outward image of his boredom and the meaningless run of time. I meant it when I said that it hurt me, too. But I think he was mournful now that the pain he suffered was not as simple as the rain. He hated the weather now for its indifference and no longer believed in its willful furies and cold shoulders. And he couldn't admit the change.

"I lie to you sometimes," I said, "so you won't know I agree with you."

"The difference between you and Aldo," he went on, as if

there hadn't been a break in that conversation, "is that you insist that you know Madeleine best. His act is different. He thinks she'd be out on the street if he didn't keep his hand in."

"No one knows Madeleine very well," I said, thinking to begin modestly but about to make it clear that no one knew her better. I understood her best is how I would have put it.

"No one knows about Phidias," he said, but I didn't know what he was *trying* to say. I thought he must be telling me that he, too, knew someone better than anyone else. Or it was an oblique remark about Mrs. Carroll and how, with her dead, Phidias had lost the person who had him by heart. As with the rock stars and the pornographic film, it seemed a forced and inadequate comparison to Madeleine, and so I ignored it and looked out at the gray, low-roofed world.

"You don't either, do you?" he asked.

"We get along all right," I said, not caring a whole lot. Why were we going on about Phidias? "I haven't spent much time with him."

"Rick, they were married."

Please don't let him mean Madeleine and Phidias, I thought. But there wasn't anyone else he could mean.

"How do you know?"

"He told me. Way back at the beginning, before the two of you came here." From the look on his face, he seemed sorry he'd told me, though as I went back over the confusion of the last several sentences, I felt how firmly he'd wanted to teach me a lesson. That wounded me. It seemed to be fighting dirty to use the truth like a weapon when the truth hurt all by itself.

"Isn't he married to the woman on the farm?" I asked, feeling off balance. But who had ever seen her? If this had been a Hitchcock film, the farm woman would never have existed at all.

"Now he is," David said. "I mean he and Madeleine were

married in France in the twenties. For three or four years. When they came over here, they broke it off. She went to Hollywood, and he came to work for the Carrolls. I don't know where he met the farm wife."

"What about them meeting in Paris during the war?" We lounged in the doorway and spoke these lines out into the mist. There were spaces between everything we said, and we didn't look at each other. David and I had nothing to do with what we were saying now.

"I gather that's true," he said. "But I think it started with Madeleine recognizing Phidias. I don't know whether Mrs. Carroll ever knew about them. Phidias and I only talked about it once, and I didn't think of all the right questions until later."

This conversation was so surreal that it seemed to me we had at last broken through the looking glass. We were having the conversation that happens at the end of a comedy, when it turns out that everyone is everyone else's brother. Some are in drag, and some know and some don't, and some have been taken care of by kindly shepherds. But usually there is some-one who has all the facts, and David was plainly half-informed. I wanted to shake him and demand a full chronology. It oc-curred to me that David and I were amateurs at the past compared to Madeleine and Phidias. And no wonder there were problems in her memoirs far back in the beginning. Madeleine had a good reason for keeping it from me, no doubt, though I couldn't see quite what it was. I had a sudden, irrational pang, hoping that Aldo didn't know.

"And she hadn't seen him for thirty years between then and this summer," I said, trying to sort out what it meant to her. What it meant to *me* was that I had some final illusions to put away. I had not known until now that I had so many left. Well, I thought, it's your own fault. I got a kick out of blaming myself. It was very gutsy and pragmatic and General Mac-Arthur of me. I squinted into the future. Blaming myself and getting it over with was palpably more interesting than feeling sorry for myself.

"What are you thinking?" David asked, half-convinced that I had gone into shock.

"It's amazing, isn't it, how for some people nothing ever really goes away. I don't ever expect to see anyone again. I've *slept* with a hundred people I wouldn't even recognize. That's the one thing I like about the past, that it doesn't rise out of the grave."

"Except me."

"Except you."

"Hey, you guys," Aldo called. We turned around, and there he was again at the door to the hall, the Dewar's half-gallon in hand. The hourly bulletin. I hoped he was going to say Madeleine wanted to see me first to talk about Tony, but instead he said: "The jig is up."

"What do you mean?" David asked.

"Tony blew her cover. He guessed. We are all wanted upstairs." Nothing was going right, I might have thought, but instead I thought, nothing is going according to plan. So we needed to make a new plan. And I was all ready.

"I'm bringing up a peace offering," Aldo went on, waving the scotch. "I wish I could give it to him intravenously."

"What's the mood upstairs?" David asked.

"I haven't been there yet," he said. "She called me on the intercom. She didn't sound as if he had a shotgun trained on her, but perhaps a small automatic."

As we trooped upstairs, one behind the other, me bringing up the rear in my coal miner's slouch, I realized that David was scared and I wasn't. He was asking Aldo questions Aldo couldn't answer, about what might happen and what had. David had been the first person, after all, who went along with Phidias's plan, and it fell out for him that he then turned the moral subtleties over to the rest of us, trusting us to carry on.

His job had been to dig a grave. After that, he proceeded with the summer he had promised himself. No wonder he paid no attention until now. It was his view, I think, that there were so many of us against a little-boy, whiskey-rotten schoolmaster that it was no contest. But now it was out of his hands, and he was getting jittery, like a passenger who notices that the pilot seems stumped about what's the matter as the plane nosedives. He wanted us to *do* something. As for me, reaching up the stairs to take his hand as it swung back, I was feeling more in control at every revelation. Perversity is going to win in the end with me. Each pricked balloon, each shock of context was bracing me like a long walk in a cold woods.

I caught David's hand, and he turned. "Don't worry," I said.

"That's not what you said last night."

"I know. I just wanted you to know that *one* of us is all right. This time it's me."

Aldo paused at the door until we caught up, and then we all walked in. I was surprised to see Madeleine out of costume. Her face was severe, and her hair was combed straight back because she had taken her makeup off. She wore the chiffon robe, and it only emphasized how gaunt she looked. I supposed she decided to get out of Mrs. Carroll because it had come to seem a bad joke, and she probably felt she needed her own wits about her, in her own incarnation. She sat in a straight-backed chair near the bed. Tony stood at the dresser. Phidias had stopped just inside the door, just as we had, but when we bunched together behind him, he moved forward. I realized that he was the one who was going to speak and that everyone, including Tony, watched him tensely, waiting for a way out.

And, certain of his audience, Phidias was clearly prepared to settle in for a lecture. Soon he was pacing about on the persian rug between the bed and the french doors while we all watched from the sidelines. He started back in the previous autumn, explaining how Mrs. Carroll felt as the winter came down. From the beginning, at the first north wind in October, she promised him it would be her last winter. And, having made the decision, she seemed to savor the rainy, lightless days that in the past sent her into bitterness and rage. For the first time in anyone's memory, she canceled the winter invitations from Palm Beach, and all along Worth Avenue, the linen-hatted grandmothers must have assumed something terminal was at work. Christmas was as grim as ever, but Phidias found her full of mirth when he visited in the late evenings. In the face of her bloodless, censorious children, she took untold nourishment from her secret death. It was set ticking like a bomb at the end of the next summer.

A lot of this was just between Phidias and Tony. I think that Phidias had always maintained the fiction of the feudal-lord-and-farmer manners where the children were concerned, so that even the mention of those nightly meetings was evidence that he wasn't going to mince words. He was establishing his power by means of his intimacy. Tony should have been doubled up with loathing at the speech, but I couldn't read him. I think David expected Tony to be weeping and inconsolable, on account of his mother being so suddenly dead. I knew better. Because he was a drunk, I knew he would save his tears for his late-night, iceless scotches. His mother's death would be the right sort of material for a tantrum. And yet I felt sorry for both of them, sharing the death and without a way to bridge the distance between them. I remembered our first day here in June, thinking as they went off after lunch that Madeleine and Phidias would bargain back and forth with their separate versions of Mrs. Carroll. Phidias and Tony were not likely to strike that kind of bargain.

I looked us all over as Phidias went on. Mrs. Carroll had made the decision about the land and the new will just as the first spring winds blew in off the ocean. Mr. Farley was summoned in Easter week and given his orders. When the garden was in full flower in May, she told Phidias her wishes about the burial. I had heard the next part before, about the night she died, and I tuned it out. It seemed none of my business, even if Phidias and Tony could not come clean about it and make it *their* business. I had compared us all before to a family gathered for the reading of a will, but the image had never made more sense. At that moment, I had the exact snapshot of the situation that Madeleine had an hour or two before, that we were the family in residence and not the Carrolls. If that was so, I thought as I looked sideways at Aldo and David, so different from each other they could be of different species, then the family we composed was still another mixed blessing. What family feelings still persisted in any of us from the dim past were a mess of false faces and doomed tests of affection. A family is a place where the fear of abandonment has turned all the human habitations into caves and cages and islands with treacherous approaches. We could do without it.

Lastly I looked at Madeleine, who had put on a face keyed to the gravity of the occasion. I wondered if she saw her husband when she looked at Phidias gesturing and chronicling in front of us. I knew the *second* husband's name was Peter Jackson and that he was the heir to a middling fortune and a slice of real estate in Arizona about the size of Connecticut. They were married for two years in the late forties, before anyone consented to live in Arizona, and Madeleine left for LA and told the weird sisters, Hedda and Louella, that marriage was not her game. Peter Jackson still surfaced in the news in his own right, a vulgar, toothy man who wore a white cowboy hat when he got dressed up. But the first husband, the child-bride marriage in Europe, was left behind in another world. When you thought of Madeleine, you had to think of her in a one-to-one with Boyer or Robert Taylor or Joel McCrea, because she had abandoned real-life men. For different reasons, of course, Boyer and Taylor do not live in the barrens of Arizona.

"Phidias?" Tony asked, interrupting the narrative, "I don't see what this has to do with me."

Phidias faced him and studied him for a moment, seeming reluctant to yield the least detail of the story, since he had no one else to tell it to. Perhaps he should have begun by begging Tony's pardon, and yet Tony didn't appear offended. He looked genuinely confused.

"Doesn't anyone want a drink?" Tony asked, turning again to the tray. "We can't have a proper wake without something stronger than Phidias giving a speech. Aldo, we need more glasses."

"Tony," Madeleine said in a tired and husky voice, "you have to decide what you're going to do."

"Oh." He took a drink. "I don't think you need *me* to do anything. I really don't want to be involved."

"All of this is against the law," she said, throwing up her hands to take in the summer and the house and what we could see of the coast from the bay window.

"You think I'm going to *tell* someone?" he asked her, and then it seemed to dawn on him that he was the center of our attention. He appealed to all of us now, and his eyes kept darting back to David's face. "What do you think, that I'm going to call Donald Farley and blow the whistle? I don't care what you do here. If you want to sow the ground with salt or cover it with cement, go ahead. I don't just *hate* this house. I'm really unreasonable. I don't like trees or the ocean or anything. I started out hating *those* trees," he said, his voice full of self-mockery, pointing over his shoulder and out the window to the woods, "but I hate everything now. I was telling her" — he nodded at Madeleine, not yet able to name her — "that I've never forgiven this house."

"Don't you see," I said, turning his attention from David, "you're the one we're disinheriting. This is a crime against *you*."

"But since I don't want my mother's land," he shot back at me, "I don't accept the crime. Now if John and Cicely were here, they'd swarm all over you." He was cheery and ingratiating, and he so much wanted us to believe he was one of us that I could have throttled him. "There are these killer bees, you know, that just keep stinging and stinging. That's Cicely. John is more like a scorpion."

"So you don't care," Madeleine said.

"Well, I'm *interested*," he replied. "I saw you all through the kitchen window, before I came in last night. I watched you all eat. It made me jealous, because we always took our meals in the dining room. If I hadn't seen you then, you know," he said to Madeleine, "I might have been fooled. You were just like her, except you were too nice. My mother wasn't nice."

"You're no damned good," Phidias said, and we turned back to where he stood in front of the french doors. He had been left hanging just at the end of his story, and he had not been given the proper time to draw the moral. In the interval, he scrapped the temple of reason. He was white with anger, but he spoke in a low corrosive voice, as if·everything were a suppressed shout. "You don't even ask how she died. Or if she died easy. She'd laugh at me if she was here, because it's a waste of time, but I want you to know something. She stopped talking about you and your worthless brother and sister as soon as she saw the lawyer. David, did you ever hear her talk about the children?"

"No," David said as if he wanted to crawl under the carpet.

"So she died clean, Tony." He was magnificent, rocking back on his heels and huge with scorn. "You'd turn on us in a minute, but you're afraid to make threats because we might laugh at you. You're just like your goddam father, except that he had the excuse that he was a fool. You know just what you sound like, and you don't care." As he wheeled around to the doors, his eyes swept over Aldo and David and me like a firestorm. But he didn't see us, arguing as he was with the whole departed family that ghosted the house. When he pulled open the doors, I remembered David's telling me about his coming in the same way on the night Mrs. Carroll died. To him, I suppose, all of us violated the room he visited after dark for forty years. Before going out, he flung back one more dart. "No wonder you drink," he snarled. "I don't know how you stand it." And then he clanged down the iron spiral stairs and away.

Now that the doors to the balcony stood open, the pearly light and the rain-washed air came in, and we had a moment to catch our breath. I had the oddest sense that, one after another, each of us would have an explosion just as Phidias had, and one by one we would leave the room. If that happened, I thought, who would be the last one left? Me, I figured, because I was so calm I could land a DC-10 on a tennis court. Calm because I had known all morning that Tony was going to react just as he did. David was right that I was jittery the night before, but that was before I knew how he and I saw each other as possessed of the same devils. When I threw myself on top of him and began to fight, without a clue about where wrestling ended and sex began, I became devoted to contrary behavior. I have lived my life (that thing I think about all day long) being sure of everything, but I had coasted through the last day on something new, that everything was at least the opposite of what I was sure of. Put another way, I thought of myself now as having stopped getting older.

"He's always told me that about my mother," Tony said, a little apologetically. "You shouldn't think it's something new. That's the sort of thing we would say in this house."

"Remind me that I'm busy next Christmas," Aldo said. He

seemed quite serious. He cradled the big half-gallon of Dewar's in the crook of his arm as if he were holding a baby.

"What are you going to do?" I asked, and I didn't hear the question throbbing in my own head like an echo. I wanted to let him know that we could keep to the flight plan even if the captain was knocked out. For once I was not asking the question of myself, as if I understood that I could not be both the questioner and the questioned. Because the one does not wait for an answer, while the other burns all inquiries.

"I think I'm going to make a break for it," he said, and I wondered if we had the same taste in television movies. "Is my mother — when is my mother going to die? I mean, is my brother John going to call me on Labor Day to break the news?"

"In September," Madeleine said evenly. "Phidias knows when."

"You're not leaving now," Aldo said, as if enough was enough.

"In the morning," David said, and Tony locked eyes with him. David was as innocent as ever, but the moment was lousy with crimes of passion.

"I'll stay tonight," he said, turning to Madeleine, "if you'll sing."

"Oh sure," she told him. What the hell was this? Madeleine must have agreed to sing for him, as if he were the scrubbed-up kid soldier in *Sea to Shining Sea* who goes into the canteen and hears Madeleine's voice in the smoke, and she's singing "As Long As You Come Home." She hadn't been good enough in the play that just closed in the middle of the second performance. So, to shake the rheumatic old woman and the flawed bit of acting in a single stroke, she meant to show Tony how good she could be. I wasn't sure he would know it if it bit him.

"I'm going to take a walk up to the field," Tony said. "I'll see you all at dinner. I'm invited, I guess."

He walked out between me and David. It took me a moment to realize that he meant to go visit his mother's grave, which Phidias must have pinpointed in the course of his story, when I wasn't listening. It was queer of him to do it, almost in questionable taste after what he had said in her bedroom. And now we were four.

"He doesn't want to be alone," David said. Inevitably. He turned to me, and only the sense of expectation in his eyes betrayed the anxiety that once would have been there at a time like this, when he wasn't sure I saw how urgent something was. He had rid himself of it, but the space it left wasn't yet filled.

"You'd better go see," I said, bringing my hand to the small of his back. I had been standing next to him all this time, and my hand homed in like sonar so that I touched him without thinking on his thin flannel shirt. In front, he wore it unbuttoned halfway down, a gesture to the cooler air the rain brought with it. I knew what he was thinking, that he could help Tony with the gay part. Maybe so. I thought it more likely that his knowing the grave well might be of more immediate help, but it was between them.

"When I get back," he said, I suppose so that I wouldn't worry that he mightn't, "we'll get dinner ready."

The door had barely clicked closed behind him when Aldo went over to the bed, put his scotch on the floor beside it, and fell forward onto the quilt with a groan. He buried his face in his arms.

"I'm going to have a peptic ulcer when I leave here. You know what I should be doing on a day like today? Sitting by the pool having a haircut and a pedicure."

"His barber makes house calls," Madeleine explained to me. "It makes him a big shot."

"That's not true, Madeleine. I know three men in Beverly

Hills who have their own barbers. *Live-in.* That's what a big shot is. But I mean, on a day like this at home, I wouldn't move from my bed without a consultation with someone in authority. I could tell it was that kind of day when I woke up."

"I had a live-in dressmaker once," Madeleine said. "In the thirties."

"Didn't you get your clothes in Paris?" I asked, aware that this little chat was an island and glad of it.

"Yes, but they can't fit you by mail. They'd ship things over, dozens of things, and we'd choose. I found her in a village in Mexico when we were on location. She didn't know what a Worth dress was, but she was a genius at a fitting. She did the final work in my bedroom, sewing by hand, and it would put me to sleep to watch her." Madeleine paused and stared into space, the autobiographer at work, trying to get the full arc of the anecdote right. "Later she got a job at MGM. She's very wealthy today. I think she's titled."

"See, Rick," Aldo said impatiently, turning over and drawing up his knees, "that's a story you can really sink your teeth into. Not like the way they treat each other around here. Since they make no *progress,* why do they still bother?"

"Well, Phidias and Tony bother in particular because they're jealous. They think the other one has something of Mrs. Carroll that they don't have."

"So it's a complex," he said with a shrug. "All right, Madeleine, what happened? Start at the beginning."

"Move over," she said, standing up from the bony, eggshell chair. "Let an old lady rest." I smiled at the irony and at the circuitous reference to Beth Carroll. It used to turn me inside out when Madeleine mentioned growing old, but I could see she was not afraid of jinxing herself when she said it. She plumped up the pillows and lay against them in her robe, then beckoned me. "There's room for you, too," she said. Aldo had pulled back to make her a place, and now he sat cross-legged at her head like the palace eunuch. "Did you know, Rick, you've been standing in the same place since you walked in?"

It was true. I stood frozen to the spot, relishing my safety from the storms that blew about the room. Afraid to take a step, perhaps, because I might jar the set of my nerves that kept me warm and dry. But it was time to go forward. I had stood still long enough and taken in all that went on with the others, so I thought I would launch forth now like a spider on his own length of rope. I jaunted over to the bed, kicked off my shoes, and sat on the end with my back against one of the posts. Above me the canopy swayed like a sail. I leaned against the post, my hands around my knees like Huck Finn on the raft. Madeleine and Aldo and I were as curious a group as the house held, and as we went through the story of Tony Carroll and his artificial mother, we played a curious group for all it was worth. We sat on the four-poster like people in a lifeboat or bent around a campfire, and we gossiped and theorized and did over the scene in a dozen different ways. We didn't make fun of Tony. Aldo and I had to hear every detail and every symptom, I think, because the three of us were so appalled by the way in which Tony was gay. His was the fate the rest of us had escaped, and we spoke of it with all the fascination of veterans and runaways telling stories of those who didn't make it.

Meanwhile, with missionary zeal, David tracked down Tony, fleshing out the plot as he went along. David believed that, as long as the genitals still had a dream of their own, there was no one who couldn't make it. He liked the challenge to his erotic energy, and he could transform himself in bed into a creature full of kinks and folklore. "Blood from a stone," I used to tell him on bad days, when I couldn't get it up, and then he would get me laughing with some swank little dirty trick with his tongue or his tireless cock, and then we'd be off and running. So I wasn't discounting his ingenuity. But when he finally cornered Tony in the butler's pantry, he didn't have the advantage he had in bed, with his body heat and the smell of him sweating close.

"Are you looking for the scotch?" David asked from the door to the kitchen.

"I'd like to have a nickel for every time I've been asked that," Tony said without turning around, opening one cupboard after another. "Do you practice temperance along with the farmer in the dell?"

"No, not in anything," David said. "Today I've already had too much rain and too much family. I only asked because Aldo brought the bottle up with him. It's in the bedroom."

Tony snapped his fingers.

"Of course," he said, grinning broadly at David. "I knew I'd seen it somewhere. I thought I was having hallucinations."

"There's gin."

"It reminds me of shit perfume."

"Or wine."

"You mean the twelve percent stuff they make from grapes." He shrugged. "I suppose if it's that or Sterno. Where did you go to school?"

David let the swing door thump shut behind him, and he unlocked the wine cabinet and took out a bottle at random, which turned out later, when David and I finished it, to be a '61 Chateau Margaux and too good for the occasion. David knew, as he twisted the screw into the cork, that Tony was asking about prep school and not college.

"The Dee School, Wilkes-Barre, Pennsylvania. It wasn't very tweedy. There was a slag heap from the coal mine at the far end of the soccer field. And though we had a Carnegie in the class behind me, he was practically retarded."

"I guess you didn't like it much."

"All I wanted to do was get laid," David said to simplify the issue. "But I liked English. Who's your favorite poet?"

How could Tony not have winced? I winced *for* him when David told me the story late that night, but David swore there was no wince. He swore it turned into a cozy little seminar on Robert Frost and Emily Dickinson. David sat on the old soapstone sink, and Tony leaned against the door to the china closet, and they drank their wine. There is a tiny round window above the sink in the butler's pantry, and it looks onto the back marsh and faces west. When the sun finally broke through, they had finished off two-thirds of the bottle and had gotten on the subject of teachers and their favorite students. The late afternoon light glowed on the polished oak of the little room.

I can see David sitting there, backlighted by the window so that his head was ringed in gold, his shirt parting to show off his ripe young chest as he leaned forward. With no self-consciousness, he would bring his free hand to his crotch and rub it meditatively for a moment, as if there were a fatal itch he had to attend to.

"You become like brothers, don't you?" David asked, picturing himself playing tennis with the dean in college and, further back, camping in the Poconos with his history teacher. "And then everything goes wrong, and it ends like a bad love affair."

"Sometimes it's just the year that ends. They graduate."

"What I don't understand is, why does it end like a bad affair when there's been no *affair?*" He was full of the worst sort of sincerity. "I mean, I never actually had sex with my teachers. Do you?"

"No." Tony seemed brutalized by the question, as if he hadn't really negotiated the turn in the conversation. David kept misjudging the psychic distance between them (he says because of the size of the room), and he went on, hoping it would make them more and more comfortable to have it out in the open. And it aroused him to talk about it.

"I don't think it happens in prep school," he said. "Both people pretend that it isn't sexual until it's too late. I think the difference is that the boy's body gets turned on and the teacher's head. The teacher just wants to touch, and the boy wants to fuck. And then the boy gets scared, right? Of his own desires."

"You know far too much about it," Tony said, and I guess by now he must have been angry and starting to put up a wall. But David misread it as shyness. "Have you been on both sides?" Tony asked.

"No, but I was a prize student for an awfully long time. And I never get over my worst desires. Why don't we go to bed?"

I do not love David right if I see him as wholly ego-centered and misguided at this moment when he made his move. There was no point in his being naive and letting the moment pass, or else the scene would have become the very parody of the boy and his master that he wished to counter. You judge these things at the time because the time is suddenly right. Now, David thought, I can clean out his head if we do it now. But what he meant as honesty in making the proposition came through as a taunt. What he meant as irony — let's follow this crazy dance to where it really leads because it can't be as bad as all this dancing — must have seemed to Tony to be all cutting edges.

"No thanks," Tony said.

"You don't have to worry about Rick."

"I'm not planning to. He's the mastermind behind all this, isn't he? I'll bet he's a professional crook. That's just my mother's type."

"Is it because I've talked too much? I just wanted you to know that I've been there."

"But only in the boy's role, don't forget."

"Well, why don't we put them together?"

"Because you're not really a boy."

David's mind went blank at the thought, and in the pause that ensued, the swing door swung open, and Aldo said "Oops." Tony took the advantage, crossed the room in two strides, and slipped out. David guessed he should have taken the other route and talked about the digging of the grave, but since sex was more his subject philosophically than death, he chose the firmer ground. Now Aldo told him to go take the sheets off the furniture in the living room and circle the chairs around the piano.

"You know she always has a bowl of violets on the piano," he said, picking through a shelf of vases. "There isn't a florist in fifteen miles. The garden is all junk and roses. What the fuck do you use instead of violets?"

"They grow wild," David said, corking the last of the wine. "They're all over the place. Just go out the kitchen door."

"Thank God," Aldo sighed. "I thought they only grew them at the florist."

Madeleine and I were still upstairs. Aldo had leapt up as if something stung him when Madeleine got to the part about Tony asking her to sing. We had been taking our time over the story because it ended well. And because I finally believed we would not be languishing in prison come Labor Day, I liked having someone else to talk about besides the lot of us. All at once, as I sat on the bed, I seemed to recover the time I lost when the deer bolted. I willingly accepted us all at face value, neither holding back because the summer was bound to go nor waiting until I trusted us more. Perhaps that is what makes the cheer possible that people are said to feel in happy families. The metaphor still grated on my nerves, us as a family in the Carroll house. What made me happy, I think, was that we didn't appear to need a metaphor to say what we were like. Out the bay window, I could see the sun break through over the trees. If a person had done it, it would have been tacky.

So Aldo jumped like the White Rabbit and said that, as he

was all Madeleine had in the way of a manager, he'd better go manage the concert. Madeleine protested that it wasn't a proper concert at all, that he shouldn't fuss just to fuss, but he didn't pay her any mind. He flew into the closet and emerged after a bit with a black velvet tuxedo over one arm and a pale gray woolen jacket and long skirt over the other. He held them up as if to say, "Well, which?" She made a face.

"Why do we have to be so funereal, Aldo? The dead are all buried now."

"That's not why," he said, all professional bustle. "The living room is burgundy and dark green, and if you wear a bright color, you'll look like a Christmas tree. Or a hooker."

"All right, smart-ass," she said. "We'll go with the black-tie."

"Is the piano in tune?" I asked.

"Tune?" Madeleine replied in some disbelief. "Who cares? I gave up the tune ten years ago."

Aldo laid out the clothes on the chaise in the bay window. He said he would send up a pot of hot chocolate and a wedge of his honey cake. She would not be taking dinner. Some of the singers whose style is traceable to Madeleine won't walk on-stage until they have had enough bourbon or Dexamil, but Madeleine seems to favor a mild form of insulin shock. In every city where she sings once a year, she knows the pastry shops and the best dipper of chocolates. In Boston in June, I have to have in her dressing room a box of jelly babies that takes me a half-hour back and forth on the subway to buy. Lastly, Aldo couldn't believe that Madeleine hadn't thought to set a time. I couldn't believe that it mattered, but I didn't say so. We all decided on ten o'clock because, as Aldo said on the way out, a late show is better than an early show if the audience drinks.

Now we were just the two of us. I didn't say anything for a time and was content to keep sitting against the bedpost. What

I had when I came here suddenly flashed in my mind as a neat little list: a Chevy, half a dozen plants, and three common goldfish. Madeleine had drawn the arm of her robe across her face, and I thought she was taking a nap until she spoke.

"What are you so happy about?"

"Am I so happy?"

"I can tell by how still you are," she said, not moving her arm. "If you were a cat, you'd be licking your fur, and you'd fall asleep with your leg up in the air and your tongue still out."

"I realized today that I don't know who I am, and I don't care."

The arm came down.

"That can't be right. Why wouldn't that depress you?"

"I don't know, Madeleine. My secret used to be that I knew who I was, even if nobody else did. It got me in and out of a lot of bedrooms in one piece." I stood up and went and stood in the bay. I had the notion that it was really my favorite place in the house, and not the porch. The porch hadn't really been very nice, just safe. "But if you always know who you are, then you can't do anything new. Like Tony."

"Well, it sounds very teenage to me. But as long as you're not depressed. Can you bear to hear me sing twice in a single year?"

"Sure. I'm tough."

"This illumination you've had. Do you still know who other people are, or are we all going to come in for an overhaul?"

"No. You're all new already because of this summer."

"I guess that's all right," Madeleine said, turning on her side and closing her eyes. "I'd rather be new than old."

"You're not old."

For the rest of the time we were quiet, and I didn't leave until Aldo brought the chocolate up at seven-thirty and called me down to dinner. Madeleine did sleep, a half-hour one time and later again. When the sun went down, I went over and closed the doors to the balcony. Mostly, I sat on the windowsill and saw the whole estate as a map of the last month, like a board game with baffles and penalties and windfalls. There I found David and the gardener. There I met Phidias under the tree. There I go walking with Madeleine. It was altogether a lucky view, and for once I saw time as a place. It is not strictly true that *nothing* was said in the couple of hours I was there. At one point I said, "I know about Phidias," and she said, "Oh?" But it really wasn't that important.

10

MADELEINE COULDN'T stop laughing. She sprinkled the song with notes, but in fact she was right — the melody was long gone.

> The only men I go with
> Have money up to here.
> They like to give me emeralds
> And eighty grand a year.

She can't sing American, and so she pays no attention to the jokes or the local ironies. She laughs because the audience has always found it funny and dirty. The song has a story that I can't follow. I can only be certain that it comes from Broadway in the late thirties, but it is by no one anyone has ever heard of. It is famous because Madeleine sings it. One verse is just a list of foods that begins with hot dogs and ends with candy canes, but Madeleine could be singing Hindi for all you can understand of the stuff in between. It closes with the whore knowing more than you do, but it isn't clear *what* she knows, not the way Madeleine sings it.

I make them laugh at breakfast
And serve their coffee hot.
You'd love them when they're loving me
And steal them when they're not.

But watch yourself. When I give them up,
They've lost their golden touch.
They'll take you out in taxicabs
And order dinner dutch.

"Watch yourself" could be "wash yourself," since I have never seen it written down, and "touch" comes out "tush." It doesn't make sense to me. Nevertheless, it has been the third song on the program for the thirteen years I've heard it.

Madeleine does a dozen numbers, the same dozen whenever she sings. Some people are jarred if they've heard them once and then again five or ten years later. In every city, one critic or another has said that Madeleine is finally so old that the love songs and the street girl's come-ons are shameless, and then the next year the same man turns around and writes a rave. It's the same as it was after all, he says, and he tells about a night on Corregidor, a lull in the shelling, when the lieutenant put on a scratchy seventy-eight of Madeleine singing "The Only Men I Go With" in a blacked-out officers' club. And everyone stopped shouting and drinking and playing poker as if it were a telephone call from home. I have heard them all too many times to hear much difference from one year to the next, like someone who lives with someone else and so can't see them age and change. And because I love opera, I don't think of what Madeleine does as strictly singing anyway. It's a one-character play about love and time in a language made up for the night on which it is performed. And then it is lost into thin air, like the dialect of an island or the tongue of a Mayan tribe whose only echo is the wind riffling the palms on the beach. Since nobody else does Madeleine's dozen songs (nobody

would dare to), they exist all by themselves, indistinguishable
from the instrument that sings them.

No one was in a very good mood. While we set the table for
dinner, David had whispered a sentence or two about his sunset talk with Tony in the butler's pantry. When Tony came in,
he and David said nothing, and the silence got thicker and
thicker throughout the meal. Aldo took up the slack because
he was so nervous about the singing, fretting about the acous-
tics of the living room as if we were recording. Phidias ate up
at the farm. I still wanted Tony gone, no matter how neu-
tralized the threat of him was, because he was so self-indul-
gent. Not that the rest of us *weren't*, but at least we had all
been invited. All in all, I was probably in the best shape to
listen to Madeleine sing. I realized that Aldo didn't believe
Madeleine had it in her anymore, and he brooded because he
couldn't summon enough illusion to soften and control the
effects. He wanted rose-colored gels and pinpoint spots and
the lilac sequined gown. We had the dress in the car from the
Boston concert, but it wouldn't work in a room-sized room.
David was too young to have gone through enough stages of
Madeleine's career. Tony looked like a relentless listener to
classical music who doesn't like songs unless they're called
lieder and finally can only bear to hear one record, Schwarz-
kopf say, doing the "Four Last Songs" of Strauss. Perhaps
that, or perhaps he had no interests at all beyond the Dewar's.
Either way, Madeleine would be too supper-club for him, her
heart too pinned to her sleeve.

Our overstuffed chairs were drawn up in a semicircle
around the piano, and we sank back into them and nearly
disappeared into the upholstery. We four had not retired to the
living room as the Carroll ancestors must have done, jocular,
florid, anticipating a two-dollar cigar and a cordial. And talking about whatever it was men talked about when, the dance at
dinner ended, the men and women retreated into different

rooms to be with their own kind. Because we were gay, we were accustomed to sitting through the hours after dinner without women, and we had rollicked into the library a few times during the last couple of weeks, Aldo and David and I, to spend an Edwardian hour over brandy, though we talked rather more about buggering even than the Edwardians. But not tonight. While we waited for the singing, each of us kept his own counsel. It was cool enough that David had laid a fire, and we stared into it until Madeleine came.

I have seen her make each of the entrances she makes in her thirty-one films, as well as several walks onstage in theaters. Her unrecorded entrances into dining rooms and train compartments and hotel lobbies are even more riveting. Particularly if you catch them from the beginning, because you watch her size up the place in the first moment and then move through it as if she'd met a lover there long ago and they'd had a crazy time, or she'd said good-bye to one and left him there. But tonight I didn't know she was in the room until I heard the first chord from the piano, and she began "I Miss You Most." The piano was close enough to the fire to catch the light, and she never turned on the lamps that stood on both sides of her like obelisks. So we peered out at her from the darkness of our chairs. I do not know if the others saw her come in and sit down or whether she nodded and smiled at them first, but I don't think so. She seemed unconscious of us, as if this too might be private and she was thinking aloud to get it right in the memoir. She always did the sappy little intro to the first song as if it were a letter to a lover she's well rid of. Tonight she did it fast, as if she hated herself for wanting him back.

"I miss you most in London," she said, playing the piano behind it, "because I get lost in the fog. I get to Paris and don't know where to eat, and you would. You're better with native guides than I. But I don't travel anymore. I miss you most in things I can always do without."

So she sang "I Miss You Most" in English, then in French "Don't," and then "The Only Men I Go With," in American. She brought the longing and smolder of the first two songs to an end with the laughter that roused the third. She was magic tonight. The phrasing was all honey and butter. The quality of being distracted from us by the music only made her come across more intimately. That is the paradox of the lover she most embodies, as if she has her head buried against your neck while she stares out across the ship's rail. It is not sure which irony dwells in her eyes (and, when she sings, in her voice), the slapstick of the past she is forgiving or the loss of illusion about what comes next. When she launches into the whore's tough and comic song, you find yourself relieved to take a break from the hurt, laughing because she shows she has the other side in her that shrugs it all off and knows what it wants and gets it.

> But watch yourself. When I give them up,
> They've lost their golden touch.
> They'll take you out in taxicabs
> And order dinner dutch,

she sang, and she finished with a bang and a swipe at the keyboard and tipped her head back and let out the one-syllable laugh. Then she swiveled a quarter-turn on the piano stool and faced the four of us.

"Am I supposed to do this for free?" she asked. She was talking about applause.

"You're fabulous," Aldo said. "What do you want? Four people clapping hands sounds like a bridge party. We're taking it in like *Zen*, Madeleine. We're letting the outside become the inside."

"I don't like it," she said, drawing up one knee in her folded hands and looking at him narrowly. The tuxedo was the darkest thing in the dark room, and her white, studded shirt lit up her face like a footlight. "It's like amateur night. No no," she said as the breeze of protest began in my chair, "I'*m* not the amateur. But it's been too long since I've played a small crowd. I don't know what to do."

She meant it. What seemed so private as she sang, a dream she was having at the piano, where the music was as muted and as even as the breathing that comes with sleep — all of that aura of removal had two sides too. She didn't want to be apart from us, neither as pure performer nor mythological beast.

"You see?" Aldo said triumphantly. "These things matter after all, and you can't sing in a bad room any more than you can sing in an apron. But it's all right. Sing."

But he was wrong. She wasn't having anything like a tantrum, and she wasn't pretending to be modest. I think she was ready to sing the rest of the dozen songs and keep working at the texture, finding the right size for the room and for all of us. But she wanted us to cooperate. She seemed not to know what to do with our preconceptions of her. She must have felt that we each saw her so absolutely and secretly, not even sharing it with one another, that she couldn't begin to be herself and take care of us at the same time. She didn't have to worry about me tonight, because I was on her side. But Aldo especially thought we couldn't stop working on the creation of the authentic Madeleine Cosquer who went on and on singing and falling in love, because she was more real than the world she sang in. Not Madeleine. She was unencumbered right now by the myth of herself. She was ready to release us from our service to it.

Oh, I thought, I am going to be just as much of a moralist on this side of the mountain as I was on the other side. The deer wouldn't flee from me now, but the weather was as changeable here as there.

"I'll sing," she said, letting go of her knee and swiveling

back to the keyboard. "But I want to be looking at all of you. Get up and come over here. You look like a board of directors."

David rose first, as if he had been waiting for the chance, and went to stand in the curve of the grand piano. Then Tony and I got up at the same time and moved to the other side, so that we were between the piano and the fire. Aldo hedged a little by standing next to her, as if he might turn the pages of the music, except she wasn't using any.

"You too," she said ironically, looking at David. I thought it was David, but he must have seen that her eyes weren't focused on him, and he turned around. Then I saw Phidias at the far end of the room, just inside the french doors. His unobtrusive entrance seemed more pointed because of the stormy exit through the doors upstairs. She began the fourth song as he came across the room: "Who Was the Man without the Hat?" But she stopped short in the third line when he joined the group, standing next to David. He looked at her but not at the rest of us.

"What do *you* want me to sing?" she asked him. She was breaking the order. "Who Was the Man without the Hat?" came next, something she could talk as much as sing, and it rested her voice, and then there were only two more numbers before she took a small intermission. "I only sing three notes," she told me the summer I met her, "and singing the highest one gives me a sore throat." Even before she embarked on the second career, she knew it was going to have to work by illusion and preconception. She didn't *blame* us for the expectations we brought to her. She had started it.

"You should ask *them*," Phidias said, meaning us. "I never heard you sing before."

"Not *ever?*" she asked. It genuinely fascinated her. Her fingers just rested on the keys while they talked.

"I don't think so," he said, a bit puzzled now. You could tell he didn't spend much time in the past, or that he didn't keep his eyes open when he was there. "Did you used to sing?"

"I think so. I sang when I was a little girl. The nuns taught me."

"But not these songs," Aldo said slyly at her shoulder. Aldo was all right. He probably gave up and decided that at least the press wasn't covering it. No one need ever know she changed the order of the songs.

"Can *you* remember what you sang to me?" Phidias asked. "I can't."

She squinted for a moment at the challenge, then smiled and turned to her right, to Tony and me.

"He doesn't realize," she said, very pleased with herself, "I'm a regular encyclopedia of the period. My subject is ancient history." She turned back to Phidias. "How about this?"

It was a song about a girl in the city who dreamed of having a farm, and there were fey little puns in every line on the names of the animals in the barnyard. This was to show how naive she was. It sounded like nuns and had nothing to do with the rest of the program; that is, with love and time. Madeleine sang it through on its own terms, neither cynical nor sentimental. Because her voice took on some of the earnestness and concentration of a child's, she was out of character as much as the song was. She finished it up in about thirty seconds.

"It's pretty," Phidias said, "but no, I've never heard it."

"Damn you. One of us is being senile. And it's not pretty, it's crap. I must have done my singing by myself." There was a small snap of dismissal in her tone. Again she turned to us, but it was really Tony she spoke to. She had not forgotten that this was his concert. "That's how I learned to act, too. I took Racine out into the vineyards and recited it. And then I sang."

I had never thought of Madeleine learning *how* to be Madeleine. The picture she drew sounded a bit like an operetta, with the peasants in the field breaking into song, and I guessed that the story had suffered from having been overremembered and heightened some in the memoir. Also, it confused me that Madeleine and Phidias were referring so openly to the past. I thought: nobody's supposed to know about it. And then I thought: why not? And couldn't come up with an answer. Neither, I suppose, could they.

"You must have heard her sing in a *movie*," Aldo said, mildly amazed.

"I only saw a couple, and all she did was talk. Hey, Madeleine, I remember how much you used to talk."

Madeleine smiled and started playing the melody of "Who Was the Man without the Hat?"

"Didn't I talk your ear off, Phidias?"

"All night long."

"What about?" David asked Madeleine.

"Becoming a singer," Phidias said. Then he looked over at Aldo as if to apologize. "She *talked* about it."

"But I wouldn't sing for you?" Madeleine asked in a curious voice, as if she couldn't believe her own perversity. "You know, I think you're right. I didn't dare sing. I was saving it up for the producers." She shook her head. This time she looked exclusively at me, and she seemed startled by the trick of her memory. "What if I'm making it *all* up?"

"It wouldn't matter, would it?" I said. "It isn't going to hurt anyone."

"I knew I could sing," she said, seeming to remember it right for the first time, "but I wouldn't do it until I found someone who could discover me. I never sang for free. It would have been unprofessional."

She had stopped playing, and she started again and then began the song.

> *Who was the man without the hat,*
> *The one who didn't come back?*

As she went through it, I saw her young again in France, full of her secret future and making plans. She was a professional from the beginning, even before she was admitted into the profession, and the improbable farmer husband was kept in the dark. I couldn't imagine what the two of them had been like, but too much had probably intervened for them to be sure themselves. Here they were, with different stories. It happened that Phidias's version had prevailed for the moment, but it would go back and forth. And if the scene of the secretive farmer's wife saving up to go to Paris to meet Lindbergh sounded as much like an operetta as the scene with the girl who recited Racine in the fields, then it went to show that the past is always an operetta if it is seen from far enough away. But it was hard to say what was going on in Madeleine's mind. No one had asked her to tell the truth in her memoirs, but it was what she appeared to be pursuing.

Then she sang "The Next Morning." Tony was listening politely, as he had all along, a smile frozen solid on his face. He had left his drink beside his chair, and he seemed withdrawn from all the attitudes we had about Madeleine. He was the rapt audience, and that was odd because you would have thought the rest of us, so possessive in differing ways of the woman we seemed to stand guard over; would have been under a spell while the music played. But I knew what it meant. Tony was responding as Madeleine's fans are accustomed to, and somehow it was the measure of what an outsider he was. Everyone else in the room was working secretly to make this concert something different.

And finally "What Do You Want?" — the song among the dozen that I thought of as David's and mine. He didn't know it, since I had always in the past avoided all mention of Madeleine and hid her records in the bottom of a trunk. I loved it for its pugnaciousness, for its warning to the lover not to overstep the boundaries. Just give me one good reason, it said, to give up what I've got for you.

> *What do you want? I told you no,*
> *I'm busy Saturday night.*
> *My friends have tickets to a Ziegfeld show,*
> *And all we do is fight.*

At the same time, the singer seems to yearn for the one good reason. I looked over at David, and my insides shook with desire. The song reminded me that I used to hate David for keeping me captive sexually, for turning me off to anyone else as I fell more cruelly in love. I did not need to be told that it was my fault and not his. I had lived with a paradox of my own, loving and hating and loving and hating until they were much the same. And by then, I suppose, I had worn us out. It did not fill me with anger anymore to love David, though I had a twinge while Madeleine was singing that you can only love that way once, and I missed it.

> *Why do we always fight like this?*
> *Don't call me again, all right?*
> *I'll just come over and give you a kiss.*
> *Don't let me stay the night.*

Aldo allowed for a small pause so that the ambiguous last line could break our hearts or rattle them at least. Then he called: "Intermission." We relaxed and began to move closer to talk to her, shrinking our circle, but Madeleine put up her hand and touched Aldo on the arm.

"That's enough, isn't it?" she asked. A chill brushed the base of my spine. She turned to Tony. "Do you get the idea of it now? The second half is just more of the same, only my voice gets weaker and weaker. I do the last number in sign language."

"Thank you," Tony said, letting her out of the full contract. "It was much more than I hoped for. They don't exaggerate about you. There's no one to compare you to."

"The others have all retired," she said. "But thank *you*."

For a moment I was so upset, upset out of all proportion to what was going on, that it was as if she had pleaded with Aldo: I can't do it, I'm too old. I had always known she would have to say something of the sort some day, and thinking about it made me hold my breath every year at the concert in June until it was over and they were on their feet applauding. This was the crisis Madeleine and I had been heading for all along, and it was the point of the changes we had made in the evening's concert. It was an inevitable result of the open-ended visit she had paid this summer. Though I loved her with no qualifications and felt unabashed and self-important at having a star of my own, I paid dearly for it, with a terrible case of nerves that lasted from April to June. For thirteen years, I dreaded that she would be old, more than I ever dreaded she would die. The three days I spent with her would serve to reassure me, and then I would forget about it until the next year.

But here it was. I couldn't avoid the moment now. I was holding my breath even as it happened, so I forced it out like a long sigh of relief and then plunged in, for once not testing the depth or the temperature.

"You'd better *not* sing anymore," I said. "If you do the whole concert, we'll feel obliged to pay you, and we can't afford you."

"I'm cheaper than Frank Sinatra," she said. She wasn't ready to be agreed with quite so fast. "Or since it's a small crowd, I could give you a discount."

"No dear," Aldo said. "No deals. As your manager, I can't let you give it away. I have to think about my ten percent."

"You see," I said, "you're a natural resource. I think your price is regulated by law."

"What do I know about money?" she asked with a shrug of her velvet shoulders. "I still think in francs."

"Money is the stuff you give away," Aldo remarked.

"Well, what shall we do now?" she asked, closing the lid on the keys. "I'm overdressed for everything." She looked up at David. "Do I look like a maître d' in this getup?"

"You look fabulous," Aldo said. He never missed a cue.

"Why don't you let us sing the rest?" David asked.

"The rest of what?"

"The rest of the concert," I said. How can it possibly work, I thought.

"Oh no," Aldo said. "We'll sound like the munchkins."

"So what?" Madeleine trumpeted, and she opened up the piano keys. "I think it's a marvelous idea. Can any of you play?" We all shook our heads no. "All right. *I'll* play."

So, without an intermission, the second half began. I looked across the piano at David, wondering where he had learned it. He was going to know the words as well as I did, I was sure, and I had always assumed she had no meaning for him. Until now, I thought he had heard of her the way you've heard of a first-class writer you know about and never read, like the non-Americans who win the Nobel Prize. I guess I took it in for the first time, what Phidias said about David taking care of Mrs. Carroll. He didn't patronize Madeleine, didn't diminish her wishes and fears, and he zeroed in on what kept her strong, tuned to the things she took pride in. Madeleine picked out the spare and lonely music of "When We Were New" and waited for David to take up the lyric. I suppose she had no doubts that Aldo and I would chorus along, so she didn't have to look at us. We looked at each other and agreed it was the best thing anyone had come up with.

David began in a shy and muted voice, and Aldo and I took

up the backup after a line or two. It was a very sultry song with the three of us singing it, ripe with midseason and the constant sun. Neither Phidias nor Tony had a clue how to keep up with us, distracted as they were by inexperience. They watched, and they watched each other, too. David, it turned out, didn't know all the words. His enthusiasm carried him along far enough, and Aldo and I filled in the rest. Aldo sang as if he were caricaturing Madeleine, dropping an octave and even hinting at the remnant of a French accent. I probably did too, but I couldn't hear myself in the general din.

"You just need a little training," Madeleine said excitedly. "Why don't we all go on tour together? We'll buy a gypsy's wagon and sing for our supper and never come home."

"We can sing at weddings and feasts, like minstrels," David said. "And set up a stage at county fairs."

Madeleine nodded. She seemed delighted by us parroting her, and in the next song, "*Quant à Moi*," she joined us for the choruses and exaggerated the Madeleine effect e.en more than we did. The only French the rest of us could really speak was the French in Madeleine's songs, so we sounded weird and broke up laughing when our eyes met. Aldo was doing his French with such an air of seriousness, his lips pouting and his chins sunk down into his neck. David had faintly raised his eyebrows, and he looked like the young Boyer, casting a disapproving eye on the human lot.

"No one ever sang along with me before," Madeleine said at the end. "Maybe it's because I'm off-key half the time."

" 'The Marseillaise,' " I said, correcting her, because it is a story that is central to the myth, a set of concerts for the French army in 1945 that ended with everyone singing the national anthem.

"Well, besides that," she said, acknowledging the reference with a glance straight at me, but too intoxicated by the present to go into the past.

"Will we all wear tuxedos and bleach our hair?" Aldo asked.

"It doesn't matter," I said. "but will we stick together through thick and thin?"

"Yup," said David, hoisting himself onto the piano and sitting there like a boy fishing on a dock. "And we won't want fame or money."

"I think you'd better count me out and be a trio," Aldo said, and then he folded his arms. "But you'd better save some money for your old age."

"What old age?" Madeleine asked, who loved to tease Aldo for being a prig. "That's a sissy's way out."

"If we ignore it," I said, "it will go away. Start the next number."

And we did the last four in a row, with barely a pause between them. We were really pretty terrible, and as we got more enthusiastic and full of the muse, all our showstopper fantasies coming true, we got more terrible still. In the end, it only made it seem more perfect, that we were good enough for this one evening and that we had better get it out of our systems once and for all. As we tore up the ninth number, a barroom song, I had a fleeting wish that we had decided earlier that this was what we were going to do, not so we could have rehearsed but so we could have savored the event and worked up a stage presence. Of course, we couldn't have projected this far ahead when we were upstairs in Madeleine's room. The turn of events that had three of us crooning while Madeleine played demanded the flash of the moment. Take this hour for what it is, I said to myself. I let go, and I had to get louder and put my feet wide apart and gesture with my hands to reach the undersea passion the songs welled up with. Aldo and David and I had all stopped laughing at ourselves. We just sang.

About then, Tony went back to his chair to pick up his drink, still smiling. He seemed grateful to withdraw. He wasn't intimidated, it turned out, and he liked our maniac program. But he didn't want to be involved. It was ̀too gay, though I don't think he articulated it to himself that way. He would have called it too group-conscious, the sort of thing he had enough of at school. Phidias, who had become accustomed to the yammering of his summer guests, didn't appear the least bit fazed that we had begun to do it to music. He followed Tony and then drew him away to the opposite end of the room to talk. When I next happened to look in their direction, they were gone.

When he got going, Aldo had a voice the size of Kate Smith, and he was so irrepressible that he jigged a little in the drinking song and flattened his hands against his heart during the final ballad. Madeleine egged him on, and in the end David was doing a closer imitation of him than he was of Madeleine. That left a space for Madeleine and me, one we had not asked for or planned any projects to fill. I sang along with Aldo and David, but my own exaggerated, ritual parody had begun to subside. Madeleine paid as much attention to me as to them, but not much more. That is what kept it from being soupy and over-wrought. Well, it was and it wasn't. I bent over from the waist and rested on my elbows on the brink of the piano and sang exactly to the measure she was playing. A *little* bit like Dick Powell, though I suppose that gives the wrong idea about how really full of myself I was.

There is a reason why we can't say what it is about this song or that side of the street. To know some things, we have to be nameless. The way to say it lies too much through a forest of what things mean. I would be the first to agree that Madeleine Cosquer is an elaboration of meanings that nest inside each other like Russian dolls, but this evening's finale was not limited to her. I had an attack of immediacy about a jaunty lyric I never paid attention to before.

What would the sky do
If it did what we do
And changed its mind fifty times a day?

Aha, I thought, the good news is that we don't have to have anything particular to say. When I asked Aldo the next day what it was like for him at the concert, he said, "You think I don't know? We were just like the four of them on their way to Oz. I mean, who would have thought our condition was in that direction?" That too.

When Madeleine seemed to be dreaming again as she played, as if she had discovered the Northwest Passage through time, I finished up with David. His version of the last song was rueful and winded, as if he were in bed enjoying a cold, while mine was crisp and heavy on adrenalin, like a bootblack buffing a shoe. We were fabulous together.

But I woke up alone. The sun had already passed across the bed and now lit up the dust that coasted in the air in one corner. It must have been eleven or even later. David had left the sheet and bedspread on the floor when he got up, whenever that was, and the sweat had poured out of me when the sun was on me, and now I was dry. I felt stranded, too far above sea level or way below. I was streaked, grimy, and thirsty. I wanted to swim. Five or six bathing suits hung on hooks or lay draped over the furniture. I took down and stepped into an electric-orange pair of baggy trunks that said GUARD on the right thigh. Then I stood at the window and scratched the hair on my chest and waited for my head to clear.

I made my landowner's survey, getting all manner of assurance from things that had stayed in the same place — the sea and the marshes, the woods and the rocky fields. It was a small relapse after the previous day, when I was so wildly in love with change, and it only lasted as long as the groggy feeling, a little like sunstroke, wrapped me in blankets. I snapped out of it when I looked down at the courtyard below Madeleine's room, which I could only just see a slice of because of the angle of the roof. I saw the back end of Tony's station wagon. It was open, and there were suitcases on the gravel waiting to be loaded. Wait for me, I thought, don't do anything until I get there. I didn't have anything to say to him when I was with him the night before, so I don't know what I expected to do now. But I got a sudden goose of energy and leapt into action like Popeye. I thundered down the stairs in my bare feet, the cool of the house breezing over my bare body after the heat of the tower. My orange suit glimmered in the halls.

Coming through the library and out into the courtyard, I guess I expected to find the whole group assembled a third time. But it was just Tony. He leaned against the car in a jacket and tie, all ready for his first class. Except he was having a morning scotch. The bottle and an ice bucket were perched on the hood of the car. He looked me up and down.

"So you do have a job," he said.

"What do you mean?"

He pointed at my cock, and then I realized he was pointing at the suit. "Shouldn't you have a silver whistle around your neck, and a coat of white chalk on your nose and lips?"

"I've never been a lifeguard," I said. "David traded suits with a hunky number in Malibu. It's a souvenir."

"Like an Indian's scalp?"

"Like a silk stocking. Are you leaving now?"

"Yes. When are you?" Not hostile, just interested. Just making conversation.

"I don't know. Labor Day, I guess."

"That's when we all used to. It about killed me."

He drank at his drink. He didn't seem concerned that he wasn't being given a send-off. I was here, I realized, for only one reason, to see him out of sight and watch the cloud of dust settle on the gravel drive. Late last night, David and I had spoiled the pretty feelings that followed the concert by arguing about Tony. When we retired to the tower, I asked for the full story of the butler's pantry and made a mistake then and said the equivalent of "I told you so." I said he couldn't take care of people who made a career of hurting themselves. David told me to shove it. He thought he had helped Tony, even if it wasn't evident. He turned away from me to sleep, and I cursed myself in the dark.

"Did we sound like cats in heat last night?" I asked.

"You mean, when you were singing? I thought it was charming. A little precious, perhaps. But if you'd lived with my family in that room, you'd have thought last night how far the human race has come since men lived in caves. If my father had walked in, he would have killed you all with his bare hands."

"Then why did you leave?"

"No, I have it all wrong," he said, caught in a sudden reverie. "He would have killed *himself* with his bare hands. I've always thought my father must have died like Rumpelstiltskin, who tore himself in two. But in my father's case, they called it a heart attack."

"Did you and Phidias go somewhere and talk?" What business was it of mine?

"Yes and no. We went somewhere, and we didn't talk. To my mother's grave, in fact."

"Oh."

"Yes. They do that a lot in *Wuthering Heights*. But maybe you're not a reader."

"I've read it," I said. Then, with terrific patience, "What happened?"

"Nothing." He turned around and splashed another ounce of scotch in his glass. "I didn't offer you a drink because it's before breakfast for you. It's before lunch for me." He looked out to sea and spoke as if he had been a mere witness and not an accessory to the crime. "I didn't fall down and cry and hold on to Phidias's skirts. I thought it was strange up there, and it made me lonely. I suppose it made Phidias feel better." He took hold of the car's aerial and bent it toward him as if he were stringing a bow. He knew he wasn't getting it right. "I suppose I'll remember it some Saturday night this winter, and I'll spend an hour making drunken phone calls to John and Cicely. Or maybe to you, Rick." He let go of the antenna and looked at me. "In a word, nothing."

"What do you do, beat it against a wall to get it off?"

"Are you going to yell at me like Phidias?" he asked, suddenly alert to the fact that he might have someone new to play with.

"No. I'm going swimming. I only came this way because I thought my friends were here."

"Your friends. What a quaint idea."

He took the glass between his teeth and held it there while he picked up the bottle in one hand and the bucket in the other. He leaned into the car through the driver's door and set up his little bar on the passenger's seat. He took the glass from his mouth and wedged the scotch-on-the-rocks between the windshield and the dashboard, just over the steering wheel so he wouldn't miss it. While he went around to the back of the car to load his suitcases, I paraded across the courtyard like a lifeguard. I was making my way to the water, intending to leave him as robbed of farewell as the others had done. Of all of us, I sure as hell was the last holdout about Tony. Being my own age, Aldo had at last made me feel how wonderful the differences were between one man and another, as if we had been shaped by different sculptors in different styles. Tony made me base, made me feel superior to him and critical and, in the cankerous faults of my heart, glad he was a mess and not I. As if he were some kind of pariah who would take all the bad blood and bad faith with him out of the world I had just caught the rhythm of.

"I'll think of you on Labor Day," he said, and now it seemed like a taunt. I stopped at the corner of the house, one bare foot still in the gravel and the other in the wet grass that started here and went around into the deep front lawn. "And don't forget to answer your phone when it rings this winter. By then I'll have figured it all out."

He swung himself into the car and slammed the door. "I'm unlisted," I said, which wasn't true, but I don't think he heard me over the starting of the car. "I'm not going back there," I said, a little louder this time, and now he didn't hear me because he backed up with a jolt and a little screech. He braked when he was almost on top of me and then put the car into forward gear. I crouched so that I was level with the car window, and I meant to announce as he pulled away that there *wasn't* anything to figure out, that that was the problem in some things. But he looked so sad when he took his last look at me. I think it had more to do with the summer place he couldn't come to grips with, but it knocked the wind out of me as I stood there ready to spring. "Take care," I said, and I put on a cockeyed smile.

"I will," he said. "I travel light. The medicine and the disease go in the same bottle. Good-bye, Rick."

I travel light too, I thought. I would have told him what an acute remark it was, but it got lost in the joke about the bottle and then in the cloud of exhaust that he burned off as he sped away. He waved at me in his rearview mirror, and I waved back. I went on through the grass, but I found myself shivering in the shade when I was parallel to the porch and face to face with the whole ocean. The grass was icy with yesterday's rain and made me squeamish. I canceled my swim. Still traveling light, I went up the front steps and stood at my perch by the porch table.

I don't know why I let Tony off so easily. Probably because he didn't have any friends of his own, and he couldn't sing or fuck, or cry at his mother's grave. I think he really believed he would figure it all out and that the expectation of a final equation or strategy made him rosy when he was drunk. I had always been the same way, but without the technology of heavy liquor. Figuring things out was my hedge against the self-evident. It was easier for me to control my life by being a student of it and not a professor. Anyway, this summer had stopped all that. But I couldn't tell Tony: just open the door and walk out, it isn't locked. When they hear that angle, people like Tony tell you you don't understand. That may sound the same as what David says, but it's worse. Besides, unlike David, they don't usually even tell you. They wrap their cloaks about their heads and go off and figure it out some more. And they get nowhere.

"Anyone would know where to look for you."

I turned to the voice and saw Phidias farther down the porch, dressed in the clothes he had worn for fifty years. Literally the same clothes. He walked toward me from the railing that overlooked the crossroads where Tony and I said goodbye. So Tony and I hadn't been alone after all, though we didn't know it. And then I thought: Tony might have known it. Maybe he was talking to Phidias before I came out.

"I wouldn't know where to look for you," I said. "If I went up to the farm, I'd lose my way and ask all the wrong questions. I may have to stay in this house forever, because I don't know the way to the outside world."

"Some people," he said, taking the chair at the head of the table and motioning me to sit down, "do the looking, and the rest get looked for. You and David are the second kind."

"Why are you looking for me?"

"I'm not. I wanted to tell Tony something, but I didn't. I watched him pack his car from the end of the porch, and then, when you came out, I got tongue-tied and ducked around the corner."

I wanted to ask what, wondering too what Tony would say in return when Phidias tried to tell him something final. But I didn't ask. I had gotten good this summer at finding another question to take the place of the one I couldn't ask. I found I was much more likely to get an answer to the unasked question if I changed the subject right. Sometimes, when we were all together, the subject changed at every third or fourth remark, like a mad dance where the orchestra wants everyone dancing with everyone else. Phidias let Tony go without a last word. So what was I after? I knew Phidias wasn't shy, and I expect he'd never wasted a moment in his life ducking around a corner. He *decided* not to say what he might have said. So I wanted to know how he and Tony had left it last night. It didn't really matter how they might have left it if they'd talked again.

"Things didn't go so well when you were out walking," I said. It was about forty percent a question.

"You mean last night? It was fine."

Really?

"What happened?"

"Not much. I showed him where the grave was — did he tell you that? — and he cried a lot." Phidias shrugged. It wasn't much of a story.

"Oh." That's not what *Tony* says, I thought, wondering if anything would ever stay the same for ten minutes. It seemed more and more likely that the phone would be ringing next winter, and Tony would have a final go at me.

"I guess the two of you made up," I said.

"I shouldn't yell at him. Beth always said he was the only one in the family who couldn't help it. And he was the only one who ever wanted to know me. He used to write me letters, you know."

"When he was young?"

"When he was in college."

"What did he say?"

"He talked about women. I mean, he made them up."

"Oh." There was no disdain in his voice, and no pity. Phidias didn't feel sorry for Beth Carroll's children, as if he knew that in that direction lay the accusations that she was a lousy mother. He treated her best by knowing her as nothing more than the woman he loved. He wasn't asking that anyone in the family understand him either. He probably didn't blame the Carroll children for calling him the enemy. I had the idea that his own children knew nothing of his fifty years in Beth Carroll's bed. With them, I bet he was a private man. He was none of his sons' business. So it was easy to see that he saw no reason to look out for Tony or his brother and sister. I couldn't figure out if he had *answered* Tony's letters, but by then it was time to change the subject again. We could only go so far.

"How do we know Tony will keep his promise?" I said. I wondered if Phidias cried at the grave too. "It doesn't seem as if he's ever told the truth. He could be turning us in right now."

Phidias shook his head.

"Not Tony. Don't you see? You're right — all he can do is lie. He's never found a good reason to tell the truth, and so he never has."

"What if we turn out to be the good reason?" I wasn't worried. I liked this conversation for its own sake. We sat at opposite ends of the table like laborers at dusk, as if we were about to be served a beer.

"Ever since he was a boy, he ran away. That's what he's doing now, and it's the only thing that makes him happy. I bet he's forgotten about us already."

"Okay," I said. "I'd just feel a lot easier if he'd never shown up."

"No, Rick. He's the one we needed. He proved we wouldn't panic."

"I panicked for a while," I said, not a shred of pretense left that I was the lifeguard.

"No, you didn't." Statement of fact. He didn't let me get away with affecting a hysteria like Tony Carroll's.

We had not talked again about David and me. I wanted to let him know my friend and I were doing fine, but I also hoped he had noticed himself. It was hard. My sharpest memory of my own father finds us in his smoky study, me telling him I was a whiz at arithmetic or reporting my viola teacher's praise or something, just so he would notice me. And my father says tautly, "A gentleman doesn't talk about himself." Consequently, of course, I can barely be relied upon to say my own name, even when asked. I was shy about telling Phidias now that everything was going to be all right with me. But I wanted to badly, because he'd complimented me.

No time. He stood up and moved along the railing to the stairs.

"You know when I stopped being scared?" he said.

"When?"

"When Arthur Carroll died. He's the last person who could have made things bad for me." He went down the stairs, and the rest faded into the language I was used to in him. "I have to go see about the paint. You know how to paint? We're going to start painting in a few days."

He walked away across the lawn without waiting for an answer. I did not in fact know how to paint, but I wouldn't have said so then for anything, because I could learn. I fancied at that moment that I would go around in my flame-colored trunks till the end of the summer and never wear anything else except a splotch here and there of white paint.

I went on into the house. In the kitchen, Aldo was sprawled

at the table, cookbooks open all over. He was as absorbed as a pure mathematician, but he came out of it to talk to me.

"I hope you're not hungry, because there's nothing to eat. Why are you dressed like that? Are you going to a masquerade?"

"Don't I look like a lifeguard, Aldo? My pecs are as good as David's, and I'm a whiz at mouth-to-mouth."

"You're a dream, honey, but that suit is too Jones Beach. It doesn't work." He sighed and buried himself again in the recipe. "You people just don't understand the class of this place."

I fried two eggs. I silently called on the gods of the house to bless Aldo, who had such a feel for what was classy there. He had spent his life shuttling from one manicured Beverly Hills dollhouse to another, from ersatz colonial to ersatz Tudor, and Mr. Carroll and Donald Farley probably would have hated him the most of all of us interlopers. He was candid and racy with jokes about money and power the way other people are about sex. He was such a booster of the California life that you figured he should be on the state payroll. If he had been straight, he would have risen to the top of the Jaycees and died of happiness. But in spite of being an alien in New England, he had the fullest appreciation of the stature of Mrs. Carroll's house. He didn't demand that we eat in the dining room or mind our language, and he didn't really care what I wore. But like a fugitive from Tara, he knew the use of every nut dish and copper pot, and he broke out the wedding linen and the French crystal. David had had a mild case of manorhouse manners just after he arrived, but it had to do with getting his mind off Neil Macdonald. Aldo sighed over the oak and petit point embroidery and fell in love with the old world of the house as he sifted its artifacts. You would have thought the place was Venice, where all the old queens go when they die. Mrs. Carroll would have loved his sense of values.

I ate my eggs out of the pan. Every bite was so hot that my eyes watered, but I needed the one-to-one connection between me and the food as much as Aldo needed four separate recipes for crème caramel.

"Where's Madeleine?" I asked.

"Her Grace is at work on *A Star Is Born*," he said, bringing one of his books close to his face. "What kind of a fish is a blue?"

"It's just a fish," I said, not prepared to talk about the earth's dumb creatures. "The meat is dark, and it tastes strong. Is she writing about the thirties?"

" 'Santa Monica, 1935.' That's what she wrote on the top of the page. I expect it will be lists of dinner guests and poolside games, which is just what we want. But she acts as if she's been asked to write the *Psalms*. She doesn't want anything from the outside world until the sun has set. Except her lunch."

"The singing last night jogged her memory, I bet."

"We remind her of everyone," he said. "Don't you think you and I remind her of each other sometimes?"

"Yes."

"Does it bother you?"

"No."

"Me neither."

"At this rate," I said, changing the subject because we were both a bit embarrassed at how affectionate we'd been, "she's going to let it run to several volumes."

"She wants to do it up fat, like Churchill on the Second World War. And he didn't know *anyone* compared to her."

"I wonder where David is," I said, because I was still, as I had told Tony, looking for my friends. I had ascertained about Phidias and Aldo and Madeleine. Now David.

"In there," Aldo said, pointing at the butler's-pantry door. It threw me off balance that he was so close, just the one door separating us. But we were going to have much less trouble putting Tony to rest now that he was on the road. I was feeling once again that David and I were safe. We were not bound by the nooses of the past, and if our being human led us back to old errors like looking after drunkards, then we had better learn all we could about making the passage safely back and forth. Six or seven years ago, in our golden age, I called us safe because we were connected to nothing besides one another, and I was probably right, as far as golden ages go. Time can stand still now and then. But we did not connect now like the bodies on the beach or the herded deer who leapt as one. We verged on each other like the sea, the beach, the marsh, the pines, wild with contrasts at the shared edges. We were living peaceably on our common borders, and we would only be as safe as our safe passages.

I put the frying pan in the sink and walked over and swung open the door. The room was darker now than it would be in the late afternoon, and it was empty.

"He's gone," I said.

Aldo looked up and fixed me with a suspecting eye.

"Why don't you let him alone?"

"Why should I?" I asked, not angry but surprised. It was odder even than Phidias's saying I shouldn't let David take care of me. Here, Aldo seemed to have more information than I did. But he must have thought I was saying it was no affair of his, because he gave it up and shrugged at me.

"He's fooling with the china," he said.

I walked into the pantry and let the door swing shut behind me. David shouldn't be so angry with me, I thought. He should have slept it off. To my right, the door to the china closet was closed, and I almost knocked before going in. But that seemed too damned tentative, so I just said "David" to let him know it was me and then opened the door.

He had taken his shirt off because of the heat, and the raw smell of his sweat filled the high, shelf-lined room. He did not turn around right away but tilted his head to the side instead, as if he were listening for something. With all those stacks of porcelain, the tureens and Toby jugs and tea things, it was like the Victorian version of an Egyptian tomb. There was hardly room for two, but I stepped on in and closed the door as I said my breezy line: "Once you've come out of the closet, you know, it's bad form to go back in." I said it as lightly as I felt it, determined to be rid of Aldo's caution. David and I would arrive at a truce. Barring that, I thought, I was amenable to surrender.

When he turned, I noticed three things, and in this curious order: that he was red-eyed, that he held in each hand the unequal halves of a broken plate, and that one cheek was puffed with a bruise that ran, blue-black, the length of the jawline. Well, I *know* I saw the wound first, but I must have willed the violence away and sought out something homely. He has broken a plate, I thought, so we will have to fix it, and then he won't cry. Then he put his arms around my neck and cried hard, the kind of crying that shouldn't be stopped. It was Tony, I knew, who'd done it, and my next thought was that I'd track him down and kill him. I raged at myself for having relented and waved good-bye. I went at the speed of light from mending a dessert plate to shooting Tony in the abdomen. He had not turned us in to the police, but the bastard had gotten back at us.

David's tears stopped after a while, but he still held on to me. His face was buried in my neck. He had his arms around my shoulders, and now and then I could hear a tiny clash as the two parts of the dish hit against each other. In the interval, my anger changed too. I felt sure that I didn't have anything to accuse David of, and so it was hard to be angry at all. The absence of that censoring reflex in me made me dismiss Tony as something terrible that was over with. He wasn't worth my fury. As long as David and I were holding on to each other, everything was going to be all right. The enemy was not us. I held David close until he was ready to talk, and I looked up meanwhile at the goods that towered over us. We could have been in the hold of a ship. The old Carroll captains had once sailed back and forth to China, and we were in the middle of the loot.

"Is he gone?" he asked, an inch from my ear.

"Yes. You don't have to talk about it."

He pulled away so that he could look at me, and his eyes seemed quieter now, though the sight of the bruise sent another jet of violence through me. He started to talk, but he was distressed by the broken dish, which he didn't seem to know where to put down. I took the two pieces from him and held them in one hand.

"Don't worry about the plate," I said.

"Oh, I didn't break it," he said, as if this matter needed to be attended to first. "I found half of it in May when I was arranging the dishes. It was cold in here then. I found it at the back of a shelf. And I just found the other half in this drawer. When you came in, I was wondering who put the pieces in two different places. And why."

"When I came in, you were crying."

"It made me sad."

"Is that all right?" I said, my fingers fluttering close to his cheek. He didn't flinch.

"It aches, but it's all right. Listen," he said, putting his hand up to make contact, and his fingertips lighted on my breastbone and rested for a bit. "I went into his room this morning to talk. Because I didn't want him to leave feeling bad about yesterday. He was still in bed, so I sat down and started talking."

"About what?" I said, because he paused. I wanted it out fast, and so did he.

"You and me. I tried to explain how it isn't just one thing to be gay, that everything doesn't fit. I talked about us fighting."

I could have said just then that we would never fight again. It would have turned out to be a lie, of course, but I wouldn't have been lying when I said it. We had moods that could have shaken all these dishes into dust, and in an opposite country we went with the changing weather as if we had been designed for it, like windmills or cactus. The wonder was in the completeness of each mood. I would hate David, or he would be out to protect me, or we would be sitting in the same room racked by the loneliness in it. Very specific scenes. And, watching us, you would not believe there had ever been or would ever be anything different from the present configuration of language and the light and two grown men.

"He *saw* us fight," I said.

"I meant the kind that goes on and on," he said with the curl of a smile that flattened out on his bruised side.

"What did he say?"

"Nothing, but he let me suck him off." There wasn't any transition in the sentence, as there wasn't in the event, I expect.

"What happened?" What happened, I thought, was still another conclusion to David's youth. It had ended a hundred times for me, too.

"He came in my mouth," he said, "and then he leaned over to the bedside table and picked up the lamp. I didn't believe it, so I didn't duck." He shrugged. There was nothing further he could think of to say. It was an event wholly without details or subtleties. The damaged vision that mixed up sex and pain was what men risked when they lived in the closet, and David and I could have come up with a list of the bad loving of sick men. They were a weird given of gay life. They made love a couple of times a year, and they boiled with guilt.

"When I came to," he went on, "He was out of the room, so I ran away. Should I have stayed and beaten him up?"

"I don't know."

"Would you have?"

"Maybe. Then he'd have called the constable, though, and we would have had the case of Mrs. Carroll."

"You're not mad."

"At you? Christ, no."

"Do you think I did the wrong thing?" he asked, just a shade of ambiguity in the adjective.

"It turned out that way. It could have turned out differently."

"Last night you said I was wrong," he said, not willing to let it go.

"I was wrong," I said, and I liked the force of the echo. "Come here."

He didn't have far to come, since we were only a foot apart. It seemed best to keep holding on. I wrapped my arms around him and spread my hands along the muscles of his shoulder blades. He told me in my ear where he had run, down the beach to the boathouse, up the field to the quarry, then through the woods and into the pasture with the cows. So the sweat on him was the sweat of miles. He said that for hours he couldn't stand still in one place, and he didn't see the irony in that and how he stood now, resting against me. I had had the notion from Madeleine's window that the whole estate was a board game. As I thought of David running out the knot in his heart, I had a different notion. This was the deer's habitat. It needed the range of the whole territory it was born to own, since it was meant not to stand still. Mrs. Carroll, I thought, must have felt that people had the same need, though they only knew it by a wave of suffocation filling their heads like a migraine. All summer, then, the land had been right for us, because it fit the shape of our running away.

"Do you know why I like it in here?" he asked. He began to

gently squeeze my sides and run his hands up and down, but very slowly.

"I think so."

"Tell me."

"Because it makes you sad."

"You mean, I'm like Aldo," he said, laughing at the thought. "I want the house filled with state dinners and balls and five-course lunches."

"No. This is the place where nothing is touched, isn't it? And now that you've put it all in order, it makes you sad that you can't protect it forever. You'd hide this room under a mountain if you could."

"It's crazy, isn't it? Tom Swift and his treasure. It doesn't even matter that it's china. It could be a lot of anything."

"Are you really all right?" I asked, and I opened my mouth against his neck and tasted him.

"I'll feel a lot better when you fuck me."

I held him out at arm's length, this guileless boy in the blue jeans, and said no.

"You fuck me," I said.

No doubt about it. You come to an impasse now and then. But wasn't he too shaken up to make love? He thought not. He said it would clear his head. You could say that he hadn't learned anything at all from the nightmare early in the morning, because here he was again, still out to prove that a tumble in bed was a miracle drug. But I didn't say so. The kinds of desire are as various as the kinds of running, and we would never know either without the range. I admit it: I still wished I could make the connections. Between David in Tony's bed and David here. Between the singing last night and standing half-naked now. But I didn't dare go into it too far, because it was *all* contrasts, wherever I looked. The china closet and the whole outdoors. Madeleine and Mrs. Carroll. Midsummer and after. It seemed that the answer might be in the question, in contrast itself, but I was not ready to follow that out.

"What do we do, flip a coin?" David asked, reaching over and tugging at the waistband of the orange suit.

"Let's go to bed," I said, "and count up as far back as we can and see who deserves it."

But it was not what you would call an insoluble problem. We both deserved it. So all we had to do was do it twice. When we burst out of the butler's pantry and into the kitchen, Aldo was fixing a tray with Madeleine's lunch. "Don't fall for lifeguards," he said to David as we passed. "They get lost at sea." But who was listening? We ran through the house and up the stairs, and all the pictures on the walls tilted as we thundered by. Madeleine bellowed for quiet. We locked ourselves in the tower, stripped, and fell to it like sailors wrecked on an island. You could tell that we weren't really thinking, because we didn't of course have to bolt the door. We were safe enough.

11

Now that I live by the sea all year, I only bathe in it for
two weeks, at the end of August. The water is too cold
before that. The air is too cold after the beginning of
September. I have always swum as well as I walk, but it
has been my fate to live in a place where swimming is a
sometime thing. It is certainly my own damn fault, but
for most of the year I am a fish out of water. Well, who
isn't. I have been a bit bedridden in the last few years, and
I would like to end by being "sea-ridden." So, on the last
nice day of the summer, I am going to swim away and not
come back. If I get washed up, I want to be buried on my
own land. But if I am lucky, I will stay right out there
and get picked up by the Gulf Stream and be warm
forever.

IT WAS UNSIGNED and unwitnessed, so it probably wouldn't
have held up in court, but it made a lovely will all the same. It
would not convey the right idea to call Mrs. Carroll's written
plan of action a suicide note. It was more of a wave good-bye.
I liked the head-on settling of accounts and the gaiety of it. A
flirtation with a great adventure was at work, and thus the

drama of the gesture was a romance and not a low comedy. Though I was hard put to decide who the audience was meant to be. I knew, of course, who the audience *would* be — Phidias, the three dead-end children, and Donald Farley. But the relish of it, the peculiar good humor with which she held herself up to take stock, were directed farther away than at those who were her circle. In part, I think she was talking to someone like me, to someone newly drunk on changing places. And then I think she was talking back to the land, both the brute New England earth and the iron winter sea.

The page had been torn out of a diary so forcefully that threads from the binding still clung to one side of the paper. I was the one who figured out, one morning while I sat in the bay window reading through the years, that the pages were not from the current year. I had first seen the note a week before, a few days after Tony left. When Madeleine finished reading Beth Carroll's journals, Phidias brought the note out of the safe to show to her, as if she were now ready to see it in context. She showed the rest of us. And we all assumed that Mrs. Carroll had written it out at some point during the last winter. But I found the place where the page had been torn out, and it was the day after Labor Day, four years ago. So Mrs. Carroll had had the idea rooted in her mind for a long time. And we would never know now why she waited four years. When I told the others, I didn't tell them what was really on my mind. I wondered if perhaps she wouldn't have done it this year either, even though she had broadcast to everyone that this was her last summer and handed the note over to Phidias in the spring. Maybe it was only an act of defiance against the winter, a dream of freedom that she would put off from September to September. It bothered me. I paid attention now to the difference between doing something and talking about it.

Madeleine read the diaries from beginning to end, starting

where they started, in 1922. I went the other way around, starting back from the present. And it surprised me how much I liked them, considering the bad press Madeleine had given them throughout. They were quirky and spare and full of self-definitions. When she dropped names, she let them bounce a little on the boulevard because she didn't have any patience with fame and pretense. It took a while to get used to the flavor, but it got to be delicious. At the same time, I was willing to believe Madeleine when she said the voice in the diary and Beth Carroll were entirely different. But when I went back over their meeting in Paris, it didn't seem as flat and badly blurred and dumb as it did the day Madeleine read it to me up at the quarry. Then I understood. It was Mrs. Carroll's portrait of Madeleine that stung her. The tone was high-strung and overblown, as if for once she lost her balance and fell in love with a star. She hid her schoolgirl reactions beneath her usual rough style, and Madeleine hadn't noticed anything odd when they were together. Now, reading the real thing, Madeleine was offended and acted betrayed, taking out her disapproval and wounded sense of proportion by hating *every* page of Mrs. Carroll's diary.

It all had me wondering again about The Truth and The Past, those creatures I kept hoping I had put behind me. Madeleine let me lie back on the chaise for an hour or two in the midmorning, as long as I didn't disturb her. So I was keeping it all to myself, which was all right because I forgot all about it by lunchtime. I got involved in Mrs. Carroll's narrative mostly in the summers, when I would read about the overnight guests and the fireworks on the Fourth and the weather. She noted the last with unbelievable attention to detail, massing up a private language ripe with meaning. *July 10. A June rain all morning. The children in sweaters. You could smell wool in the dining room at lunch, and outside you smelled the grass, which is usually brown by now. I like it brown.* I was content to drowse over the import of "a June rain" and managed to get The Truth off my mind. I wouldn't have mentioned it if Madeleine hadn't brought it up.

"Tell me something," she said. She had turned the vanity table into a desk and did her writing there, among the powders and pots and ointments. There was a mirror over it, and I don't know how she stood it, catching glimpses of herself for six and eight hours a day. Perhaps that is how she kept a good grip on the present.

"What?" It was the first time she had spoken in all these morning sessions. I came and went without a hello or goodbye. We did our talking on our afternoon walks.

"Rick, was I any good in *The Fork in the Road?*"

"You want the truth?" I asked, turning so I could see her. She was looking into the mirror and tapping her pencil lightly against her cheek. "It was a mess. You were forty-seven, and you looked thirty-five. But they dressed you up like Carmen Miranda. You made a lousy gypsy."

"You know, they all seem about the same to me," she said. She stood up and came over to the bay window. She wore a Chanel suit when she was writing because it made her feel like a working girl. "I've heard that people laugh at *The Fork in the Road,* but you know, it didn't *feel* like crap when we were making it. And *Bad Dream* didn't feel like a breakthrough either — they talk about me as if I invented the thirties in it." She wasn't sure where this was going, but she wanted to make it simple. "Listen: it always felt good to work and get it right, but it always felt the same."

"What are you trying to say, Madeleine? You think the critics are full of shit?"

"Some are, some aren't," she said, as if she didn't care one way or the other. "I'm talking about the public. And they all agree. After all these years, they say one's good and one's crap."

"And you wish they were all good," I said.

"No I don't." She walked around the chaise and stood in the bay window, her hands on her hips and her elbows thrown back. "If you know it's crap when you're doing it, you learn a lot from it. You get to know the direction it comes from. If you don't know crap, what you don't know can't hurt. But later on it's different. The years go by, and you see there are two separate things, what it was like and what people say a long time afterwards, when they've put it all together."

The years go by is a line she sings in half a dozen songs, or it seems that way.

"There's a third thing, isn't there? What *you* say when you put it all together. That's what you're doing over there," I said, jerking my thumb in the direction of the vanity.

"I guess so."

Silence fell. It was about the end of my hour at the diaries, and I wanted to walk before lunch, find David, get *moving*. I kept guessing wrong anyway. I couldn't say how she was. Not unhappy. Her antennae were crackling, and — unusual for someone whose two feet were planted firm on the ground — she could have talked on and on, I think, about what was real. She appeared to be struggling to work the key to her book into the lock on an old satin album. I had had two versions of the past myself, David's and mine, but this summer I had brought them together. Her versions were not disparate for lovers' reasons. Then, when I thought she must be unhappy after all, she went on, and I heard the mirth rising in her voice. Honestly, she seemed to feel that those who had analyzed her work and boiled her life down to obituary length were just as right about it as she could be. It even amused her. She realized that she was an irony in the flesh.

"Nobody wants new material from me," she said. "The best I can do with this book is give people what they already have, tell them the stories they tell about me."

"You're right, Madeleine," I said, standing up and moving next to her at the window. I shut Mrs. Carroll and put the book on the wide sill. "The fans don't want to hear that that's not how it was. They'd all feel, I don't know, cheated."

"Old," she said, calling a spade a spade.

"You're not old."

"I know," she said, swatting my arm with the back of her hand, "but a lot of *them* are."

Her book was proving to be the limit of the summer. She was coasting along at eight or ten pages a day now, and she expected to be done with a draft before the end of the first week in September. "I was up to two years a day until I hit 1930," she told us, as if she were sewing a quilt every night in front of a fire, "but I'm lucky now if I can do one." So it seemed that the rest of us could settle down for another month. Madeleine's progress on the book seemed to dovetail nicely with the timetable of Mrs. Carroll's farewell swim. If Madeleine had a stretch of writer's block, of course, we would still have to leave in the first week of September, because setting the stage for the last of Mrs. Carroll took precedence over everything else. But as long as Madeleine's book was likely to conclude at the right time, we liked the idea that we were waiting for her to finish. It seemed to make the waiting more real, because Madeleine's book would at least go public, whereas Mrs. Carroll's passage would have to remain a secret.

"Where are you and David going to go?" she asked. It was the first time she let me know she understood that I wasn't going back to Boston, though she probably knew it way back in June when I packed the plants and the dime-store fish.

"We don't have to decide that yet."

"*I'm* not rushing you, so don't sound like you're holding a gun."

"David and I haven't *said* we'll leave here together," I said, and I thought I was being waggish.

"Stop it."

"Stop what?"

"Sounding so cautious. You both know you're together again."

"All right, we're together." She was being much more exacting than the occasion required. Of *course* we were back together, David and I, but since everything was going to be all right, we left a lot unsaid. David and I had arrived at a strange economy. We were forgiving the past as fast as we could recall it, but I didn't think of us as putting it in words, or having to. Madeleine had the wrong idea. "But I can't speak for him," I said, "about after the summer. I don't want to make too many plans."

"Because you're afraid to?" she asked. She turned to me with the question and looked straight up at me. She asked it so mildly that she seemed to say, "I don't blame you, anyone would be." It touched me, but I just didn't need the protection it offered.

"No, Madeleine. Because I'm spending my time as I go along."

She took it in with a neutral look on her face. She nodded as if to say she'd heard, though not necessarily that she'd understood or agreed. Then she walked back over to her desk, sat down, and patted her hair in the mirror. She talked to me through it, the way David had in the bathroom.

"Since when have you been *spending* time instead of doing it?" she asked.

"Just lately," I said, smiling broadly because I was on good speaking terms with time. "I don't save it up much anymore."

"Good. Get your fill of it. Later it costs more and more." Madeleine and I had enough sermons between us for a month of Sundays. "I knew a girl singer in France who waited twenty years to get a coat made of martens, and then they went extinct before she got it."

"What's a marten?" I asked her.

"Some poor little beast. David and I have started to talk about things other than movies, you know."

"Did he run out of questions?"

"I ran out of movies." She picked up her pen and got set to write, as if she were being photographed doing it, then paused and froze in a profile. She had one more thing.

"He's more flexible than you and I are," she said admiringly. "He doesn't disapprove of life having stages."

"He's in an easy one."

"Oh no," she corrected me, "nobody is. You know that."

It was true. I knew it. I have never felt much kinship with any of the phases except the one I happen to be going through. David was curious about all of them, but I think he was specially awed by the very old. I could imagine him here in the spring evenings, smoking a Gitane with Mrs. Carroll and getting a look at things through a wide-angle lens. Until this summer, I kept my contact with the aging to a minimum. Madeleine was my one exception, but only because she took good care and stayed young. Of course it was self-defeating of me. I had ended up being the oldest person I knew, and the very young were as young as ever. Meanwhile, I suspected that the "other things" they were talking about were David and me.

It was a few days later that, leaving Madeleine's room just before noon, I bumped into the gardener. Actually, David and I both bumped into the gardener, but from different directions. David was coming up the stairs, and I was coming along the hall. As to the economy of gesture that grew up between us, his eyes widened a fraction, and mine narrowed about the same. Or it may have been that we both just slowed up a bit when we caught sight of each other. It is hard to say which way we did it, but that it was done by fractions I am sure. I could pick out the hairbreadth ripple of attention in his face, the strokes of concentration that would in time sink in and line it. The day took shape from our accidental meetings. We did not hold our breath for fear of anything in each other, though the weather we brought about when we were in the same room had about it the quiet of extremes, of hot or cold or the hour after a long rain. Put it this way: it was no particular time or place in the hall that morning, but because the moment threw us together, we were bent on meeting gently at the top of the stairs. And just as he reached the landing and I gripped the ball on the newel with both hands, a door opened at the opposite end of the hall from Madeleine's room, and the gardener stepped out.

Well, well. If my first, fast reaction was a tight-lipped whistle of outrage too high-pitched for human ears, my second was much more discreet, since I saw he had come out of Aldo's room. David saw him a moment later than I did and so missed which door had shut. "What the hell are you doing in the house?" he demanded. And the gardener swaggered up to us as if he were walking through a locker room with a towel at his hips. He wore a pair of dirty white overalls and seedy engineer's boots. He put his face close to David's and answered tightly.

"I still don't work for you," he said, "so fuck off." Then he went down the stairs. He hadn't so much as looked at me. He had caught on that he wasn't my type, so he had adopted a policy of cutting me. He made a big show of going about his pruning or his digging if he happened to meet me in the yard. He was, as I was fond of telling David, a real creep.

"He came out of Aldo's room," I said suggestively.

"Come on," David said, and he flew down the hall before I could stop him. *His* first thought must have been that the gardener was picking pockets, and he expected to find the drawers spilled and the closets ransacked. I knew better, that Aldo and the gardener must have been fucking, and I figured it was none of our business. I didn't know what Aldo was into. I didn't want to burst in on him while he was putting away his toys.

But he was sitting in his easy chair reading the real-estate section of the LA *Times* when David threw open the door and we both tumbled in. Someone in Beverly Hills sent him the *Times* every day, which meant he read it three days late. But he said it was better than nothing, by which he meant the New York *Times* and the Boston *Globe*.

"Am I late for something?" he asked, looking up.

"We just saw the gardener sneak out of here," David said, and I could see that what had dawned on me about the fucking had just dawned on him.

"Sneak?" Aldo asked delightedly. "That's just his Portuguese blood, David dear. It comes from thousands of years of skulking about in fishing boats. I gather that it takes thousands of years to produce that physique as well. All I can say is, it was worth the wait."

"But I bet you'll sleep safer at night, knowing our security unit is so alert," I said as I boxed David's ears and grabbed him around the neck to pull him out of the room. "Come on, Inspector. This case is closed."

"Wait," Aldo said. "It's darling of you both to look after me. Tell me what you think of this: I'm taking John out to the Coast with me."

"Who's John?" I asked.

"The gardener."

"Oh. How nice," I said. Was I supposed to say congratulations? I still held David's head pinned under my arm, and I let him squirm loose. He peered over my shoulder at Aldo and plunged on, not leaving well enough alone even now.

"Are you and he a thing?"

"Goodness no, David. That type is just a cowboy in LA. You buy them by the dozen. It's a *gardener* I need."

"I never thought ot him actually gardening," I said. "Is he any good?" I couldn't believe we were going to talk about this. What I meant was that his gardening seemed like strictly stage business, the excuse that put him in our path day after day. I couldn't imagine him in connection with flowers. In my mind he was connected with sex, and not the flowery kind.

"He's fabulous," Aldo said.

"And he's going to go with you, just like that?" David asked. David had never done love for money, and he adored the details of how it was done. He wasn't sure yet that this wasn't a hustling arrangement.

"Well," Aldo answered, "I said to him: 'Look, how long is this job going to last? She's an old lady. Big gardens are passé in the East.' And then I offered him twice what she pays."

"Do you get all your help this way?" I asked.

"But my dear, you can't trust the agencies. In Beverly Hills, we always steal them from each other, and it all evens out in the end. My first acquisition was Madeleine's driver. He's a hundred and ten, and he grew up on Pierce-Arrows. I'd *die* without him."

"Will you pay the gardener extra to do indoor work?" David asked.

"In my old brass bed? No, I never fuck with the servants. I pay considerably more for that sort of service, and it doesn't get in the way of the food getting cooked or the grass cut. If you fuck the servants, they take it out of your breakfast. Now don't go. I want to talk to you."

David sat down on the end of the bed, facing Aldo, and I did my usual trick of standing at the window, here an open casement facing north to the marshes. I still gravitated to windows as if I needed as much light as I could get. At least I no longer did it in order to protect my rear flank and have an easy escape.

"I have two things on my mind," he said, stuffing the newspaper down into the chair beside him. He glanced at the table next to his chair, on which were gathered a box of cookies, a quart bottle of Tab, and several packets of gum, and he seemed to waver about offering us something. He wanted to, but there wasn't anything good enough for guests, so he let it go and went on. "One is that I have to leave."

"You mean, leave here?" I asked, feeling a little foolish because I sounded like Heidi.

"I've stayed too long as it is, Rick. My telephone bill would pay off the national debt if I didn't get to write it off my taxes. My friends all think I'm at a fat farm, no matter what I tell them, so they're going to expect me thin. I will be utterly humiliated."

"When?" David asked.

"In a few days. Frankly, I'm so sick of fish I could shit. I'm going to go home and eat beef forever, like a good American."

"We'll starve without you," I said, to tease him. "I thought we were one for all and all for one."

"Which brings me to the *other* thing on my mind," he said, as if there were scarcely room for two. "What are you going to do at the end of the summer?" He looked from one to the other of us expectantly.

"Beats me," David said and then turned to me. "*You* tell him," he said, wondering what I would come up with.

"We'll decide that then," I said, curbing my impulse to float away out the window and be done with decisions.

"You could come west," Aldo said. "I mean, I don't want to be a spoilsport, but in a couple of months it's going to look like Hudson's Bay out there."

I darted my eyes out the open window once and, because the sun cast the sea into sapphire, refused to believe him. It was warm enough now for me to swim as long as I wanted, no matter what Mrs. Carroll said. I felt closer to the sea just then than I did to either David or Aldo, and I saw how the feeling sprang up because I feared their control. I may not ever know, I thought, why this wave of suspicion comes over me that I don't know who I am. I think everyone is going to take advantage of my momentary lapse of self and enslave me forever in who they think I am. Then the other side hit me. I *threw off* people who left me free, who had no version of me at all — they were the population of my bedroom for fifteen years, the men in jeans and flannel shirts who came for the one night only. Go after the contrasts, I said to myself. Don't say it will still be summer when you know it won't. If you don't remember who you are, play for a while with the opposite.

I knew then, I think, that the specter of control had nothing to do with them. It was my own shadow on the windowpane. I had always made the Chinese boxes I got locked in, and when I had no one around to blame, I accused the passing of time. In Aldo's room it was going on noon, and time was suddenly as actual to me as the window. I mean it was open.

"Am I talking out of turn?" Aldo asked, and when there was no answer from David, I turned back from the view and saw the question was meant for me. I had reached for a split-second look toward the sea, and I had gone into a little trance. David and Aldo didn't know where I was, and they waited for me to say.

"The end of the summer is not taboo," I said, to reassure us all. "What do you have in mind for us, Aldo? Do you need more cheap New England labor?"

"No," he grinned, "but you can stay with me while you look around."

"What would we be looking around for?" I asked David.

"Work, I guess," he said. "What would we do with the Chevy?"

"Drive it?" I just threw these answers out, but they sounded all right to me. It was like running on the beach in the fog: you can't see a foot in front of you, but on the other hand there isn't anything there to bump into.

"What about Boston?" David asked.

"What about it?" I said. "I've got everything with me." I

hadn't actually *told* David that Boston was over with, but he must have known.

"That Chevy will be worth a pile on the Coast," Aldo remarked. "It's so kinky."

David looked over at me, and we both shrugged as if to say, "Why not?" Because it didn't hurt the way my decisions always used to, I would be hard put to call it a decision. It was just the way things happened.

We had never made any plans to do anything on a particular day before, so we were lucky to have the sun. It was the day before Aldo was leaving, and instead of dinner around the table, we had made up a sunset picnic and taken it down to the beach. We filled a wicker hamper with the best of everything, the china and crystal and linen, and we kept Aldo out of the kitchen and made him pack his suitcases while we cooked up the dinner and cooled it off. Cold chicken and potato salad and pickled eggplant, and Madeleine baked cream of tartar biscuits for strawberry shortcake. Phidias brought up champagne from the cellar. We didn't pretend to be doing other than what we did. This was the picnic that was stolen from us when we were children, by rain or measles or the disinclination of our long-lost families.

We were spread out on the sand below the house. The sky was still a faded rose, but the night was coming down. Aldo, in a caftan, had compared the Pacific to the Atlantic in a long toast to the sea. Just now he was setting out the dessert on the damask cloth, arranging the strawberries one by one on the biscuits, as if the photographer from *Gourmet* were on his way across the dunes. Then he set to beating the cream with a wire whisk. We had successfully kept him from cooking, but he had placed himself next to the hamper like the captain in a lifeboat. Throughout the meal, he had dispensed the food at his own pace, calling our attention to the proper presentation of each dish. In fact, he had by him a small covered basket of his own, so that when he appeared from among the dunes at sunset, he had told us with a brief curtsy, "Call me the Little Red Riding Caterer." And out of it had come the parsley and paprika and whatever else was needed to tart up our humble fare.

"Why whip cream at all if you're not going to give it guts?" he asked rhetorically of Phidias, who sat next to him. "I think an ounce of Grand Marnier is *crucial* in cream, but I added a little brandy, too, to tone down that orange-lollipop taste. You don't want it tacky."

David was stooping at the water's edge, maybe ten feet away from the picnic. He had been given charge of the half-case of Taittinger's, and he held a bottle in one hand and his tulip glass in the other. All of us were dressed up tonight, but to me David was the most incongruous in fancy clothes because he never wore them. These were probably all he had, a white silk wedding shirt embroidered with flowers and black silk trousers done up in a drawstring. Erotic pajamas. He and I had spent the last few days taking in the idea of LA, and we did it by spending our time in bed and in the sea, talking less and less. If the Chevy broke down in midpassage, he told me, perhaps we would settle down on the prairie for a while. I took him to mean that we didn't want to be too tied to a calendar. The way I was feeling, I would have liked to take the Chevy and go into orbit on automatic pilot, setting up house in transit. So LA was fine, but in our own time. We had to get there first.

Phidias had sited our picnic blankets at the exact spot where the Carrolls used to eat on the beach, and he had told us during dinner about the outings that took place in Tony's youth, with the children attended (and spoon-fed, one assumed) by a nurse, and the cook and butler serving. Since I never got the impression that Beth Carroll was happy pointing the finger at servants, the scene here evoked was rife with tension. It sounded very like *Mr.* Carroll's picnic, proper and

sober and dead. Meanwhile, Phidias never talked at all about
cows and the dairy business, and if he hadn't appeared every
second morning with a crock of milk and a bottle of heavy
cream, I would have forgotten about the farm entirely. It was
another way in which he wouldn't talk about the present. I
didn't, of course, expect him to fill us up with anecdotes about
his taciturn wife and the beefy sons, though I had read my
share of master-servant stories and had an inkling of the gossip
I was missing.

But he wouldn't talk about himself in a day-to-day fashion.
He had expressed in my presence exactly one crystal-clear feeling, his rage at Tony in Madeleine's room. He wasn't living
wholly in the past, because he still gave us our daily orders for
knocking together the house. And I knew he wasn't dumb
about who we all were because of our talk about David under
the apple tree. David said it was because he was the only
straight one among us, an old Greek lover in a houseful of
faggots. Not that he did any flinching about any of us being
gay. But David said his own close contact with Phidias had
ceased when he and I became lovers again. The rhythms were
different between gay and straight, David said idiotically, and
Phidias proved it by going his own way now that we were three
to one, four counting Madeleine. I thought it had more to do
with him being a man with things to do. He did them by himself, whatever they were, and they were the inner equivalent of
getting the mildew off the lawn chairs, so they didn't occur in
the external world. From what I had read of her journals, I
guessed Mrs. Carroll had things to do herself. What luck, I told
David, that they happened on each other. I was sounding idiotic, he said.

"You're going to turn it into butter if you don't quit,"
Phidias said to Aldo.

"I don't deny you're a whiz about cattle, Phidias," Aldo
said, not missing a beat, "but dessert is more important to me

than people, and I'm as jealous as a sorcerer. I don't make mistakes, and when I do, they're a revelation."

Madeleine meanwhile paced up and down the beach, writing her book in her head between dinner and dessert. Everything was fine, I told myself, as if I had to take our temperature and reassure myself. I wouldn't have dared to tell *them* that everything was fine, because they would have accused me of tying us up together and throwing away the key, implicating us all in a mixed metaphor. It was my most secret failing, that I had to keep looking to see if we were all right, and the summer had not done away with it. I did as I promised I would and took the present at its word, but something else persisted. The apples on the tree in the drive were crabbed and tart, but you could eat a bite or two before your lips puckered. If I was walking with Madeleine to the woods, for example, I would sometimes bring down a couple and chew and spit them. Some gauge in me, no doubt, was checking to see how far along the season was, no matter how much it seemed as thoughtless to play with apples as to draw in the sand.

What I wanted, I knew, was to say what we were, even though the four of them, the only ones who might have cared, didn't. I hadn't anyone to compare us to, and now that we were splitting up, I expected we would seem like an optical illusion when we had gone, since no one would remind me of us. I got what comfort I could from taking our measure one by one. Aldo and Phidias bickering like old vaudevillians over the shortcake. David suspended in a Zen intermission at the shore like a fly in amber. Madeleine rampant. I kept it a secret that I wanted more, wanted something to take away with me that would group us all together in a metaphysical snapshot. I had to be content with the image we had all made real, of Mrs. Carroll swimming east toward Bermuda. A sensible New England freestyle until she got beyond the breakers, and then a lazy sidestroke as she made it out to sea. It was vivid to me, like a scrap of film.

So what we *did* this summer was what we were, I said to myself on the beach. The sentiment made me queasy with its moral uplift. It made us sound like the bugger fringe of the Eagle Scouts. Not that we hadn't had terrific results, having kept a whole suburb off the face of the earth and won one for Mrs. Carroll's deer. It's hard to describe what I ached for. You could say I just wanted to stay on in a safe place.

I jogged over to Madeleine and fell into step beside her. "What year are you up to?" I asked. We tended now to talk about her book first, and today our afternoon's cooking had preempted our afternoon walk. She had asked me more and more questions about her films in the last few days, putting her trust in the passion of the myth. Because she had scoffed so long at its balmy prose and its excess of relics and ceremony, she probed its contours now with the cool of a social scientist. A myth and a self, she seemed to decide, were not mutually exclusive.

"Nineteen fifty-eight," she said.

"Oh." The year we met in France.

"You're having a relapse, aren't you?"

"Of what? Nineteen fifty-eight?"

"No," she said sharply. "You're mooning at all of us. The next thing you know, you'll be wringing your hands."

"I was being sentimental about the summer," I admitted, my hands in my pants pockets as still as the twilight air. "I'll get over it. Am I in it?"

"In what?"

"Nineteen fifty-eight."

"No," she said, hanging her head and shaking it thoughtfully. "As these things go, you're not important enough. Isn't it stupid?" She stopped and put one hand on her hip in the concert position, as if she were about to sing a café ballad. She looked worried. Something was on her mind. She had never had anything on her mind long enough to furrow her brow and make her frown, because she put whatever it was into words with a lightning touch and got rid of it, or at least it had always been so between her and me. Since she didn't embarrass herself, since her genetic makeup didn't include the need for approval, there was nothing she wouldn't say. And yet, as we stood face to face on the beach, she was struggling with words as much as I was, though I couldn't guess the reason. Nineteen fifty-eight was a big year, working out as it did the shift from movie star to chanteuse, but the years had not brought her to grief so far in her memoirs. I couldn't imagine they would start to hurt her now. The years that started in 'fifty-eight were her most triumphant. Everyone agreed about that.

"I don't care," I said about the memoirs. "But are you mad at me about something?"

"What would you do if I were?"

"Tell you to go to hell."

"Then I'm not," she said, and the one-syllable laugh came out at half volume. "Why would I be?"

"Because maybe you feel the same way as I do about the summer, and you don't want to start mooning at your age."

"*My* age?" she asked, hooding her eyelids.

"It's just an expression," I said.

"Oo-hoo!" Aldo called, and we turned to see him waving us back to the picnic for our shortcake. I noticed for the first time that it had gone dark on the beach. Phidias had lighted the pair of lanterns he brought down, and Aldo would have faded into the landscape except for the scarlet of his caftan in the circle of light. It seemed the right time to go back, since Madeleine and I were just idling away the moment, teasing one another but fighting clean. I looked at her to make a joke about Aldo finally taking charge of the meal, and she was doing the most curious thing. She peered at them in the distance as if she were making calculations, then looked at me appraisingly, and I felt that I was the one variable factor. She was like someone sketching a getaway route in his head the instant before he makes a break for it, and she made you understand that they are the only kind who ever get away. But I couldn't understand what she was figuring until we started to walk. She took my arm and kept our pace slow, at the same time talking low and fast. Before I quite began to take in what she was saying, I realized she had a speech to make that would last as long as it took us to reach the others. There wouldn't be a moment left over for me to reply.

"You want it not to end," she said, going back to the summer, "because you're afraid the future will shoot you in the back the way the past did. You can't help it that you break time down into pieces. Even I do, but at least I know they're all about the same. The past isn't the enemy. In fact, I've had an even better idea this summer. There *is* no past."

Maybe it was a hundred feet, but I am not good at distances. David stood up at the water's edge and started back to the others. Of course there was a past.

"Not the way we're used to thinking of it anyway," she went on, the "we" as preachy as the ones I was partial to. "I mean, the past *happens* in the *present*, when it crosses our mind again. Most things never come up again at all, and so they don't exist. Nothing would have happened, I've always thought, if you and I had never met, and yet that meeting was an accident. Another mile one way or the other, and you never would have walked into town that day." It was curious, but I could have sworn she was as angry as she was grateful. "We're not taught to love accidents, are we?"

"No," I said. I couldn't get a handle on it. I guess I thought she was apologizing in a roundabout way for not putting me in the book. But since I really didn't care, I only half listened. It didn't mean I didn't like the theory, or what I could understand of it at least. But it was too absolute. Sometimes there was a past, and sometimes there wasn't, I thought to myself equanimically. It depended on who you were at a given time, and what proof you had and what proof you still needed. None of us here, for instance, needed more proof, and I wished we could walk a little faster and get back to the group in the lamplight.

"You have to throw out all the facts you think you know," she said, "and even if you could, it will still seem more like a story than something real. But I ought to tell somebody." She stopped again, and I waited with her. We were so close to the others now, maybe twenty-five feet, that she lowered her voice to tell the story. She still held my arm. "I met Beth Carroll in France in nineteen thirty and not during the war. Phidias didn't know. When I left him in 'thirty-one, I knew I was pregnant, but I thought I could have an operation over here. It was too late. So I called Beth Carroll from New York, and she kept me here in a maid's room until it was over. I didn't want it. It was just like being sick. Beth took the baby, and I went to Hollywood. Then, a few years later, I got Phidias a job here, and then we got divorced. He never knew."

"It sounds like a soap opera," I said, and now she had started us walking again, just as I realized we had to stop and finish this. I had no idea how either of us was feeling.

"I know," she said. "That's what I mean. The truth is *true*, but it isn't *real*. I hadn't thought about it in twenty-five years, and then that day when you walked into town, I was all alone in the hotel, I was broke, and it started to hurt again. We had that week together. I realized I didn't know anything about my own child, except I remembered it was a boy. It's the only time I ever missed him. I got busy again."

Now wait a minute, I thought.

"Are you saying that Tony's *your* son?" I asked her.

"No," she said impatiently, as if I were being stupid and mawkish. "Beth put the baby up for adoption."

But then it didn't make sense at all. And then, when we were almost on top of the picnic, it all came together.

"Aldo?" I said, and she let go of my arm to walk around the blanket to her own place, between Aldo and David.

"Sit down," Aldo said to me. I was standing up at my place, and Madeleine had reached the opposite side. She looked over at me as if she had already dropped the subject. The others were all sitting down and waiting.

"Not me," I said, swaying a bit, and she shook her head no and then tilted it to the side and smiled, as if to say she knew what I meant. "It's no one," she said. "I don't know who it is. I never will now. Forget it."

But what if it were *me*, I thought as I sat down. Just suppose it were. Suddenly my mind swept over us all like an airborne camera zooming in, and I knew I was finally in a scene in a Madeleine Cosquer film. As luck would have it, I had drawn a fragment of thirties melodrama. But there are no small parts, as they say in the theater, just small actors.

You keep certain things about yourself like money in the bank. I always expected to be terrific in an emergency. I may not have actually *waited* for one, for the pilot, say, to slump over, and the stewardess to turn to me and tell me, *"You* fly the plane." But I've thought about them, tremors in the earth and wildfire and storms, and I've known in my deepest place that that was how it might be given to me to take care of people. It was the very impulse that set me up as the group moralist at the beginning of the summer. I was the one who would have been the troubleshooter if the cops got called. I would have done the plea bargaining with the DA. Or if worse came to worst, I would have black-marketed the cigarettes and whiskey for my gang and me while we languished in jail. In other words, I had a real feel for movie emergencies and the measures people take who take charge. Since I had always lived so hermited a life, I never expected to be myself the center of the crisis, so the wind was knocked out of me for half a minute as I danced among the possibilities here. I spooned up the first big berry and bit into it, and the sweetness of it stung my eyes with tears. But I swallowed it and recovered, because there was nothing else I *could* do. You have to rescue the survivors so they won't die and make matters even worse. The dead are already dead.

It couldn't be me, I thought. There were too many problems. I looked too much like my mother and father back home, for one thing, and it didn't change the facts of my bloodline that I had sloughed them off and become just like my friends at Mrs. Carroll's. Besides, my parents were too dull to have hidden the business of an adoption from me. But I was not interested in the truth, which had a habit of getting me nowhere. I was flying. I couldn't imagine what I used to *do* all the time, but I was damn sure it didn't used to happen in the air.

I was between Phidias and David, and when I made a sentence out of it and thought to myself "What if I'm sitting for the first time next to my father?" I knew I was on the wrong track. Madeleine was a pure evangelical who believed our survival lay in choosing what was real over what was true. It was still a distinction that sounded too good to me, but I was doing what I could to applaud us for how far we had come. I shouldn't get too lost in the confection, I thought, watching us gobble up shortcake for all the world as if we could get away with being like everyone else. They were all talking. I waited for a good place to jump in and swear we were pals at least, if not blood kin, and ready to defend our right to believe the sheerest lunacy.

"I knew you wouldn't chip in and buy me a present because it's tacky, and I have everything already," Aldo said, going into his picnic basket. "So I brought my own bottle to crack over my bows and launch me," and he pulled out a cobwebbed bottle of Mr. Carroll's cognac. "Eighty years old. Worth its weight in carats."

"I don't understand why Tony doesn't haul it away by the case," Phidias said. "It's practically his."

"Drunks can't stand good liquor," Aldo said. "It makes them edgy." He drew the cork and passed it to Madeleine, who breathed in the perfume and narrowed her eyes as if she were a medium and we were a séance.

"Why not?" David asked.

"Because they like to swill it," I said, "and it makes them ashamed to waste it."

"You have to be a connoisseur to like it," David said.

"Oh, wine queens don't like it either if they've had to buy it," Aldo said, who was a connoisseur of queens. "They hate themselves for it, but all they can think of is how much it cost. Whether it was worth it or not."

"I never think of how much something costs," Madeleine said, as if we didn't know. She was on another wavelength, like a foreigner who has misread the idiom. When she was in a good mood, she spoke to the interviewer she carried around in her head and judged everything she touched until you knew damn well what was first class and what wasn't. She was no age at all to me anymore, and since I wasn't either, it was all one to me what hour it was or what season. A voice in *my* head said, "This is who we are, who we are right now," over and over, and I mentally put a match to the diary I never wrote down but kept in perfect chronological order. I let the voice try it out: there is no past.

"I bet nobody gets to like it if it's that old and it costs that much," David said.

"Wrong," Aldo answered brightly. "*Thieves* get to, if they've stolen it. And con artists and song-and-dance men love it after a caper. People who live from job to job get into the vintage stuff, right, Madeleine?"

"What do you mean 'that old'?" Madeleine said dryly to David. "I'm almost as old as this myself."

"You're not old," he said, and she lifted her glass to him and smiled as if she had never heard it before.

The cognac didn't have what you would call a taste at all. When I took a sip, the top of my head lifted off, and a warm breeze blew in from the south. It didn't make you drunk exactly either. After a minute or so of it, though, I could have kissed the whole lot of us, cavorted around the blanket planting wet ones on everyone's face. But I haven't sat through Madeleine's films in vain. I knew we were at the climax, when it could all fall over into spun sugar and mush. This was the scene where Madeleine would step back and survive the narrow, sentimental valentine that movies used to end with because they didn't know how to suggest how life went on after the credits. Only Madeleine, of all the actors, would get it across that she kept on going beyond the frame of the film, that every passion of her life was as arresting and inevitable as the one the movie chronicled. Things are at their most cruelly sentimental only at the end, and if you can get it across that things don't end, the moment won't curdle. Oh had I studied it.

"Listen," I said, a touch of the senior officer in my voice, "since this is the last time we'll all be together, we'd better sort of synchronize our watches about the end of the summer. I've got a timetable." I hadn't one at all, of course. I was going to make it up now as I went along. They all leaned forward to make sure they'd heard me right, since I was the one who had always held them back from making plans. I came up into a crouch and laid out a master plan, restraining myself from fetching a stick and scratching in the sand while I talked. I spoke with a little reluctance, as if I hated to spoil a party, a shade world-weary at having to think of these things, but resigned to it too because someone had to. It went like this: Aldo and the gardener would leave tomorrow. Then, in about three weeks, David and I. Madeleine, I said, had better be alone at the end and do a swan song as Mrs. Carroll. Perhaps a phone call to Farley or even to John or Cicely. She should be seen by some of them up at the dairy. Then, a day or two before Mrs. Carroll's ocean swim, Phidias would smuggle her out during the night in a milk truck and get her to the airport. Then it was up to him. Leave the note on the bed on the first nice day and then find it and call the authorities.

It didn't take Caesar to plot this strategy, and it was, after all, what we had been expecting to happen, give or take a tactic. But they murmured their approval and nodded alertly when I spoke their names. They looked so unexpectedly relieved that for a moment I thought I'd come up with something clever. And then I realized, as we broke up into small and easy conversations, that they were relieved about *me*. By putting off the talk about September, it seemed they had been taking care of me. Am I all wrong, I wondered, and didn't I take care of them at all? But then I shook that thought as sniveling and trapped in time. Oddly enough, and I felt this very specifically, I didn't believe it was too late for me to claim Phidias and Madeleine as father and mother and grow up all over again. Besides, they deserved the son they had lost too carelessly, and I was as good as anyone. It was too late for them, though, so I had to let it go. I laughed out loud, a single-noted hoot, because for once I wasn't going to get anywhere splitting hairs. I gave up the past I wanted to invent along with the one I spent my life burying. It was like buying champagne with my last ten dollars.

David was tugging at my sleeve. I looked at him and thought: I wonder if we're together now for good. Once we got it balanced, could we ever get it to stay that way? But the bells rang, and the flashing went off in the tilt mechanism. Dopey thought. Wrong attitude.

"I just wanted you to know," he said, locking eyes with me, "you're not a romantic anymore."

"Why?"

"Because you don't want to cling to the past, and that's what they do."

"What am I now?" I asked. How did he know? Where was he getting his information?

"Beats me," he said. "But Madeleine and I agree. It used to be you couldn't wait for the present to become the past so you could cling to it. You're a *post*-romantic now. You're going to have to wait for civilization to catch up."

"They'll catch me. The Chevy doesn't *go* over fifty-five. Fifty uphill." He stretched back from the blanket into the sand and propped on his elbows. When I turned to him, we were removed from the lights of the picnic. We were not removed from the scene I was in, since I brought it with me. "Are you sure I won't have a relapse? What if I start asking again why you left me?"

"I'll say I already told you."

"The weather." He meant the question would never deserve more of an answer. "Well, how can we be sure we're going to stay together now?"

"Because there isn't much time."

"Why not?"

"Don't you see," he said, as if he wished I knew it already, without him having to tell me, "*I'm* the romantic now. Everything's going to die, and I can't stand it. In a minute you're old, and before you turn around you're lying in a field." He seemed to find it maddening to talk about. "I'm thirty. Madeleine says that's the oldest you ever get, and then you get over it. I don't believe it."

"But wait," I said, wanting to let him know there was nothing to worry about *there*. I was all rosy about the ten dollars and the bottle of champagne. Once you've gone and bought it, I thought, anything can happen, and you're free enough at last to go with whatever it is. But I didn't know how to say it and still be the bittersweet senior officer, rueful and in charge. And I had to stay in the part. David didn't want me sentimental any more than Madeleine did.

"It's just a phase I'm going through. I know." He smiled wanly, and he looked too young to be visited bv the dark phases. "So is a bad cold, but you still blow your nose and cough a lot."

Why did it hurt so much that he reminded me of me? Had he always? When *I* thought everything was going to die, when we used to make love and be like two men in a mirror, it was not each other we resembled but a third man charged with life, and I imagined him as the one man I knew who was fully free. Now that everything was going to live, I was full of ordinary thoughts. I thought that nobody was so smart about me as David and nobody but me knew quite what he meant about himself. I put my hand on his stomach and stirred the silk as if I were rubbing a Buddha's paunch for luck. The million things I had to say to him about time would take all the time we had. But I didn't say so now because he would think it proved him right. He couldn't know we had all the time in the world, because that was the next phase. By then, I suppose, I might be back in the glooms myself. So it would go, back and forth between us like the urge to make love.

"Where did you get these dreamy clothes?" I asked him. "Did one of your lovers in high places used to dress you up?"

"They're Aldo's, and they don't fit him. He got them cheap at a studio auction. They were in a movie called *China Captain*. I never heard of it, but the guy who wore this outfit was Aldo's first man. He never made it big in pictures."

"It's like the six-thousand-dollar gloves," I said, thinking of Aldo buying up the golden age, piece by piece.

"Oh no it's not," David said, not understanding, thinking I was comparing Madeleine to a co-star. "These are just souvenirs. The glove with the cigarette burn is history, like the pens they signed the Constitution with. Or Washington's wooden teeth."

"What if nobody ever heard of *The Ambassador's Lady?* And what if *China Captain* starred Errol Flynn in your silk pajamas?"

"Then it would be the other way around," he admitted, but he wasn't really interested. "What are you saying?"

"I was wondering what's real."

"You were?" He started to laugh as if I were irresistible. "You sound like Madeleine. And you both sound like a B-picture."

We were interrupted by the tweet of a whistle, very close. It must have to do with some peril at sea, I thought, because it is just too late to call the cops. David sat up, and I turned around, and Madeleine and Aldo stared across the blanket at us as if to say it wasn't *their* fault. Phidias was standing downwind from us, facing south, and when he blew a second blast, we at least knew where it was coming from.

"He says he's got a present for me," Aldo said. "Isn't that European? I hope it's not something to wear because I can't stand anyone else's taste. Why is he blowing a whistle? Madeleine, say it isn't an animal."

"What if it's a cow?" she asked him. "What would you do with it in Beverly Hills?"

"Too much milk gives me pimples," he said.

There was a sound from beyond the ridge like a muffled gunshot, and then the sky broke open in white and gold over the water. Fireworks. Phidias turned back to us and grinned, the whistle still in his mouth. Aldo, who was so comfortable about being sentimental that he threatened to turn us into a boy-and-his-dog story, started laughing and sobbing and took hold of Madeleine's hand for support. The aftershock of the rocket crackled up the beach. Phidias was antic and cocky, as excited as he must have been when he produced these shows for the Carroll children and shook the starch out of their lives. He couldn't stand not being with the production crew, though. The next one burst bright green, and the sound it made was like a bomb. "I better go see if they need help," he said, though I don't think they did, and he trotted away. The difference between him and us, it occurred to me, was that he worked like a cameraman and we worked like actors.

Then a red one. It was sent up even higher and bloomed open like a flower. We all gasped in chorus, and in between firebursts we looked at each other and agreed it was the perfect thing. It was even more perfect than champagne, of course, because it was wilder and more fleeting and seemed to end with a sizzle of shrapnel out in the dark water. Madeleine told us that Phidias found the fireworks cache in the boathouse, where they were stored after the last lit-up Fourth, twenty years ago. In all that time, I figured, if anyone had dropped a match, the place would have blown like a powderhouse. But as it didn't it would have been a waste of time to worry about. Phidias's boys had set up tonight's display on the boathouse beach — all his boys but me, I thought wryly, but let it go — and they were having their own farmers' picnic between the ridges. I suppose Phidias felt more at home there with them. Then I had a picture of him and Beth Carroll and guessed he was about as close to home here as there. I thought of the mid-ocean floor where Mrs. Carroll would officially lie, and the warm night breeze blowing in off the water was full of ambiguous powers.

Aldo got up and went to the water's edge to watch. He hugged himself gleefully and did a jig on the lip of the tide and

got the hem of his caftan wet. David, whom I wanted to promise he wouldn't die, lay back down again and looked up at the
fires in the sky. Madeleine and I were sitting across from each
other now, and she motioned me forward as if she had a secret
to tell. She couldn't have *another* secret, I knew, but we both
leaned across the littered blanket and said what we could
about the one we had played with.

"Are you having an Oedipus complex?" she asked.

"No more than usual," I said ruefully. She was lit up in the
white light of the next firework, and I raised the following
words to get over the noise: "Pretend for a moment it's me."

"But it isn't."

"Just for the sake of argument." Because it was the end of
the scene, she didn't want us getting lost in sentiment. "Would
we tell Phidias? We wouldn't, would we?"

"No," she said approvingly, and as if the decision were
really mine to make. "Because he has enough sons as it is.
They're not what his life is about."

"Would we tell David and Aldo?"

"Not Aldo," she said, brushing my shoulder with her fingertips. "It would make him jealous. But David, yes. He senses it
already."

"What do you mean?"

"It wouldn't surprise him," she said. "It's the sort of thing he
appreciates."

"And you and I would go on as before," I said.

"Of course. How do you feel?"

Fine, I thought. But the moment had reached such a pitch
that I saw what the question must mean. When I said "Fine," I
was taking my temperature again, telling how I was as if I
were caught in an epidemic or a pitched battle, some situation
where everything else was emphatically *not* fine. What I was
being asked was how it felt to be who I was.

"All grown up," I said. "How about you?"

"Me?" She shrugged so deeply that her shoulders lifted up to her ears. "The same as ever. Like a movie star."

I couldn't whisper at great distances as Madeleine could, so I leaned even closer. I would never tell her this, but she looked just then like none of the women she'd played. She looked like their mother. As for me, I wasn't worried at all that we'd blow our best lines. We've survived, I thought, because we don't remember to be afraid.

"How do movie stars feel?" I asked, and a rocket went off that, for the space of a held breath, threw off the night. We were unearthly bright, like a summer day.

"Fabulous," she said.